ANN SIMKO

THE DARKING BOOK ONE

DARK

CROSSINGS

DARK CROSSINGS
By Ann Simko
Copyright © 2015 by Ann Simko
...

Published by Coyote Moon Books
through Createspace
November 2015

ISBN-13: 978-0692587751

Published in the United States of America
Cover Art by Fiona Jayde
Edited by Judith B. Glad

COYOTE MOON BOOKS

"I am terrified by this dark thing
That sleeps in me;
All day I feel its soft, feathery turnings, its malignity."
—Sylvia Plath, *Ariel*

"But they can't know how the dark space inside me is growing. I lie to them. I can't get out of the dark hole. 'Peace is here' it whispers."
—Lurlene McDaniel, *Breathless*

"God is evil. Sometimes he lets you live."
Stephen King

Acknowledgements

The author wishes to thank a whole lot of people;

Judith B. Glad for her friendship, support, amazing editing skills, and psychotherapy when needed.

Cynthia Koons, grammar Nazi extraordinaire.

June Kramin, for formatting this puppy and pointing out all those annoying mistakes and for keeping me from hitting delete like a million times.

Tirzah Goodwin for endless hours discussing plot holes, characterizations and incredible suggestions to make this so much better.

Cindy Amrhien for reading the first very crappy edition of this.

Nancy Matuszak for squeezing me in between traveling.

Jen McConnell for talking me down off a ledge and her fabulous husband Scott McConnell for chapter by chapter giving me his valuable impressions of each scene and character.

I know I missed people. It doesn't mean I didn't appreciate your help. It means the author has a crappy memory.

Stephen King said, and I'm paraphrasing, a book is written alone. It is never published alone.

CHAPTER 1

Cross Delancey didn't want to die. He also didn't want to live, at least not like this. This wasn't a life. It was barely an existence. He tried to suppress a groan as he turned on the narrow cot and failed. His twin brother, across from him, pretending to be sleeping.

"I know you're awake," Cross said. His bruised ribs pulled as he spoke and he couldn't quite keep the pain from his voice.

"Shhh, keep your voice down. Do you want them to come back!" Kale's whisper was louder than Cross's normal voice. Cross knew his brother was scared, hell, he was scared. But anger was quickly replacing the fear. He liked the anger way better.

"I don't care if they come back." Cross braced his side and rolled to his back. The anger dissolved as quickly as it came leaving hot tears rolling down his face. "I can't take this anymore, Kale." He swallowed hard and wiped the hated tears with the back of his hand. "We gotta get out, they're gonna kill us if we don't."

"They'll kill us for sure if we even try!" Cross heard Kale slide off his cot to sit next to him. "I know it sucks, but you're making it harder than you have too. Just give them what they want and they won't beat you." Kale was crying now too.

Cross hated that. They weren't kids anymore. They were fourteen, practically grown men. They shouldn't be balling to each other like babies, but Cross didn't feel grown up. He hurt from the beating Tanya's goons had given him earlier that day. His one eye had almost swollen shut and he was pretty sure a couple of ribs were broken. Those guys sure weren't treating him like a baby.

"I can't," he said.

"No, you won't. There's a difference." Kale sounded all pouty now, but Cross felt the frustration in his brother. "I don't get you man. All you have to do is show her what you can do. She knows you're lying when you say you can't do anything. I know you know that. Why can't you just show her? What's the big deal?"

Cross sat up with a little difficulty and a grunt of pain. He swung his legs off the side of the cot to face Kale. "What's the big deal? You are so dense sometimes, Kale. Tell me you haven't been inside her head, you know what she plans to do with us. We are nothing more than freaks to her. Something for her to use until she can't use us anymore. I know you know that!"

"So what then? You let them beat you to death? What do you think you're proving? That you can take a beating? Come on man, I can get in your head too, you know. We can't leave here, Cross. What would we do in the world if we ever got out? I'm not dense. Maybe I just have a better sense of self- preservation than you do."

The anger was making a comeback, partly because Kale was right. As much as Cross hated to admit it. They had been born and raised within the walls of the Department. Tanya never failed to let them know they were nothing more than property. They had no say in what was done to them. No rights. They were things, not people.

Freaks.

Cross disagreed.

"Why do you think she wants to know what we can do?" Cross said.

Kale picked at his clothes. "I don't know. I just know what happens when we say no."

"You can make people do whatever you tell them, you don't think she wants to use that?"

"I told her I wouldn't use it to hurt people. I won't."

"She'll find a way to make you, Kale. You're lying to yourself if don't believe that. If she found out what I can do, you better believe she would use that too."

"You don't know that!" Kale said. "You don't."

Cross tapped the side of his head. "Like hell I don't. She wants to bottle us up and sell us to the highest bidder. I won't pretend to understand why, but I understand one thing. If we let Tanya use us the way she wants, then she will truly own us. Body and soul."

"So what do we do? I don't want to die."

"Not exactly on my list of things to do either. But let me ask you something. Wouldn't you want to do the things we talk about? All those dreams we planned in that crappy treehouse they built for us when we were little?"

Kale wiped his hands down his face and sat cross-legged on the floor next to Cross's cot. "Sure I would. But they were just dreams. Stupid dreams. They're not real."

"What if they could be? Think about this for a minute. All those things Tanya wants us to do. She thinks she knows what we're capable of, but only we know the truth. What if we did it Kale? What if we showed her exactly what we can do?"

Kale's eyes grew wide and terrified. He shook his head and backed away from his brother a little. "No, we *can't!*"

"Oh we sure can. You just don't want to."

"She'll kill us for sure if we try."

"Not if we get out. I can't take this anymore, Kale. We are not property. We deserve a real life, but I can't leave without you. I won't."

Kale's eyes glimmered with unshed tears, his whole body vibrated with fear. "You'll never give her what she wants." It wasn't a question. Kale knew the answer as well as Cross did. They could read each other's thought as easily as reading words on a page.

"She'll kill me first."

Kale took a deep breath and let it out slowly. "Then she'll have to kill both of us. When? When do we do this?"

Cross felt a grin spread across his face. Despite the beating, he felt light. A weight had been lifted from him. He had no idea what the future held, but he thought, they might actually have a chance at one.

"No time like the present." Cross stood. He pushed the pain down and did what Tanya had wanted him to do for her.

With both hands he made a scooping gesture in the air around him. The room temperature dropped as a glowing light grew between his hands. It grew until it was a seething ball of energy waiting to do as Cross commanded. He turned and saw Kale's face brilliant in the light.

Vaguely aware of the alarms his actions had caused he felt far more confident than he should. Confident? Hell, he felt invincible. "We can do this, man."

Kale gave him a tentative nod. "I won't hurt anyone, I won't."

"Not asking you too. Come on, we got company. Just help keep me on my feet, I'll do the rest. Stay close." Cross felt Kale's hand grip his arm. At his brother's touch, the energy he had called up doubled in intensity. They had linked their powers and together they were stronger. Cross sent all that seething energy toward the locked metal door that kept them in a cage.

All that power at his command. Cross knew what he could do, he had just never done it before. He had never had the chance. With every step out of that room his power grew. As did his arrogance. A part of him understood he killed people as they navigated the maze that was the Department. The larger part didn't care. Kale's voice was a small annoying buzz inside his head. He felt his brother's fear, his distress, but Cross was drunk with power. All the times Tanya had him beat, tortured to try to make him show her what he could do.

What do you think of what I can do now, bitch?

Instinct moved him forward. Anger was his motivation. He would take as many of them down as he could and when they were dead and this Department was nothing more than smoldering debris under his feet, he would take Kale and they would both get out.

Giddy with power, he heard Kale's warning too late. Cross focused on the sight in front of him and tried to make sense out of what his mind was telling him.

A man appeared with a gun in his hand. Cross's attention had been on finding a way out, he hadn't sensed the danger until Kale's urgent scream and the sharp jolt of pain as he was pushed.

He was floating. He was nothing. Darkness smothered everything.

CHAPTER 2
TEN YEARS LATER

Finn Doyle's voice was calm, rational even. It was the voice he used when nothing else worked. The voice he used when the situation was about to go tits-up, out-of-control bad. Cross tensed in the back seat of Crown Vic and waited for the bad. He gripped Niko's harness with one hand and the back door handle with the other as he tried to determined just how screwed the situation had become.

"Danny, I don't want to hurt you, I mean does it look like I could hurt you? Come on, we just wanted to talk to you and your sister. What's with all the drama?" Finn's voice held the right amount of sincerity, the perfect lilt of honesty with a dash of contriteness thrown in but Danny King wasn't buying the bullshit. Finn was out of the car walking toward the teenager. Cross could read Danny's terror from where he sat inside the car.

"Finn, this kid isn't interested in having a conversation, you do know that, right?" Cross said.

"Relax, I got this," Finn's voice was quiet. Danny and his sister were deep in the cemetery now, they wouldn't hear. "Besides, Vic is circling around to the other side. Between the two of us, we can handle this."

Cross didn't have to be psychic to understand the kid was unhinged, but it helped. "I think you're underestimating the hell out the situation, partner."

"And I told you, I got this, *partner*."

As if to emphasize Cross's concern on the escalating conditions, a soft whoosh accompanied by a rush of heat blowing through the open car windows stressed exactly what Danny thought of Finn's pleas for rational actions.

"Danny, stop! You have to stop it now!" Sybil, Danny's younger sister screamed at her brother.

"I'll stop when they fucking leave us alone!" Danny was seventeen, scared out of his mind and playing with fire. Literally.

The problem, however, was Danny wasn't quite up to the challenge. He could almost control his fire abilities. It was the *almost* part that scared Cross. He felt the instability in the power Danny was trying to calling up. The situation was getting out of control and he wasn't at all confident Finn understood the danger they were in.

"Finn, we need to get out of here," Cross called from the car. He wasn't even sure Finn could hear him anymore.

Super-heated air rocked the car sideways. Exposed skin on Cross's face and hands tightened in the heat. He smelled singed hair and hot metal and knew play time was over.

"Finn?"

If Finn answered him, Cross didn't hear it.

Time to scramble. He was sitting in what amounted to a metal roasting pan and the kid had just lit a fire under it.

Danny King was out of control. Cross opened the car door, barely keeping hold of the dog as they jumped out. A moment later the driver's side burst into sudden searing flame.

A few feet from the car he tripped. As he slammed into the ground he lost both his wind and his grip on Niko's harness. He lay flat and breathless in the tinder dry grass of the ancient cemetery trying to coax air back into his lungs and hoping he was far enough away from the burning car. He smelled the stink of burning leather and scorched electrical circuits. The pops and crunches of the car as it was consumed by the flames filled his ears.

Too close.

He whispered Niko's name and crawled forward. He tried to call again but only inhaled acrid fumes and smoke. He choked and coughed. Tears streamed down his face as he fought just to breathe. His searching hands found a headstone and he hoped it was big enough to shelter him. He used it to pull himself to a low crouch while feeling for more obstacles with outstretched hands. Niko was gone and his cane was in the car, dammit. He hated feeling helpless. He hated being afraid. But right now he was both of those things.

He tried once more. "Niko! Come!" His voice was hoarse but it had more volume to it this time.

Where is she?

Sudden fear for Niko gripped him. Did the heat get her? Did the flames? With everything happening so fast, Niko could've easily become confused.

Danny and Sybil were yelling at each other. Somewhere close. Sybil sounded terrified. Cross could relate. Both kids had fire talents but zero training. That made them more dangerous than a toddler with a machine gun. Cross stumbled forward, putting another headstone between himself and the car. The grass would soon catch, if it hadn't already. Grass fires spread faster than he could walk.

Where the hell is Finn?

"Niko!" he yelled once more, and the hot air scorched his throat. This whole acquisition had officially gone down the crapper. The only thing he could do now was try to get clear. He just remembered the two way and pulled it from his jacket pocket. After fumbling with the controls, he tried to call Finn but all he got was static. He tried to find Finn's unique aura, but he couldn't calm himself enough to accomplish that relatively simple task.

A wet nose, a soft whine and the next moment Niko was frantically licking at his face. She had overcome her instinctive fear of fire and came back for him. Sweet relief flooded through him as she nosed under his hand. Cross reached for the familiar leather grip of her harness and followed her lead. He had no idea if she was leading him deeper into the cemetery or toward the entrance. He tried to put the heat at his back but everything was hot.

He stumbled over another low headstone. Niko was doing her best but Cross wasn't listening to her cues. He was scared and he knew Niko sensed it. They were both moving as fast as they could, hopefully in the right direction. Cross did the best he could without his cane as he shuffled his feet over the uneven ground. He didn't want to fall and lose Niko again. He hoped Finn was safe.

An unnatural silence replaced the fire's roar.

He was out of time.

The gas tank blew up.

CHAPTER 3

Cross had a killer headache. The loss of his dark glasses in the stumbling dash across the cemetery and the annoying play of shadows, across his visual field didn't help. Neither did Jenner Coben's annoying rant. Cross's boss and the director of the Paranormal Containment Unit, was in the middle of ripping everyone on his team a new one. Cross sat across the desk from Coben wishing he was home in bed. Wishing he was anywhere other than here. Medical had cleared him with first and second degree burns and some minor scrapes and cuts. Niko, her fur slightly singed, sat at Cross's feet as if nothing out of the ordinary had happened a few hours ago.

"Not only did you ignore standard operating procedure," Coben yelled at Finn. "You failed to even call the situation in."

Finn paced in front of Coben's desk. "The heat messed with the reception, and even if it hadn't, exactly when would you suggest I should have called it in? When Danny sucker punched me at his parents' or as we were chasing him across town? Or maybe when we cornered them in the freaking cemetery and he tried to fry us with the flaming ball of death?"

"It should've never gotten that far. Cross, what the hell happened out there? I thought you profiled these kids."

Cross wiped a hand over his face and leaned back in the chair while trying to ignore the escalating pain in his head. "I did. Nothing in their profile suggested they would run. Danny is a classic bully. Loud but basically unorganized and easily intimidated. He should've backed down, he shouldn't have run." Sharp needle like spikes in his head made him wince.

Coben oblivious to his pain continued his rant. "Well, they ran and guess what? They're still running. Now I have, not only the parents flipping out that we lost their kids, but Tanya is breathing down my neck asking why the hell these two are not in our custody. Do you want to tell me why, instead of a nice quiet acquisition we have two extremely volatile, and unpredictable, pyro kinetic teenagers on the run?"

"You okay?" Finn had finally sat down, and now leaned over to whisper in his ear.

A sudden image of his dead brother flashed in Cross's head. Kale giving him that stupid half smile like he used too. It was a flash. There and gone again but the pain it brought with it, stayed. Cross grunted in answer to Finn and hoped Coben would get to the point soon.

"This isn't Cross's fault," Victor Harris, the third member of the acquisition team said. "We all thought they would come in without a problem."

"The parents were on board with all of this," Finn said. "They were relieved when I told them we would take the kids in."

"Then what the hell happened? Cross is your profiler and far be for me to state the obvious but he's also your *psychic* profiler." Coben was working it now. He was pissed and Cross was his primary target. "You told me these kids weren't a problem. You told me this would be a routine acquisition. Exactly which part of this would you consider routine? Someone explain this to me."

The voices around him grated on him like grit in an eye. He knew Coben asked him a question but damn if he could remember what he had said. Another image slammed into his brain. This time it stayed longer. He saw two boys. Kale and him as kids.

Did you ever wonder why they keep us like this? What did we do that was so bad? He heard himself ask his brother in his head.

"What?"

The images evaporated. He realized it was Coben asking him the question. But in his mind Coben was the one he was trying to explain things too.

"Why do we do this?" Cross asked. "Why do we hunt these kids, these people? What did they do that was so terrible they deserve to be locked away, studied as if they're specimens. Freaks."

Cross put a hand to his head as the pain cranked up. He was a ten-year-old whispering in the dark to his brother. He was fourteen, the sole survivor of an accident that had claimed his twin's life. He squeezed his eyes tight, but the pain was all hot and furious trying to bite its way out of his head.

He thought maybe he stood. "It's not fair the way you keep us." He grunted and a hand clutched his arm. He leaned into someone. Niko pushed under his hand and he gripped her harness. "We're people, just like you, only a little different." He wasn't sure if he was speaking the words or if they were simply in his head. He didn't think it mattered. His knees buckled, something wet and warm leaked from his nose. "I can't live like this anymore Kale, I can't." His hands went to his face.

There was only the pain.

Taking bites out of his mind.

More images flashed in agonizing slideshow. Kale. It was just Kale, now as everything else faded.

Out! I need to get out!

Kale grinned at him from inside his head. And then, even the pain stopped, and Cross had a brief moment to wonder- *is this death*?

CHAPTER 4

Finn had asked him once if the blind dreamed. Of course, Cross replied. But the dreams varied. He'd lost his sight at fourteen. Cross only remember bits and pieces of that day. It almost like looking at someone else's life.

A friend of theirs from school was showing off his dad's short-barreled revolver. "It's not loaded," Joey had he said as he aimed at Kale. "I checked, the barrel's empty. Bang bang, you're dead." Joey sneered like he was a gunslinger and pulled the trigger. The barrel was empty, but Joey forgot to check the chamber.

The bullet struck Kale below the breast bone, killing him. It had missed his spine and had gone straight through him, hitting Cross sitting just behind him. They told him he was lucky. The bullet had spared his life taking only his sight.

Cross disagreed. Losing both his brother and his sight in one day didn't feel especially lucky.

He didn't dream often. Maybe he just didn't remember them. But when he did dream, they were either auditory, from his life after he lost his sight, or they were from before the accident. He liked those dreams best because in them he could see like he used to. But he hadn't dreamt of Kale in a long time.

In his dreams his brother was always forever fourteen. Tousled brown hair, dark eyes and a cocky half grin that Cross never could imitate.

This dream started off no differently. Kale sauntered through the door of the hospital room where Cross lay on the bed. That's when he understood he had ended up in the medical unit of the Department.

"Man, when you crash and burn you do it in style," Kale sat on the end of the bed and cocked that grin.

"I never was known for my subtlety." Cross studied his brother. "I've missed you."

"Sorry. I've been keeping an eye on you, so to speak, but it's been a little tricky trying to talk to you."

"It's a dream Kale, my subconscious. You have no control over that. I don't even have any control over that."

"Well, see that's why I'm here now. This isn't actually a dream. It was easier, safer for you to believe that before. Things have changed."

Cross narrowed his eyes. "This isn't a dream?"

Kale shook his head. "Remember when we were little, we would talk to each other up here?" Kale tapped his head.

"Telepathically?" Cross remembered. The psychic abilities he used for the department had been shared by his twin. But he still didn't understand. "You're dead, Kale. I can't telepathically communicate with the dead."

"And this is where it starts getting weird. See, I'm not dead, man."

Cross stared for a second or two. "What?"

"Yeah, look, I know I'm asking a lot of you right now, but I'm short on time. I need you to remember two things, okay?"

"I don't understand." And what an understatement that was.

"Just listen. All we ever had was each other, I know you remember that much. That hasn't changed. That will never change. First, don't trust what anyone tells you but me, not Finn, not Coben. Especially not Coben."

"How do you know about Finn and Coben?"

"Just be quiet and listen. The second thing is what I've already told you—I'm not dead, man. Things are going to start happening fast."

"What things? Never mind. Don't answer that. I must have seriously hit my head because this is whacked."

"Can you trust me? Can you just do that for me? Please?"

Cross considered his brother sitting next to him and decided what could it hurt? "Trust you? What the hell, sure why not. So, let me get this straight; you're not dead, this isn't a dream and trust only you. Is that it?"

"I'm not playing with you, just remember it. This is going to get ugly man. I wish I could help you more, but I can't. Not yet. She promised me she wouldn't bring you in, she promised me you would stay safe. She lied, so now it's my turn."

"What are you talking about?" A small pain started at the base of his skull and Cross remembered the pain when he was in Coben's office.

"This isn't what was supposed to happen."

"Kale?"

"Just watch your back. If you need me, just think about me, I'll know up here." Kale touched the side of his head then gave Cross a long hard look he didn't understand. He hopped off the bed and seemed to just walk away. Then everything when dark again as the dream, or whatever it was, faded.

Cross opened his eyes and blinked to be sure he was really awake. The familiar play of shadows greeted him as did Niko. She pawed at him and he realized that she was lying next to him on the bed. Cross roughed the fur at her neck. "At least I know I can trust you, can't I girl?"

"Hey, you're awake."

Finn's feet hit the floor with a quiet thud. Cross smelled the harsh chemical clean he associated with hospitals and underneath that, Irish Spring, the soap Finn favored. It seemed his partner had been sitting vigil over him. Well at least part of his dream was right. He was in a hospital. But he needed Finn's confirmation anyway.

"Where am I? What happened?" The last thing Cross remembered was being in Coben's office and then the nightmare quality slideshow he still didn't understand.

"Medical. You had, I don't know what you had, but it scared the crap out of me."

"I can't remember," Cross said. In light of Kale's warning be it real or not, he decided to keep what he did remember to himself for now.

"I don't doubt it. You were babbling nonsense then dropped with your hands over your face. You were screaming man, like someone was killing you, then you stopped and went limp. That scared me more than the screaming. You were bleeding too, from your nose and ears."

"Wow that sounds dramatic."

"I thought you were dead. Seriously, don't do that to me again."

"How long have I been here?" It didn't feel long, but that meant nothing. When he woke up after he lost his sight, he thought a day maybe two had passed. Then he found out he had been in a coma for over a month. That blew him away, all that lost time. He wondered what happened to time when it got lost.

"Just a day. They're still running tests and shit but I'm just happy to see you awake."

Niko laid her head on his belly and Cross contented himself by stroking her silky ears. He had no idea what strings Finn pulled to let him keep Niko here, but he owed his partner one. Niko was the one constant in his life. She was with him 24/7, for the last three years. It was a bond no one else would understand. She wasn't just a dog, she was his life, his eyes. His friend.

Something about the visions he had in Coben's office stirred to life. "Finn?"

"Yeah, I'm here."

Cross rubbed his eyes and the pressure building there. "Have you ever asked yourself if what we do is right?" A memory or maybe a feeling of being trapped like a rat in a box settled over him. He didn't like it.

"What we do?" Finn sounded concerned.

"We take people against their will and we put them in cages," Cross couldn't understood why he never questioned that before. It seemed so horrible and clearly wrong to him now.

"Dangerous people, Cross. People who have aberrant abilities, who've demonstrated they are a threat to the rest of us. We keep this city safe from those aberrancies."

"Danny and Sybil King weren't aberrancies. They're just kids. They never hurt anyone. They're just confused as to what was happening to them. All they need is someone to explain it to them. They don't need to be locked away from the world."

"The people we lock up are monsters. You know that, at least you used to know that." Finn sounded like he was speaking to a confused child.

The headache that never went away crept from the back of his skull and wrapped itself around Cross's head. "I think maybe you got that backwards. We fear them because they're different. We fear what we don't understand, so we lock them away and make them perform for us. Maybe we're the ones who should be locked up. Maybe we're the monsters, Finn.

"Cross, partner, you're scaring me a little here. Maybe I should get the doc."

"I don't think I want to do this anymore." Cross winced as the pain dug itself in deeper. "I don't think I ever did." Cross grunted and grabbed his head. Even through the pain he sensed another presence in the room. He recognized Coben's aura but there was someone with him. It had to be the pain, but Cross couldn't get a clear read on the man.

"Cross, we need to talk," Coben said.

Cross was sure he beyond talking.

"And in about five minutes he will in no condition to listen if I don't intercede now."

The man seemed as if he should be familiar to him, but Cross was sure he didn't know him. If everyone would just stop talking he could figure it all out.

"And I need answers, Gabriel. This can wait," Coben said.

"Not if you still want him in one piece it can't. I need to remove the blocks now. They're crumbling and he's receiving conflicting information. It will destroy his mind if we wait, and then what good will he be to you?"

Cross put up a hand, it was all he could manage. He wanted them to stop, wait, something, he wasn't sure and he never got a chance to ask as white hot pain stabbed at his brain, his eyes. He struggled to focus on something other than the pain but it was nearly impossible. Flashes of light exploded inside his head. He was coming apart.

Warm hands touch either side of his head. He wanted to object to the unwanted contact for about a half a second, but then sweet relief flooded his system. The pain backed down.

Relax.

He understood the man Coben had called Gabriel was speaking inside his head. Everything went quiet. All the noise he hadn't even been aware of disappeared. The sharp-edged, hungry pain dulled, and with Gabriel's soft cotton-whispered words Cross didn't understand, it faded until it was only a memory. The words soothed the hurt, they calmed the panic. Much like a mother hushing a babe to sleep, like balm on a wound, Gabriel entered the mental cacophony that was Cross's mind and left only serenity in his wake.

He opened his eyes. The normal shadows that were all that was left of his sight, greeted him. No pain. His head rested back on the pillow as he took a moment to catch his breath.

"Cross?"

He sighed in contentment. "Yeah."

"Are you ready to listen now?" Gabriel said.

"What did you do to me? I'm not objecting, but... I," Cross couldn't find the words. "What did you do?"

"You were experiencing something called a psychic intrusion. As you are aware, it can be quite excruciating. If not taken care of, it would have destroyed your mind. Torn it apart, actually. Not a pleasant way to die."

"I'll agree with you on that. I have no idea what a psychic intrusion is, but I think I should know you. I do, don't I?" There was a familiarity about the man, but he couldn't remember anyone named Gabriel. Now that the pain was gone Cross could detect his psychic aura. His energy signature was familiar but Cross couldn't understand why it should be.

"In another life, yes, you knew me. What I just did was remove several layers of psychic blocks that had been placed in your mind a little over ten years ago."

"Psychic blocks?"

"Walls, if you will. Fortresses built around your memories. They were beginning to weaken. Your past was leaking into your constructed present like a dripping faucet. Small events from your hidden past were starting to bleed into the reality we created for you. The intense headaches, the confusion, the memories that made no sense, were caused by the incongruities trying to make sense in your mind. They couldn't. If I hadn't torn down the blocks, your mind would have been ripped itself apart."

"Keep talking." Cross was calm. It was as if he had waited on this moment for a long time.

"You and your brother were born here. This Department was the only home either of you ever knew until you were fourteen. Your mother was brought in much like you bring in your acquisitions. Her name was Maria, do you remember her?"

Cross squeezed his eyes closed in an attempt to recall a face to go with the name. He got fleeting images of a dark haired beauty who he ran to for comfort. He had always been told his parents died in a car accident when he was very young. The people who raised him were foster parents. "Only bits and pieces." Cross opened his eyes again. "Nothing concrete. I was told she died."

"She died when you and Kale were thirteen."

A sudden image slammed into Cross's brain. He angled his face toward where Gabriel sat beside him. "She killed herself. Didn't she?"

"Yes. Your mother was a delicate thing, both in body and in spirit. She couldn't handle it when we took you and your brother away from her. You were more than old enough to be studied on your own. She disagreed."

"Studied?" his stomach rolled as that trapped rat feeling came over him.

"This Department exists because of people like you and your family," Coben interrupted. "You're dangerous, unpredictable.

People, normal people were getting hurt. People were getting killed so this Department was created to control people like you."

"People like me," Cross repeated.

"The freaks," Coben said with utter disdain.

"Some of us chose to help the department," Gabriel said. "We thought if we could understand what it was that made us different, we could help the others learn to control their gifts. If they weren't a threat then we could help them return and live productive lives in society again."

"You were the exception," Coben took up the thread of the story again. "The only reason for your existence was to be studied."

"Coben, please." Gabriel said. "It would be better if he learned everything from one source. His mind has already suffered a huge insult, let me take it slow with him. This is a delicate situation."

Coben clearly didn't like being told what to do but he reluctantly let Gabriel have his way. "Delicate my ass, but yeah, whatever. Do it your way, just do it quick."

Cross heard Gabriel sigh then he leaned on the bed rail and continued. "Your mother, Maria, had a unique talent. She could *push* people. She could tell someone to do something and make it seem like it was his idea all along. It wasn't the power of suggestion. From what we could figure out, she could actually rearrange a person's brain waves. We've never seen anything like it before. She objected when we wanted to see how far she could take it."

"You wanted her to hurt people." Cross didn't know if it was a memory, but he knew it was the truth. He could read that much from Gabriel.

"Yes," Gabriel said. "Technically we wanted her to tell people to hurt themselves or someone else. The military applications alone were staggering to think about. Then we wondered what would happen if her talents were mixed with psychic abilities."

"You." Cross understood now why the man felt familiar to him.

"Me," Gabriel agreed.

"You're my father." Cross didn't need him to confirm it. He understood that much. He could feel it.

"Guilty. I always preferred to call it a biological contribution."

"You *bred* her like an animal. You used her as a means to an end. You threatened her family if she didn't agree. And after we were born you threatened her with our safety if she didn't play nice." Cross got all that in one huge mental info-dump from Gabriel.

"And when we didn't need her anymore, she took matters into her own hands. I found her hanging in her quarters a few months after you and Kale were taken away."

Cross was grateful for the comforting numbness that wrapped around him. He understood that was Gabriel's doing as well. Whatever he had done to keep his mind from tearing itself apart, also kept him from feeling the outrage, the injustice, the anger he knew he should. It was as if he was learning about a fascinating story instead of his own life. A life that had been taken and then hidden from him for the last ten years.

"The images I had." Cross said.

"Memories." Gabriel confirmed. "When you were fourteen you decided you had enough of us. Or as you put it –"

"I was tired of being a lab rat." Cross could remember the words but it was as if they belonged to someone else.

"Yes. You wanted out. You convinced Kale that you could both just leave. You didn't care what the cost of your freedom was, you were going to leave. You have to understand Cross, we thought you had no abilities. Kale had inherited his mother's *pushing* abilities and believe me when I tell you he was not afraid to use them. He also was a mildly gifted psychic. We had no idea you had been holding out on us."

"What abilities? I'm psychic to some degree, but nothing more than that. Lately not even that, just ask Coben." Cross wished he could see Coben's face to see if he got the jab.

"There was that one incident with the kid in police custody," Coben said.

Cross struggled for a memory and then it hit him. "That was one time. It never happened again. The department cleared me."

"You nearly incinerated the station. You have no idea the red tape I had to go through to explain what happened. We almost brought you in then, but Finn convinced us to wait and continue to watch you."

"Finn?" Cross's attention shifted to where he knew his partner still sat next to his bed.

"And this is where this gets a little tricky," Gabriel said.

"Yeah, like it's all been fairly straightforward so far."

Gabriel ignore him and continued. "We discovered what you could do only when you used those abilities to try and escape."

"What exactly am I supposed to be able to do?" Cross asked.

"You have the ability to manipulate energy."

Cross snorted. "Come again?"

"You are able to gather up ambient energy and using your own body as a conduit, use that energy in any number of ways."

Memories slammed into his mind, shadowy images of melted metal, heat and heady power. The same images he had before collapsing in Coben's office. "We tried to get out." He wasn't talking to Gabriel. He was trying to sort it all out in his own head.

"You did." Gabriel agreed.

Cross wiped beads of sweat that had popped up on his brow away from his eyes. "I did that to them. I killed them?" He didn't want to believe that he was capable of such an act, but he needed to know.

"Yes," Gabriel said. His voice sounded calm, so matter of fact. How could he sound so calm? Cross remembered something else. "It was you, wasn't it? You were the one who shot me."

"You surprised us. We had no idea that you and Kale were synergistic. When linked together the power the two of you wielded was staggering. Over a dozen agents died trying to stop you. Some of them so badly burned by the energy you killed them with, they had to be identified with dental records. They were good men and women simply doing their job and you killed them with no thought or remorse. They were in your way and you thought you had the right. I confronted you. Kale was scared, but he would've done anything for you and you even used that."

Cross shook his head. "No."

"You can deny it all you like. I know you can feel the truth of it. You come by your psychic abilities honestly. I got in your head that day and knew what you planned, which way you chose to get out and I headed you off. I gave you a choice. You could stand down and let me take you back –"

"Or you would kill me," Cross could almost grasp the memory. "I tried to kill you."

"And I tried to kill you back. Kale shoved you out of the way. The bullet meant to take your life put you in a coma for over a month. When you woke, you were blind."

"So why keep me alive at all? You had the choice." Anger, betrayal and confusion were beginning to work through the numbness.

"If it had truly been my choice you wouldn't be here now. I would have finished what I started. Whether you remember it or not, you are a dangerous man, Cross."

Coben spoke up again. "Tanya wanted you alive, but you were unpredictable, volatile."

"Imagine that, a hostile fourteen-year-old, especially one who'd been kept hostage his whole life."

"That attitude is exactly why we did what we did," Coben said.

"And what exactly did you do?"

"We needed you alive, we wanted to study how you did the things you did, how you manipulated energy, but we also needed you to control Kale. The one thing we absolutely could not allow was for you and Kale to get together again. If you knew he was alive we knew you would stop at nothing to get to him."

"Kale is alive?" He hoped but he didn't want to believe it, not if it wasn't true.

"Yes," Coben said.

Cross let out a shuddering breath, he gripped Niko simply to have something to ground him. "You let me believe he was dead, all this time."

"It was necessary. Kale would work with us if we agreed to keep you safe. So we made a choice. We gave you a new life. Wiped all your memories and gave you new ones. Ones we thought you could live with. Ones we thought would make you complacent. Your entire life has been carefully orchestrated, Cross. From the implanted memories, to your foster parents, home schooling, colleges. Your placement in the department. All of it planned, all of it played out according to script. Even Finn."

He turned once more to Finn. "What about Finn?"

Coben's voice sounded as if he might actually be enjoying destroying Cross's life with nothing more than words. "Finn was put in place when you were hired as a profiler for the department. He is, for lack of a better word, your babysitter."

Cross felt heat spread through him. He was breathing faster than he should. He felt like he was floating. His reality had been turned inside out and upside down. "My babysitter?"

His partner remained silent. No denials. No outrage at what Gabriel had said.

"Technically your job was real. Finn and you are partners, but his main job was to watch you. He wrote monthly reports on any problems with the psychic blocks or your implanted memories. Everything was going smoothly until last night."

"Why tell me all this now?" His voice sounded hollow. He couldn't deal with Finn's betrayal right now. "Why not just do what you did to me ten years ago? Why the big reveal. If everything you told me is the truth, then you want something from me. Something I couldn't give you the way I was."

He heard Gabriel grunt. "We knew this day would come. When you collapsed yesterday my vote was to kill you before you woke up."

"At least you're consistent," Cross said. "So why am I still alive?"

"Your brother has been in contact with you," Coben said. "Don't bother to deny it. He already admitted it. He had one rule, no contact. He broke that rule because he understood what was happening to you. He also told Tanya he would refuse to cooperate if we hurt you. For the last ten years, he's done everything we've asked of him just to keep you safe. He wasn't happy when he found out we brought you back in."

"I want to be with him." To Cross it wasn't a request. Kale was alive. After ten years, he learned his brother was alive. All he wanted was to be sure, to touch him, to make sure he was real.

"Not happening," Coben said.

Cross swallowed down the sudden anger that flooded through him. He wanted to smash Coben's face. He wanted to smash something. Instead he took a breath to calm himself.

It didn't work as well as he would've liked. "Fine, it would be easier with your help. But I can find him on my own. I remember we had a psychic connection when we were kids. What do you want to bet we still do?" He flipped the covers off and put a hand on the bed rail with every intention of getting out of bed, and with Niko's help, finding his brother. He didn't know how, but if Kale could contact him, then Cross would sure as hell figure out a way to find his brother. He heard Niko jump off the bed and then in the next instant he felt cold metal encircle his wrist. A harsh ratcheting sound and then the clang of metal on metal.

He moved his hand and was brought up short. Handcuffs. Someone had just handcuffed him to the bed. Cross yanked hard on the cuff. It hurt his wrist and he didn't care. The anger he'd tried to push down flared to life. "What the fuck? Get these off me, *now.*" He didn't raise his voice. He didn't need to. His barely contained rage was in every word. Niko whined, obviously distressed.

"We don't need to do it this way, Cross. It's up to you."

"It's up to me? Fantastic. Unlock the cuffs." Panic begin to take the place of the anger. "Coben, you can't just lock me up. I didn't *do* anything!"

"It's not what you did," Coben said. "It's what you're capable of doing that concerns me."

"And if I don't agree? What then? You going to have Gabriel shoot me again?"

"I don't think it will come to that, but we do have Kale. It might be in his best interest if you cooperated."

And just like that everything changed. He didn't even consider that. Coben's words froze Cross to the core. *We have Kale.*

"You said you needed him," Cross said, hoping they really did.

"We do. I didn't say we would kill him. Perhaps we'll only make him wish we did."

"So what, you put me in one of the glass walled rooms down in the containment unit? So, I'm one of the freaks, now?" Panic definitely was winning out over anger. Cross didn't like that. Anger felt much better.

"You were always one of the freaks," Coben said. "You just never knew it."

Cross pulled on his wrist again. "Jesus, Coben. I work for you."

"Not anymore. If you behave, we'll keep you in medical until they clear you. Finn will stay with you. If you're good. Maybe we'll even set you up in one of the secured witness apartments. Call it a professional courtesy. If you give Finn a hard time, your brother will be the one to pay. That, and perhaps we might make one of those glass-walled rooms available. As I said, your choice." Cross heard Coben leave, his soft-soled shoes scuffing the floor as he walked away. He paused. "Oh and the dog..."

That got Cross's attention. "What about her?" Everything was on alert now. Coben had managed to find the one thing that meant more to Cross than his own life.

"Can't let you keep it." Niko's tags chimed on her collar as she whined. Her claws scrabbled on the smooth flooring as she was being pulled or dragged out of the room.

"Wait, Coben, no. You can't take Niko-" the thought of being without her had Cross in full-blown panic mode. Begging was not beneath him. "Coben, please. Don't do this. She's my eyes, man. I'll do what you want, whatever you want. Please just don't take Niko."

"I'm sorry, Cross. For whatever that's worth, I truly am sorry." He heard shoes on the floor, heading to the door, two pair, Gabriel and Coben he assumed.

Cross tried to jump out of the bed but both Finn and the cuffs keep him there. Niko whined once as she was being led away from his room.

"No, God, Coben, please don't do this. Finn stop him, you have to stop him." Tears streamed down his face with the pleas. He didn't care, any pride he might have had left with Niko. Cross listened, but Niko was gone. He shoved Finn's hand off his chest. "Get the fuck off me,"

Finn took his hand away. Cross gave one last futile yank on his cuffed wrist, pulled his knees up and lowered his head into the crook of his free arm.

"Cross..." Finn's voice cracked.

"Just tell me one thing," Cross said, his head still buried in his arm. "Was any of it real? I trusted you, I thought..." Cross didn't know what he thought anymore. "Fuck it, just fuck it all."

"It's not like Coben said. It was real, it is real. You and me, that's real." Cross heard the emotion in Finn's voice. He could've looked in his head to understand exactly what was real, but he honestly didn't care. He was pulled apart and didn't know how to put himself back together again.

"So Coben lied, you're not my *babysitter?* Your real job wasn't to keep an eye on me?" A sudden thought occurred to him. "Jesus, you knew, didn't you? You knew Kale was alive."

"Shit," Finn sounded miserable which only made Cross furious. What right did he have to be miserable?

"Leave me alone, Finn. Leave me the hell alone."

"I can't." The words were barely more than a whisper, but Cross heard him.

"Right. Babysitter." Cross lay back on the pillow and tried to figure out what the hell happened to his life. Two days ago he was finishing up his report on the King kids. Yesterday he was fighting for his life in an abandoned cemetery and today... *Holy hell, today...*

"What happens now?" he said.

"Exactly what Coben said. He's planning on housing you in one of the vacant secured apartments. If you were anyone else, he'd put you in containment."

Containment was where the department placed new acquisitions until it could be determined how dangerous they were. One room with a front glass wall. Security depended on what abilities the person housed there had. No privacy, no contact. Food and water delivered through an anteroom.

The secured apartment was no less of a prison, but a gilded one. A small living space with a bedroom and bath. The door opened with a key card and cameras recorded live feed from every room. The illusion of privacy was just that, an illusion. The apartments were only a step up from the containment units and were earned with good behavior. It didn't give Cross any comfort that Coben wanted him there. "Yeah, I'm lucky like that."

The spectrum of raw emotions he had just been through in the last few moments left Cross exhausted. He despised self-pity, but thought he was due one moment. "I thought you were a friend." Cross angled his face toward where Finn stood by his bed.

31

"Was any of it real? I thought..." His voice trailed off, he didn't know what he thought anymore. He wasn't sure if Finn's answer even mattered.

"That part was real. I am your friend."

Cross choked out a laugh. "I could almost handle the rest of it, but you Finn," He lowered his head and grinned. "I wasn't expecting that. I gotta give you credit though, you played the part to perfection."

"You don't understand."

That brought Cross's head back up to face Finn. "Really? What part do I have wrong? I might be blind, but the ears work just fine. So let me recap, basically I'm an experiment that went wrong –"

"Cross –"

"No, no let me finish. My entire life has been a lie. Everything I remember, my childhood, my parents. All lies. The father I remember grieving for has been instrumental in wiping my past away to keep me, what? Malleable?" Cross pulled on the handcuffs as he spoke. "And you, Finn. My friend, who turns out to be nothing more than a glorified babysitter, hired to keep an eye on me. Did they pay you extra to get me to trust you? They should have, because let me tell you, you did a hell of a job."

"That's how it started, man. I won't lie to you, but it's not how it ended. I am your friend. You have to believe me on that."

Cross laughed. "You won't lie to me? I have to believe you, trust you? That's good, Finn, that's really good. Coben threatened my brother if I don't do what he wants, that's the only thing I trust right now. That's what I believe."

He was tired and done with talking, done with lies. He turned away from Finn as much as he was able with one hand restrained, closed his eyes and tried like hell to shut the world out for a little while. He needed quiet, he needed peace. He needed to find his center to make sense out of the mess he was in. It was doubtful any of that was going to happen, but he refused to say another word to Finn.

Sometime in the night, sleep took pity on him. He wished he could have said the same for his dreams.

CHAPTER 5

Tanya Santiago sat behind Jenner Coben's desk with her feet propped on the polished wood because she knew it would piss him off. A live feed of Cross Delancey freaking out in medical played on Coben's computer. That she accessed his computer would piss the man off as well. She sincerely hoped so. Technically, as the department's director, Coben was her boss. Tanya was one step below him as the head of the containment unit. She considered it a temporary inconvenience. Someday this office would be hers.

Her chief of security wrapped his arms around her from behind and bent down to nuzzle her neck. "Think we have time for a quickie before Coben comes back?" He turned her around in the leather chair to face him. "We could do it right on his desk," his hands fondled her breasts. "The fat prick would never know."

Tanya trapped him between her long legs and considered Robert's less than subtle request for a half a second. She turned back to look at the monitor again and saw Coben take Cross's dog and leave medical. She reluctantly freed Robert and smoothed her skirt down. "As much as the thought delights me, Coben seems to be finished with Cross." She stood and was nearly as tall as Robert's own six- three. "Coben and I have business to discuss. So, go stand in the corner, put on your stern face and pretend your job is just to keep me safe from all those scary freaks down in containment."

"My job *is* to protect you from all those scary freaks. Fucking you is a perk." Robert pulled her to him and grabbed her by the hair as he ravaged her mouth. Tanya pushed him away and pretended to be annoyed. It was a game between them that she enjoyed immensely.

As Robert stood in his corner looking all tough and proper with his hands clasped in front of him, Tanya leaned back in Coben's chair and waited for him to enter.

He opened the door dragging the dog beside him. Gabriel walked behind them, then stopped when he saw Tanya.

It took Coben a moment longer. "Will you take this animal please," he said to Gabriel. Gabriel took the dog, and only then did Coben turn and notice Tanya.

"You were supposed to meet us in medical for the briefing." He glared at her, obviously annoyed that she not only blew off an ordered meeting but had come, uninvited to his office.

Tanya waited a beat, and only then did she relinquish his chair. "I didn't see the need. Gabriel was the one you needed, not me. Cross is already overwhelmed by the things he's learned. When he's ready, trust me, I will inform him what his place in all of this is. I have a feeling he isn't going to like my rules one little bitty bit." She slowly moved from behind the desk and let Coben sit in his chair. "Nice touch taking the dog." She reached down to touch the lab on the head but the dog lifted a lip in a barely audible growl. She withdrew her hand and met Gabriel's amused expression.

"Dogs are such excellent judges of character," he said.

Tanya sneered at him and moved in front of Coben's desk. "So Cross Delancey is finally back where he belongs. What I need to know now is, how dangerous is he? I won't lose any more people to him. Tell me he's unbalanced, tell me he's a threat and I'll send Robert down to medical right now to but a bullet in his head." She spared Gabriel a caustic glance. "And I can guarantee Robert will not miss."

"I thought you said you needed him not only to keep Kale in line, but for the things he can do," Coben said.

"I do. But that doesn't mean I don't have options. I can control Kale with or without Cross. It would be easier with, but not impossible without. Just tell me he's not a threat."

Coben motioned to the live feed from medical still on his monitor. "I'm assuming you watched the interaction. Right now Cross is trying to figure out what we want from him. We've effectively removed all his support systems, outed Finn to him, introduced him to a father and a brother he thought were dead, told him his entire life was a fabrication. Hell, I even took away his dog."

Tanya watched on the monitor as Cross was sedated to prepare him for transportation, as she ordered.

"All right, as long as you're certain, then I guess Cross Delancey gets to live- for now. But I'm through coddling him, Coben. He is mine for the rest of his life, agreed?"

"Agreed," Coben flicked the monitor off as Cross was being lifted from the hospital bed to a transport litter. "Cross is a smart guy. I'm sure he'll figure out his place in the scheme of things on his own. I'm assuming security is in place." He glanced at Robert standing still and silent in the corner.

"No worries, sir," Robert said. "We've managed to contain more dangerous people than Cross Delancey. My team can handle him."

"I hope so," Coben said as he tidied his desk. "For everyone's sake. Keep me informed. Maybe if he cooperates we can show him it's not so bad. Maybe we can even give him the dog back if he behaves." Coben looked at a smudge on his previously pristine desk top. Tanya glanced at Robert and smirked. Coben took a tissue from the dispenser and rubbed at the mark. "What about Kale?" Satisfied that the desk was once more spotless he balled the tissue up and tossed in the trash can.

"Leave Kale to me," Tanya said. "It seems I have been a bit too lenient with him lately. That needs to change."

"As long as everything is in its place," Coben said.

"All neat and tidy," Tanya said, a small smile on her lips. "You did well with Cross, Gabriel," she said as she walked past him. "I think he might hate you most of all." She gave the dog a wide berth and left the office with Robert at a respectable distance behind her. She could practically feel his eyes on her ass and regretted they hadn't had the time for that quickie on Coben's desk.

CHAPTER 6

G abriel stroked the dog's silky ears. He could feel Niko's anxiousness. Her world was in almost as much chaos as Cross's. She whined and cried for Cross. Gabriel rested his hand on her head.

Animals were far less complicated than human beings. They operated on a simple set of directives. Dogs in particular were easy. Gabriel soothed Niko much the same way he had soothed Cross. In a way she could understand, Gabriel imparted to her that Cross was safe, she was safe. He asserted himself as pack leader and when he withdrew from her mind, she sat with her tail wagging, looking up at him waiting for him to tell her what to do next.

He liked dogs. They were very calming. When your life existed of trying to constantly filter out other people's thoughts, when, if he let it, his world would consist of nothing but the voices in his head, a dog's loyalty and simplicity was extremely comforting. Once, long ago, Gabriel had almost let the voices destroy him. But then he had learned how to control them. He allowed only the noise he wanted, in. It was a talent that had saved his sanity. He took Niko to the fenced in yard outside his quarters to do her business, and then made her comfortable inside.

He felt Tanya's presence before she knocked on his door. She didn't have to knock. They both understood that. For her to allow him the courtesy told Gabriel one thing – she wanted something from him and she wanted it badly. He waited until she knocked, his courtesy extended to her. She hated it when he acted on her intentions before she had a chance.

"Please come in," he said from the sofa. Niko had curled up on his lap and he had no intention of disturbing her. Besides he was tired. They both knew his comfortable apartment and his lack of guards or locks were just illusions. Gabriel was just as much a prisoner at the department as Kale or now Cross. The difference was Gabriel had accepted his role, embraced it even. As a reward he was allowed this limited freedom and of course, the illusion. If he didn't think about it too hard, it was almost as if it were his choice.

Tanya opened the door and let herself in. Behind her, was her ever-present shadow, Robert. Head of security and Tanya's flavor of the month. He had lasted longer than the others though. Gabriel reluctantly had to give the man credit for tenacity at the very least. He did not make it a habit of exploring Tanya's thoughts but from the little time he had been in her head, he understood one thing about her. Loyalty was not one of her best qualities. Tanya used people for what she could get from them and when they gave her everything they were capable of giving Tanya disposed of them. Apparently Robert had a lot to give.

"I need to talk to you," Tanya said. She eyed Niko nervously. "Does that need to be here?"

Gabriel ran a hand over Niko's head soothing both of them. He felt her dislike for Tanya and liked her all the more for that. "I promise she won't bother you, but if it makes you more comfortable..."

Bedroom, please, Niko.

Niko jumped off the sofa and trotted down the hall to Gabriel's bedroom. Gabriel raised his brows. "Better?"

Tanya gave a short exhale, something she did when annoyed. "I suppose it will have to do. Robert," she spoke to the man without looking at him. "Wait for me outside."

Gabriel couldn't tell from the man's body language but his thoughts betrayed him. He was not at all pleased at Tanya speaking to him like an underling. Even if that's exactly what he was.

Robert closed the door behind him as Gabriel made himself comfortable.

"What can I do for you, Tanya?"

"I want to know your thoughts on Cross."

"I already told Coben what I thought. You were there." Gabriel wasn't about to let Tanya know how tired he was. Tanya and the paranormal division made an art form out of using other people's weaknesses against them. Gabriel knew that well. He'd lived the better part of his life exploited by his own weaknesses.

"I know what you told Coben. But I want you to tell me what you really think."

"I would tell you to relax. Cross is, at the moment, emotionally and physically compromised. He is of no threat to anyone except perhaps to himself."

"He won't kill himself," Tanya said. "He doesn't fit the profile."

"For once I agree with you. I saw nothing indicating that in my brief time linked with him. But not being suicidal does not necessarily mean he won't cause himself harm."

"So, what would be your advice concerning Cross?"

"I'd suggest to take it slow and don't push him. Let him adapt to his circumstances, to the things he learned today. He has an entirely new reality to accept. Allow him the time to do that and then you can hammer him again. You plan on developing his abilities, as you did with me, with Maria, with Kale."

Tanya said nothing. She just continued to watch Gabriel.

"If you want him, then you need to work with him, give him something in return."

"The dog?"

Gabriel shrugged. "It would be a gesture he'd appreciate. Don't make him fight you. You won't get what you want from him that way."

"You know, Gabriel, I think this might be a momentous occasion. I actually agree with you."

"I still think this is a mistake," Gabriel rubbed his eyes. They all seemed to forget that what he did for them taxed him. Removing the blocks from Cross's mind had been a delicate process. One he almost didn't manage. But what Gabriel learned in that brief time is what Tanya had come here for. If honesty is what she wanted, he would not disappoint her. "He's dangerous. Maybe not now, but once he understands what he's capable of, he will be."

"We've watched him since he was fourteen, and he hasn't proven that once. Whatever aggressive tendencies he might have had were altered by the bullet you put in his brain. I won't kill him now just because he makes you nervous."

He leaned forward and made sure Tanya was paying attention. "You're the one who's nervous and again I would say with good reason. But your need to exploit him is stronger than your good sense."

"Careful Gabriel."

"You wanted honesty? You wanted truth? Then listen to me carefully. This is a mistake," he repeated. "Cross is a sleeping dragon."

"Dragons don't scare me," she said.

"This one should."

Tanya walked around his apartment completely at ease. She was a woman used to getting her way. She didn't like being told she was wrong. A look of condescension settled across her features. Tanya Santiago was always so sure of herself. It would be her undoing, Gabriel was certain of that.

"I've waited ten years for this particular dragon of yours to show me his teeth. I don't think he has any. I think you're worried about nothing." Tanya stopped in front of Gabriel still sitting calmly. "Tell me you can control him. Tell me, regardless of how dangerous you think he might be, that you can control him."

It wouldn't matter what Gabriel told her, Tanya wanted to hear only her version of the truth. He was too tired to have this conversation. He gave her what she wanted to hear. "He's under control," he said and then added in his mind- *for now*.

Tanya met Gabriel's gaze with unnerving intensity. "Very good. I won't forget your help with this Gabriel. I never forget those who are beneficial. We will talk later about how to proceed. Right now I need to bring Kale to heel. He has been a very bad boy." She grinned and then turned to the door. "Don't worry about your dragon, darling. I believe he is toothless." She opened the door and walked past Robert without so much as a glance. Robert closed the door and Gabriel was left alone once more.

Niko came out from the bedroom and resumed her place in his lap. Tanya's last words kept playing over in his head. He had a bad feeling about the way they were handling Cross. With his hand on Niko's head he spoke to the closed door. "It's not the teeth you have to worry about, my friend," he said. "It's the end of the dragon's tail that'll get you every time."

CHAPTER 7

Cross woke with his hearing muffled and his memory shredded. There were holes in his memory he couldn't account for and that scared him. He opened his eyes and shadows greeted him as did the musty scent a place accumulates when left unattended for too long. No echoes, no whisper of soft soled shoes. There was a feeling of emptiness about this place. He didn't like it. If this was not medical and it wasn't home, then where the hell was he? A TV was on in another room and the bed he lay in had no rails. He wasn't restrained. Whoever put Cross here, didn't worry about him going anywhere.

Out of habit he reached down for Niko only to remember she wasn't there. That pang of loss hit him hard. He pushed it down and sat on the edge of the bed. A wave of dizziness rocked him for a moment and he waited for it to pass. When he searched the bed with his hands, he found a folded cane next to him on the covers.

Without Niko, the cane was the only way he had to find his way around. At least someone had thought about his needs. With one flick of his wrist he flipped the cane open and heard it lock into place. It wasn't the one he was used to, but it was a reasonable replacement.

Someone had taken his glasses off again. He felt for and found a bedside table. Next to the lamp he nearly knocked over were his glasses. He must be in one of the secured apartments, but he'd never known how they were laid out. With one hand in front of him and his cane sweeping an arc at his feet he walked in slow halting steps, trying to find the door.

He was out of practice navigating an unfamiliar environment without Niko. First he bumped into the nightstand on the other side of the bed, which toppled the lamp sitting on it. The light bulb popped when it toppled to the floor.

"Shit." He tried to avoid stepping on the broken glass, but something sharp pierced his heel. As he hopped on one foot, his cane bumped into something hard. A chair?

Frustration built. He was doing everything wrong. He stopped moving and listened. The muffled noise from the TV came from his left, so that's where the door should be. Using the bed and the cane as guides he felt his way around with one hand extended in front of him until he felt the wall. From there it wasn't too difficult to find the door. Before he had the doorknob in his hand the door opened. The volume from the TV increased and disoriented him. But then the scent of bacon and eggs made his stomach growl. He might still be pissed but that didn't mean he wasn't starving.

"I heard something break. You okay?" Finn took his elbow. Cross jerked free. The last person he wanted help from was Finn.

"Kind of a loaded question, considering the circumstances, don't you think?"

Finn sighed.

Cross took a few hesitant steps into the living area and realized as much as didn't want it, navigating would be a lot less frustrating with Finn's help. He pushed the hair from his face. "Okay, you want to help me?"

Finn misunderstood and moved to guide his elbow.

Cross shook his head. "Not like that. Mind if I borrow your eyes for a minute or two? Just until I get my bearings."

"What? Oh, yeah, sure. Have at it." They had used the technique a few times over the years. Cross had the unique ability to enter a person's mind and then literally *see* out of that person's eyes. It wasn't Cross's sight, he was limited to the other person's observations, but it did have its advantages. Like now, when he had no idea the layout of a new place. Finn could help orient him, so he could mentally map it.

Cross closed his eyes to shut out the shadows and took several calming breaths before sending his energy into Finn. When he felt entrenched in Finn's consciousness, he opened his eyes. An immediate rush of light and color overwhelmed his senses. He rocked back a little. Even though he had been expecting it, the sensory overload got him every time. Finn took his arm and this time he didn't object. Little by little his brain began to accept the stimuli and process it as his own even though the information came from Finn. The light dimmed to a comfortable level and the color spectrum evened out until Cross was seeing the room much as Finn did.

"You good?" Finn said. He turned to look at Cross. As a result, Cross saw himself. It was a weird moment when that happened. Seeing yourself literally through someone else's eyes.

"Yeah. Just walk around the room slowly." Cross stayed where he was as Finn did what he asked. The apartment was set up much like Cross had imagined. There was a small living area divided from a kitchenette and by a bar with a couple of stools. The front door was off to the left, and as Finn turned, Cross saw another door. Finn opened it to reveal a bathroom. Next was the bedroom door he had just left. As Finn walked in, Cross realized it was a lot smaller than he'd thought as he groped along the walls. The broken lamp lay on the floor, its shade dented.

"Walk the length and width of the room, will you? Count your steps." It wouldn't be a precise measurement, but it would help. When he crossed the room both ways, Finn came back to stand next to Cross once more.

"That's good, I think I've got it," Cross took hold of Finn's arm. When he withdrew from Finn's mind, there was a moment of nausea and dizziness. He steadied himself with a firm grip on Finn and opened his eyes.

"Okay?" Finn said.

Cross blinked to get used to the shadows once more. Somehow they always seemed darker when he came back. "Yeah. Thanks."

"Wow, don't hurt yourself on that gratitude," Finn said.

Cross didn't want to, but he grinned a little and changed the subject. "How long have I been here?" He moved with a great deal more confidence toward the smell of food.

"Couple hours. You were only supposed to out a few minutes. Guess they were a little generous with the sedative."

Cross found the kitchenette bar and pulled himself onto one of the stools. "They didn't need to sedate me. I think Coben's threat to hurt Kale would've sufficed." He heard Finn move to the kitchen side of the bar.

"They don't trust you. Here" Finn placed a plastic bottle in Cross's hand. "Water. Medical told me to give it to you as soon as woke up. Said you'd be thirsty."

Cross took the bottle and drank deeply as Finn put a plate of food in front of him. "Scrambled eggs at three o'clock, bacon at nine."

Cross ate without speaking until his plate was empty. He had seen the surveillance cameras through Finn's eyes. Everything he said or did was being recorded so there was no point in a real conversation. He had nothing to say to Finn anyway.

He pushed the plate away and considered Finn for a moment before speaking. "So now what? You've done your job and successfully placated me with food and water. If this plays out according to the department's standard operating procedure, that would make you the good cop. That means the bad cops should be walking in any minute now."

"Jesus, Cross, why do you have to be so difficult? I don't think you understand. This isn't a game. Tanya is in charge now, not Coben. She'll get what she wants out of you. Believe that. For God's sake don't put her to the test." Finn almost sounded sincere. Almost like he truly gave a shit about what happened to Cross.

Cross laughed. "Oh, I'm sorry. How truly inconsiderate of me to be difficult. What a bastard I am. I really should thank Coben. Oh and Gabriel, you know, the father who tried to blow my fucking head off when I was fourteen. The same guy who erased my entire life up to that point.

"And let's not forget you." Cross paused for dramatic effect and to try to contain his emotions. "Thank you, Finn. My friend, my partner. Thank you for lying to me, thank you for betraying my confidences, my friendship.

"Now tell me, who should I thank for locking me up, drugging me and monitoring me like a freaking test animal? Coben, Tanya? How about what they've done to my brother? You know, the brother everyone, including you, told me was dead. Who do I get to thank for that?"

Cross slid off the stool. He wanted to hit something, anything, but settled on throwing the cane he still held, in Finn's general direction. He didn't think it hit him but something broke with a very loud and satisfying crash.

"Trust me. I'm not playing any games. They took Niko. They took my entire life and then told me it was a lie. They took my brother. My *brother,* Finn. Now you tell me, what else could they possibly take from me?" His breath came in ragged gulps as futile anger surged through him.

A soft click and the door locks disengaged. He sensed the changed in air pressure and the scent of fresh air as the outer door opened.

"That's enough." Cross recognized Tanya's voice. The door locks clicked back into place behind her. She wasn't alone. The slide of a jacket being adjusted, more than one pair of feet moving. Subtle cologne mixing with her perfume. He wanted to send out psychic energy to see who he was dealing with but that took more focus than he was able to muster at the moment. Anger always impeded his abilities.

"And you must be the bad cop," Cross said. He was beyond caring what they did to him. If Tanya wanted a fight, he was more than willing to bring it. Let her try to lock him in a glass walled room. Let her fucking try.

High heels clicked across the wooden floor to stop a few feet away from Cross. "Finn, you can leave. Your job here is done," It was clear Tanya did not expect to be argued with. Finn did anyway. A small part of Cross respected him for that.

"Wait a minute, what do you mean I'm done? Coben told me to stay here with him until further notice."

"Consider this further notice," Tanya said. "You're being reassigned. Coben will let you know what your next assignment will be. Until then I am putting you on two weeks paid leave."

"No fucking way. Six years and all of a sudden I'm reassigned?" Finn's voice rose with every word.

"Sucks, right?" Cross said.

Finn ignored the comment. "You can't do this, Coben told me-
"

"Coben may be in charge of the department, but I'm in charge of containment. Which means, that I am in charge of Cross. I have no further need of a *babysitter* so if I say you're reassigned then you are reassigned. Leave on your own, Finn or Robert will escort you out of the building." One of the presences Cross had sensed with Tanya shifted, Robert he presumed. Tanya never went anywhere without her security.

Finn let out a growl. "This is fucked." He walked toward the door. The locks disengaged but before he left Finn paused. "I'm sorry, Cross. For whatever that's worth. I'm sorry." He walked out, the door closed and the locks clicked back into place.

"Are we done with all the drama?" Tanya said.

"I want to see Kale," Cross said.

"First rule. You don't get to demand things. You don't get to ask questions. You get a free ride one time because I understand this is difficult. But the sooner you accept your place, the better it will be for you."

That was almost amusing. "Accept my place? As what? A specimen?"

Tanya sighed. It had a sad sound to it. As if she had expected more from him. "Ten years ago, you tried to walk out of this department. In the process you killed a dozen men and woman under my command. Do you remember that?"

"No, I know that's what everyone tells me I did, but no, I don't remember. Maybe the bullet Gabriel put in my brain has something to do with that."

"That's all right because I remember it well enough for the both of us. You want to know what you did? I wish to hell you could see so I could show you the pictures but the description will have to do. As you tried to walk out of the only home you ever knew, you surrounded both you and Kale with a shield of pure energy.

"My agents weren't trying to hurt you. They were only trying to stop you. They were armed with Tasers and Co2 guns-tranquilizers. Non-lethal force.

"I don't know how you did it, but from what we could gather at the time, you boiled them alive inside their skin. Almost as if you trapped their own body heat inside them and then looped it back until they cooked. These were the same people who guarded you every day. Brought you food, kept you safe.

"We were your family Cross and you turned on us. Twelve men and women. Twelve funerals, twelve families I had to explain to as to why their loved ones weren't coming home. So you'll forgive me if I am less than sympathetic to Gabriel's treatment of you ten years ago. As far as I'm concerned losing your sight was a small price to pay for what you did."

The things she described, the things she said he did, they didn't reconcile with who Cross always thought he was. "I don't remember," he said more to himself than to her. He tried to remember something, a feeling, anything. All he got were the images of the dead bodies surrounding him.

He didn't think he was the one responsible for their deaths. He couldn't be. "I don't believe you," he said finally. He couldn't have done the things she said. He was sure of it. If he killed those people the way she described, then maybe he did deserve to be locked up.

"I don't care what you believe. I know the truth, I was there. Even as a child, you always thought you were better than everyone else. You could have helped this department achieve great things, if only you weren't so arrogant. You never cared about anyone except yourself and I can see that time has not improved that particular character flaw."

"You used us. You bred my mother just to satisfy your curiosity for God's sake, and you call me arrogant. I might not have all my memories but I think I do recall that about you, Tanya."

Cross heard Tanya's security move quickly. He put up a hand to ward off the expected assault. His arm was gripped hard.

"No, let him talk, Robert. I want to know what he does remember."

The grip on his arm tightened for a moment before releasing him. Cross resisted the urge to rub the spot. "You want to know what I remember?" Cross thought it was ludicrous. "Sure, I'll tell you what I remember. Up until about two days ago I worked for this department. I remember thinking I was protecting people from some pretty unstable forces out there. I remember thinking my brother was dead. That I grew up with foster parents because my own were killed in a car crash before I could even commit their faces to memory. I remember being shot in the head by the same bullet that killed my brother. Only now I understand that none of that actually happened. I don't remember killing those people like you said, but I do remember the anger. Most of it directed toward you." Cross gulped air as that anger flared to life inside of him. "Maybe you should remember exactly what made you so afraid of a fourteen-year-old boy that you had to brainwash him to make him safe." From somewhere deep inside of him Cross listened to that anger. He raised his hands and scooped raw energy out of the air. He felt it seething as he held it between his palms.

"I'm giving you one chance to stop this now, Cross."

"Why? So you can put me in a cage like you did with Kale?" Kale, God he needed Kale now. Kale could tell him what happened that day. He was the only one who could. He would believe Kale. "I want to talk to my brother."

Cross never heard Robert move this time, but in the next moment his entire body seized up with pain. He dropped to the ground, unable to breathe, unable to move. The energy he had collected dissipated. His entire world was pain. When he could, he sucked in air and rolled into a ball grunting out small noises he never heard himself make before.

"That's what's called an attitude adjustment. Robert just discharged a Taser into you. That was the lowest setting. Do you understand?"

"Fuck," Cross choked out the word. He had never felt anything like that before in his life. At least not that he could remember. He was pretty sure he never wanted to feel it again.

"I'll take that as a yes. Stand up."

Cross did his best to comply, but his body still wasn't taking orders from his brain. A rough hand pulled him to his feet and shoved him into a chair. All Cross could do was breath. "I've been more than patient with you," Tanya said. "That little demonstration you just provided is more than justification for what I am doing. You see, Cross, whether you remember it or not, you are one of the dangerous people you used to protect us from. You might not remember what you are capable of, but I sure as hell will never forget."

"What the fuck do you want from me?" Cross yelled when he finally caught his breath.

Instead of an answer the Taser was shoved into his side once more.

Cross sucked in air and tried to back away, but he had nowhere to go. Once more raw pain coursed through him as he fell to the floor again. It was worse this time. He was sure the Taser wasn't on the lowest setting anymore.

Again rough hands grabbed him and threw him back in the chair. His body still seized from the jolt it had taken.

"You don't ask the questions." Tanya reminded him. "As far as Kale goes, let me make this perfectly clear. You've been told your brother is alive. That's as much of a concession as you get. That's more than I wanted to give. You will not talk about Kale. You will not even mention his name again. And you most certainly will not see him, let alone speak to him. Ever. If you break any of those rules or dare to threaten me again there will be no more warnings. I will do nothing to you. I will punish Kale. Do you understand?"

Cross's body still shook with remembered pain. He might not believe the things Tanya said he did, but he sure as hell believed she would do exactly what she said she would to Kale. He swallowed and lifted a shaking hand to wipe at his face.

For the first time since he woke up in medical, Cross was afraid. He hated that. He hated that Tanya made him feel that way.

Holy fucking fuck!

"Do you understand?" Tanya asked again. He felt the Taser pushed against his side and jumped at the contact.

"Yes. Yes, I understand." He held his hands out in submission, hoping the answer would satisfy her. He froze until he felt the

Taser prongs removed. He let out a pent up breath, then slid off the chair and collapsed to his knees.

"That's better," Tanya said. "Now we can begin."

Something cold started deep inside of Cross.

Begin what?

CHAPTER 8

Cross couldn't remember what she wanted from him. Whatever it was, it was clear he was not satisfying her demands.

Tanya would ask him a question. He would answer. Robert would hit him, or if he was feeling particularly creative, he would use the Taser.

At first she wanted him to show her what he was capable of doing. She wanted him to try and call up the energy as he had when he threatened her.

He couldn't. He didn't know how.

He tried to tell her that, but she wasn't interested in excuses. Tanya wanted results and Cross failed her at every turn. Eventually he lay in a heap on the floor, crying like a child, begging her to stop, promising her things he couldn't possibly give her, if only she would stop. He didn't remember being taken to the bedroom, he didn't remember much of anything except Robert and the Taser.

He didn't want to move, for fear they were waiting for him to wake up to start all over again, but stiff muscles begged for release. He turned to his back and an involuntary groan escaped his lips. He desperately needed to talk to Kale. If he ever needed his brother to show up in his head, it was now. But maybe Cross could show up in Kale's head. Cross had told Finn the truth about them communicating that way when they were younger. But that had been before a bullet and little brainwashing had messed with his abilities. He didn't know if he could contact Kale that way anymore. Until recently he had no reason to try. He'd thought Kale was dead. As much as Tanya wanted to know what Cross could do, he wanted it more. He simply couldn't remember how.

Kale. It all came down to Kale. If only Cross could talk to him, he could figure everything else out on his own. Tanya might be waiting for exactly this. Maybe that was the purpose behind the endless questions and beatings.

Cross didn't care. Kale. He closed his eyes and tried to concentrate on his brother and nothing else. Just Kale. It wasn't easy. He hurt everywhere and he had no idea if what he was doing was even feasible. The only image he could grab onto was that of his fourteen-year-old brother. Cocky grin, messy hair and attitude.

I need you, man.

His brother had told him he was the only one Cross could trust. Kale had been the one to warn him, the only one who had watched out for him even when he wasn't aware of his presence.

But what if Kale was just another lie.

Cross couldn't write him off that easily. He'd done that once already when he believed Kale to be dead. The bond they had ran far too deep. If Kale was alive, he deserved more than becoming only a ghost of a memory.

You there, man?

Cross was too desperate to feel stupid, so he tried again. Hell, maybe he was going crazy, at this point he didn't care. A quick slide into insanity might be preferable to this reality.

Come on Kale, if you are alive, I need you now.

"Hey man."

Cross opened his eyes. Kale was sitting next to him on the bed "Hey." He didn't question why he could see Kale. He assumed it worked much the same way as when he saw through Finn's eyes. He didn't wonder why after days of silence his brother had finally appeared to him. As relief surged through him, all Cross could feel was gratitude.

"Told you they were fucking with you," Kale said.

Cross grunted out a laugh. "Can't argue with the truth." He turned his head to get a better look at his brother. He looked like he always looked, forever fourteen.

"Are you a ghost, Kale? Or am I crazy?"

"Are they still going with the whole, *Kale's dead,* thing?"

"They told me a lot of things, not the least of which is that I'm a sociopath with homicidal tendencies." Cross motioned to his eyes. "They also told me you saved my life."

"Fuck that. Fuck them. No way. This is not what was supposed to happen. You were supposed to stay safe. Listen to me. I don't have a lot of time, but you need to know, no matter what they tell you, no matter how they mess with your head, this- you and me? That's real. You trust this and nothing else. Do you understand?"

"And how do I know you're just not something else they're messing my head up with? They told me you were dead, then they told me you were alive. I don't know what to think."

"Point taken. Okay, here," Kale pulled up the sleeve on his right arm and turned it over. From wrist to elbow there ran an old faded scar. "Do you remember this?"

"I don't know what I remember anymore," Cross said.

"Just look." Kale took hold of Cross's left arm. He rested it on his knee and pushed the sleeve up revealing an identical scar.

"Let me help you remember." Kale held out his hand.

Cross took it, he had never touched Kale before when his brother appeared to him. The hand he grasped was solid, and cold like marble. A slight static shock flowed through him at the contact. Then suddenly a flood of images filled his mind. Kale was helping him to remember. He was seeing Kale's memories.

A tree house built under a sky light in the enclosed garden. It was small and they were always guarded when they used it but it was the best place a ten-year-old boy could ever ask for. For Cross and Kale it had been a refuge. The ritual had been Kale's idea, of course, but Cross had no problem with it. He wasn't scared. He remembered thinking--*this is cool.*

He didn't know where Kale had gotten the knife, let alone how he sneaked it past the guards, Tanya would have had a fit but that, too, was supremely cool. "It's a promise," Kale told him. "A promise made in blood can never be broken, understand? It's the most excellent promise anyone can ever make and is broken only on the threat of death. So, don't make it unless you mean it. Okay?"

"What's the promise?" Cross was already rolling up his sleeve.

"That no matter what else happens, we'll always be there for each other."

"I don't need to cut myself to promise you that."

"I know, me neither. But that's now. What about when we grow up? What if we forget? This will remind us. This will cover all the 'what ifs' that might ever happen, you know?"

That had made sense to Cross, but at ten he could never see how he would need to remind himself that he and his brother would always be a part of each other. But it seemed very important to Kale, so he'd nodded and he solemnly swore the oath.

Kale held the blade under a candle's flame until it was red hot and then made his little speech. "I will always be there for you, no matter what. I would give my life for you, Cross." And then without any hesitation he sliced his forearm. The blood had been impressive, but it hadn't scared Cross. It took a hell of a lot to scare either Delancey boy. Then it was Cross's turn. He'd repeated word for word Kale's speech, substituting his brother's name for his own, and then he cut his arm. It hadn't hurt nearly as much as he'd thought it would.

With both wounds bleeding freely, the brothers placed their arms together so the blood would mix. It was a purely symbolic gesture since they were identical twins. Their blood was already shared.

They'd never told anyone.

Cross remembered now. He glanced down at his arm. Faded but still visible was the thin scar. A promise made in innocence. A promise he'd meant with all of his heart. He looked over at Kale. He stared into eyes he imagined looked much like his own. He saw hope in those eyes. Hope that Cross recalled the past that still shone brightly for Kale. He also saw raw need and desperation.

Cross wasn't sure for what. "I remember." The memory was faded, but it was there. Cross nodded in thought. "I remember."

"I would still give my life for you, Cross. They're going to tell you I did things, bad things. I didn't, at least not all of it." Kale gave a quick jerk of his head, squeezed his eyes closed for a moment and wiped at a thin trickle of blood coming from his nose. He looked like he was in pain.

When he opened his eyes again his voice was quiet. "Okay, this is the important shit. You gotta go man. You gotta find a way to get out of here, because they're never gonna let you go. That was never part of the deal. If you don't believe anything else I told you, you have to believe that."

Cross examined the marks on their arms, identical but opposite, just like Kale and him. "I believe you."

Kale nodded in approval. He seemed relieved. "Good. I think I can give you something to work with here," He squeezed his eyes shut as if some external force was trying to vie for his attention. Cross felt it too. "Wait for a distraction, you'll know it when you see it."

"Maybe it's not overly apparent, but I can't see anything. I'm blind, remember."

"You can see through other people, use that. Use anything you can. They'll kill you if you stay. They'll end up killing both of us. I'm going to try and take out the generator. Everything here, the locks, alarms, all of it, is electric. If I can mess with the system, it'll give you a chance. Take it."

"What about you? How can I get to you?"

"Don't worry about me. Just get out." Kale paused for a moment. He reached out to touch Cross but at the last moment pulled his hand back. "I'm real Cross, don't let them make you believe I'm not." Without waiting for Cross to answer, Kale vanished and Cross's world went dark once more. He rubbed the scar on his arm and felt a little lighter. He decided he didn't care if he was losing it.

He chose to believe in Kale.

I would give my life for you Cross.

A part of him wondered if that was exactly what Kale was planning to do.

CHAPTER 9

Finn sat at the small outdoor café in SoHo waiting for Vic. An expresso sat in front of him growing cold. He had tried to stay away, but he couldn't get the image of Cross as he left him in that room, out of his head. For two days he'd roamed his loft, but he had no appetite and sleep wasn't to be found. Tanya had locked him out of the department computers, even deactivated his ID key card. He had no way to get information. That was what was keeping him up at night.

Last night he took a chance and called Vic. Finn figured Vic would either help him or tell Tanya what he was trying to do. He honestly didn't care either way. There was no way he was going back to work for her after this. Not after what she did to Cross. Finn had told both Tanya and Coben months ago that Cross was nothing like they thought he was. He recommended taking him off their radar. Coben had made noises like he agreed with Finn. Apparently not.

Finn glanced at his watch. Vic was late and not for the first time, Finn wondered if he was being set up. He nervously surveyed the area around the café to look for any obvious government vehicles. When he turned back, Vic was sitting opposite him at the table. His stylish gray Armani suit, crisp with seams so sharp you could cut yourself on them. Black reflective glasses gleaming in the afternoon sun.

"Shit, you scared the crap out of me," Finn let out a breath. "I was beginning to think you weren't coming."

The barista came by and took Vic's order. When she left, he turned to look at Finn for the first time. "I almost didn't. You are officially *persona-non-grata*. Anyone talking to you or seen with you is going to end up in the same boat."

"Then why are you here?" The man didn't look the least bit worried. He sat back relaxed and in control. Finn had always admired that about Vic, but right now it only annoyed him.

"Because I don't like ultimatums. I don't like what went down with you, and mostly I really don't like what is happening to Cross."

The barista came back with Vic's black coffee. Vic charmed her with a smile, and took a cautious sip.

"How is Cross?" Finn said.

"He's been with Tanya for the last two days. How the hell do you think he is?"

"Fuck. He doesn't deserve this. The worst part is he thinks I betrayed him."

"Really? That's what you think the worst part is? The way he might perceive your actions in all of this. Jesus, Finn. She spends all day asking him questions he has no way of answering and then her security guys *discipline* him with a Taser. I have the joy of watching it all on live feed."

Finn closed his eyes trying to get the image of Tanya having Cross tortured out of his head. When he opened them again he realized what Vic had just said. "You're on the monitors?"

Vic seemed to understand where Finn was going. "Don't get any ideas. I can't help him, Finn. No one can. Tanya owns that boy now."

"He was our partner. We were a team. I can't forget about that. Can you?"

"I can if I want to keep my job."

Finn played with the small ceramic espresso cup. "What did I do? What the hell did I do?"

Vic took off the sun glasses. His soft brown eyes narrowed as he spoke. "You did your job."

"My job? I betrayed my partner. My friend. I don't think that was in the job description. Can you really sit there and tell me that after all the time you've spent with Cross, he's nothing more than a job to you?"

Vic retuned Finn's glare, his expression unruffled. "I wouldn't be sitting here if I did."

Finn put his head in his hands. "Jesus, we eviscerated him. I know he started out as a job, an assignment but I swear that's not how it ended up."

Vic studied Finn for a long while as he sipped his coffee. The scrutiny made Finn nervous. "What?"

"I don't know, I guess I'm not buying the whole 'woe with me' thing. Exactly what did you expect would happen to Cross in the end? As much as you want me to tell you it wasn't your fault, you know differently. Cross was your job. There was never anything else. You were hired to profile the profiler. You can't deny that now because you like the guy."

Shame sat like a hot rock in the pit of Finn's stomach. Truth was something he had no defense against. "Yeah. Guess I was a little too good at my job."

"Did you honestly think Tanya and Coben would forget about him?"

"I hoped."

"And who the hell have you worked for? Seriously Finn, face the facts. You did the job you were hired for. Now when Tanya does exactly what you knew she would do, you're sorry? You want to know why Cross thinks you betrayed him? Because you did."

Finn narrowed his eyes and stared right back at Vic. The words stung all the more because he couldn't deny them. "I guess I thought I could protect him, shield him if I had too."

"Didn't quite work that way, did it?"

"No, it didn't." Finn sat back. Vic sipped his coffee as if he were on vacation. Not a care in the world. "Why did you come here?" Finn said. "You could have told Tanya or Coben I called, and they would have made sure I never set foot back in the department."

"I guess I could have, but then I would have missed the opportunity to make you squirm a little before."

Finn sat forward, his attention fully focused on Vic. "Before what?"

"Before I tell you Cross is not as alone as he thinks he is. That's what I came here to say."

"What's that mean?"

Vic finished his coffee and wiped his mouth with a napkin. "Do you really want to help Cross or do you just want to wallow in self-pity?"

"Do I really need to answer that? Yes I want to help Cross. I don't care if he hates me. I know he has that right. I helped to put him in Tanya's hands and I would like to make that right if I can. So I guess the next move is yours. My hand is on the table. If you are here for Tanya then I guess I'm screwed. If you're really here to help Cross, then tell me what I have to do."

"Don't do anything stupid Finn. Stay clear of the department. Do exactly what Tanya wants you to do and forget you ever knew Cross Delancey." Vic stood, put a couple bills on the table, straightened his jacket and walked away.

Finn watched his back as he disappeared into the crowd. He had no idea what Vic's word games meant. All he could think of were the images Vic had placed in his head-Cross at the mercy of Tanya and her security team. He pushed away from the table in frustration. "Fuck."

He wondered if Cross would survive long enough for Finn to tell him his side of things. Vic's parting words were not lost on him, but Finn knew one thing. There was no way he was sitting back and waiting for something to happen. No way in hell.

CHAPTER 10

Robert gave one final upward thrust and shuddered as he came. Tanya bit the side of his neck gently as she collapsed on top of him. The man might have his flaws, possessiveness being one of them, but damn, he could curl her toes in bed. He had lasted far longer than her other lovers because of that alone.

She rolled off of him and reached for the sheet that had been kicked to the floor sometime in the last hour. As her heart rate returned to normal and Robert sprawled next to her, she reached for the remote. She saw his scowl of disapproval as the monitor flared to life. Tanya turned on the live feed into Kale Delancey's cell.

"Seriously? Can't you forget about that freak for more than an hour?" Robert said.

"Darling, you forget your place. That freak pays your bills."

The black and white feed showed Kale pacing the small confines of his cell. There was no audio but Tanya didn't need one to know her charge was agitated.

"It's not like he's going anywhere. I don't get it. You got a sick thing going on with him. I don't like it."

Tanya let the feed play, but she put the remote down and turned to face Robert. The man was all hard long lines of nothing but muscle. His face wasn't bad either. His most attractive quality, however, was he did what he was told. All those things were reasons he shared her bed. But his jealously over how she chose to keep Kale in line might push him out of it if he wasn't careful. "You don't tell me how to handle Kale. We've had this discussion."

Robert clearly didn't like being dressed down but his tone changed. "Yeah, I know. I know. I just don't get it, that's all."

"You don't have to get it, Robert. All you have to do is continue to keep me satisfied and leave Kale to me. He is fragile and now that Cross is back in a cage where he belongs, Kale is going to act out. I expected this. We've made plans for this, have we not?"

"Yes." Robert sounded petulant now, which annoyed her.

"So, we follow through with those plans and we have nothing to worry about. Kale requires energy to *push.* We simply keep him exhausted. If he has no energy left, he can't *push,* he can't contact Cross and he will do as I say. Simple."

"I still don't like it."

"You don't have to like it, darling. You just have to follow orders. Besides, with Kale occupied doing busy-work, I will have more time left for non-work related activities." Her hand slipped beneath the sheet so Robert wouldn't have to think too hard about what she meant. His mood immediately improved. Tanya didn't object when he assumed the dominate position this time. He needed to be mollified and besides she had a better view of the live feed from this angle. She didn't care if Robert understood why she handled Kale the way she did.

All she cared about was the fact that she was the one in charge. She called the shots. No one would tell her how to run her unit. No one would deny her because she was female. No one would take anything from her ever again. What was hers, would stay hers. She would fight to keep it that way.

Sometimes it seemed that was all she ever did, fight just to keep what was hers. First it was her body. When her own father took that from her as a child, she fought just to live. When she grew up, she fought her way out of that life and learned, when she entered the military, that life would always be one fight after another. The trick was to win them or learn from them.

There was never defeat. This was no different. She had learned one lesson from her father that would not be forgotten.

Sex was as much of a weapon as any knife or gun. And Tanya was a fast learner. She wielded that particular weapon with practiced expertise. Even with Robert, there were no emotions involved. Emotions are what nearly destroyed her when she was young. They were a weakness, and Tanya was not weak.

So, as Robert grunted and sweated on top of her, she watched Kale and she planned exactly how she would use him to gain control over his brother. That was the real challenge, and Tanya would do whatever was needed to win. Anything less was simply not an option.

CHAPTER 11

He had never done anything like that before. The amount of energy he used was terrifying, even for him. But Tanya had convinced Kale he could do it. More than that, she told him if he wanted to keep Cross safe he would at the very least try. What else could Kale do?

Even before they had brought Cross in, Tanya had him practicing something new. She wanted him to *push* from a distance. She had talked to him about it but she hadn't had him try it until now. It had worked with the subject in the next room or even on another floor of the same building. Never any farther.

Today's plan was to push everyone in a crowd. A crowd more than two miles away. When he objected and told her he couldn't, that it would take more energy than he had, she'd told him in graphic detail what she would have done to Cross if he failed.

So he *pushed.* All of them, all at once. It wasn't a difficult suggestion- she simply wanted him to tell all those people to look at their watches at the same time. Just a quick glance at their left wrist whether they wore a timepiece or not. And it had worked. It had worked even better than he'd expected. It worked so well the results scared him.

Maybe it was good thing Tanya kept him locked up, away from everyone.

His nose started to bleed before he was even through. Now Kale lay on his back in his little room, staring up at the ceiling. His brain felt as if it was leaking out his ears. He wiped blood from his face with the back of his hand.

Getting hit by a truck might have been more pleasurable than what he had just been through. He remembered his face hitting the concrete floor of his room as the *push* ended. Apparently someone had seen fit to drag him to his bed. He didn't remember.

He opened his eyes expecting the pain in his head to increase and he wasn't disappointed. He brought a hand up to rub the pounding behind his eyes and noticed an IV tubing taped to the back. He had no memory of them doing that either.

Guess they thought I did a good job.

Normally if Kale over did it, he was left to his own devices until he healed, but then he was usually trying to piss Tanya off, not help her.

He desperately wanted to contact Cross. He needed to give him the distraction he promised. He had to help him get out. But he couldn't. Not now. He didn't even have enough strength to search for his brother's unique aura in the mass of humanity at the department. This was the closest physically they had been in ten years.

Tanya would not be happy if she knew Kale had been in contact with Cross again and Tanya was a scary person when she wasn't happy. He knew it was only a matter of time until she figured it out. He never could hide things from her from long.

But this time it was more important. He didn't care what Tanya did to him, but right now he couldn't contact Cross if he had to. He was totally tapped out. Even the hand he lifted to his head felt too heavy and he let it drop back to the mattress. Blood smeared on his arm where it had brushed against his face. When he looked down, he saw more blood on his shirt and even on the mattress.

Damn.

He closed his eyes and had nearly drifted off despite the headache, when the door opened. He feigned sleep, knowing full well who had come to see him.

She sat on the edge of the mattress near his knees.

He opened one eye. Maybe it would hurt less if he only used the one eye.

"I'm proud of you Kale. It worked perfectly." Tanya seemed pleased. One manicured hand pushed hair from his face. "You have to be more careful," she whispered. "We almost lost you. Can't have that now can we."

"Cross?" The single word cost him, but he needed to know. If he couldn't find out on his own, maybe Tanya would do him this one favor and tell him about Cross.

"Cross is none of your concern. You know that."

Kale squeezed both eyes shut. "Please." He despised the pleading tone in his voice but he was too hurt and too wiped out to even pretend to be witty or devious. What was worse, he knew Tanya knew that as well. He understood that was the point. If he was exhausted, he couldn't help his brother.

"Please, what, Kale? Please tell you that Cross is alive? That he is devastated now that he knows the truth about his life? Tell you that Coben and Gabriel totally destroyed him, that we have isolated him from everyone and everything he thought of as the truth or a friend? Or please tell you that you were instrumental in bringing him in? That now the betrayal is complete?"

Tears leaked out from behind Kale's closed eyes. No matter how hard he tried not to hear her words, Tanya had made herself understood. She placed a soft kiss on his cheek and wiped the blood from his face with the sheet that covered him. "Now why would I do that Kale, when I know exactly how it would make you feel?"

Silent sobs shook his chest at her words. What had he done? He had only wanted to protect Cross. His entire life-- that had been his singular goal. To protect Cross. He had only managed to drag him down into the pit with him. The monsters were swarming and Cross didn't even know how to identify them.

What did I do?

"Why would I tell you that in your condition? Rest, Kale, heal." A gentle hand caressed his face. "No further contact. Is that understood?"

He didn't need to answer. He hated that Tanya knew exactly how her words had affected him. The mattress moved as she stood. With his eyes still closed he heard her walk to the door and knock to be left out.

I'm sorry, man.

He knew Cross couldn't hear him, not now. But he would do exactly as Tanya told him do. He would rest and he would heal. And when he was well enough he would make strong on the promise he had made to himself all those years ago. He would keep his brother safe. Tanya might not have realized it yet, but she had started a war that Kale was more than willing to finish.

Hold tight, man. This isn't over.

CHAPTER 12

Cross made a decision. He wasn't crazy and Kale wasn't dead. Whether or not that belief was based on reality didn't matter. Not anymore.

For nearly a week he waited for Kale's distraction and when it didn't happen, Cross understood what he had to do. He could stay where he was and let Coben and Tanya dictate his actions, or he could take control of his life.

Bit by bit anger replaced the sense of helplessness that had nearly overwhelmed him after he'd learned the truth. If there was one thing Cross could never be accused of, it was being helpless. Stubborn pride was what helped him survive those first months of learning how to cope without his sight.

Even if everything Coben and Gabriel told him was the truth, there was no way he was rolling over for them.

No fucking way.

He would deal with this the way he dealt with every obstacle in his life. Head on with no flinching. He desperately needed to find Kale. His brother was alive, and Cross would find him. No maybe about it. But first he needed to find his way out of the room they had locked him in. Yeah, anger was a perfect fit for his situation. The bastards had Niko. That alone was motivation enough.

If Kale wanted him to leave, Cross had no problems with that. Thanks to Finn he now knew the layout of the apartment. The apartments were a few blocks away from the Department's main building, but were staffed twenty-four seven if anyone was staying there. Each unit was rigged with audio and video surveillance devices which fed into a command center staffed by one or two agents.

Cross had no idea if he was the only occupant of the three-unit complex. But it didn't matter. The units were all on the first floor, so no stairs or elevator to navigate. That simplified things.

No one had come to wake him yet, so it was still early. He wished for his braille watch so he knew what time it was, but apparently total disorientation was what Tanya was going for. One of the security guards had the TV on in the next room. Although they didn't have a set schedule, Cross had managed to figure out a routine of sorts.

Tanya never came to him first. It was always one of the guards. So far it had only been two. Robert usually came in with Tanya a few hours after the first guard would wake him up. Cross had heard Robert call him Bernard. He was by far the larger of the two, but Cross felt Robert was the bigger threat. Robert displayed independent thinking. That made him dangerous.

As far as Cross could figure out, Bernard's main job was to exhaust Cross before Robert and Tanya had at him. He had to give the guy props, Bernard was exquisitely good at his job. First thing he would do is turn on everything in the apartment that made noise, TV, radio, stereo, anything that could disorient Cross. It worked beautifully. Once the assault on his senses started, Bernard would begin the physical attacks.

Cross's cane had disappeared the first day, so he was left with only his mental map of the apartment. Bernard would rearrange things to purposely trip him up. It was childish and it shouldn't have bothered him to the extent that it did, but Tanya was very good at psychological warfare.

They always made sure he had enough to drink, but food was hit or miss, as was his sleep. He could pretty much count on starting the day hungry and tired. Bernard would make him breakfast, which Cross was more than welcome to eat, but first he had to find it. It could be anywhere in the apartment or even tipped onto the floor.

They were keeping Cross so mentally and physically spent that there was no way he could even think about using his psychic abilities or, God forbid, contact Kale.

When Tanya and Robert showed up, the real fun started. She was obsessed with having Cross recreate the energy he had used to escape ten-years ago. Once he had managed to form a ball of psi energy in his hands. If he hadn't already been so exhausted he might have been able to do something more with it, but it only lasted a few minutes before it dissipated.

That only increased Tanya's efforts.

By this point Cross was close to his breaking point. That morning when he heard Bernard out in the main living area, Cross was glad for the noise. Feet wedged against one wall of the narrow bedroom entry and his back against the other, he inched up until he was directly above the door. All he had to do was wait. Bernard was predictable. A few minutes after he engulfed the small apartment in noise, he barged into the bedroom.

Bernard stopped in the doorway and clapped his hands. "Time to rise and shine!" It was the same line every time.

Cross dropped. He spread eagle and let go. Gravity did the work for him. His weight flattened Bernard. Cross figured he had one shot at this. If Bernard got to his feet, Cross would never get another chance. Tanya would lock him in that glass walled room for sure.

As soon as he touched the floor, Cross rolled and came up fast on his feet. Keeping Bernard's general location in his head, Cross aimed and hoped to hell he made contact. A low roundhouse and the heel of his foot hit Bernard soundly on the side of his head. From the sound and feel, it was a direct hit. Bernard grunted, but Cross took nothing for granted.

He found Bernard's hair and used it to know where to drive his elbow down hard across the guard's nose. Bernard went limp without a sound.

Cross was breathing heavily. His hands were wet with what he assumed was blood. He almost laughed with the shock that he had actually done it.

"Don't get cocky," he muttered. "You aren't out of this yet." He felt around Bernard's neck. Finding the lanyard he ripped the ID badge off. Now all he had to do was get out before whoever was watching the monitors realized something was up.

Finn had once told him that no one liked monitor duty. Most of the time the people slept at their posts. Especially early in the morning or late at night. Cross had no idea what time it was and he was too keyed up on adrenaline to try to send out any psychic feelers. All he had going for him was speed and surprise.

It took him two tries to find the door. Then he couldn't find the key-swipe and when he did, precious seconds ticked by as he had to swipe Bernard's ID a few times until he heard the soft click of the locks disengage. He had never heard a more beautiful sound.

Sweat poured off him as he closed the door behind him. "To the left, ten steps to the outer-door." Cross had heard them come in enough times that he started counting how many steps they walked and from which direction. The room wasn't meant to be escape proof. Guess they figured a blind guy wasn't going to get too far.

He heard no alarms, no one running after him, nobody yelling at him to stop. Every step he expected either a bullet or the fucking Taser to stop him. Sliding a hand along the wall, Cross counted out the steps to the door at the end of the hallway. He almost fell out of it when it pushed open.

The air rushed over him as he opened the door and stepped outside for the first time in days. The sounds of the city washed over him as he felt for and found a railing leading down stairs. When he reached the bottom he had no idea where to go next. No cane, no Niko, nobody to help steer him in the right direction.

Everybody was moving too fast for him to get a clear lock to use anyone as his eyes. He froze in place until he heard the alarms blare behind him. It would only be a matter of seconds until they found him if he stayed where he was.

"Shit!" His heart slammed against his ribs as Cross stepped into the Manhattan foot traffic. He had never been more terrified in his life. People buffeted against him and turned him around. Twice he stepped off the curb, fumbling against parked cars. Only when he stepped on something sharp did he remember he was barefoot. They had taken his shoes when they took the cane. He found the side of a building and used that as a guide of sorts, but he had no idea where he was going or in which direction. For all he knew he was standing directly in front of the door he just left.

He heard running. Feet hitting the pavement hard and fast, Cross had no doubts that the runners were looking for him.

"He can't have gone far, I want this area completely canvassed." Robert's voice. He was close. Way too close.

Cross froze, unsure what to do, when someone grabbed his arm. His first instinct was to fight. He tried for a simple jujitsu grip but was surprised when his move was countered.

"Take it easy."

He didn't recognize the woman's voice. "Fuck you." His wrist was in a lock, any move he made only increased the pain.

"Yeah, you're a real charmer."

Cross tried to get free, but a small, sharp pain in the side of his neck caused him to suck in his breath. A moment after that, his face was on the concrete and he forgot he was supposed to be fighting back. The noise of the city muffled and then went quiet. His last thought was one word. *Caught.*

CHAPTER 13

Kale lay back on his bed and stared at the ceiling. It had been days since his last contact with Cross. It had taken him longer than normal to recover after the massive *push* Tanya had him do. But now he felt strong, edgy and very caged. Nerves tingled through his system. He needed information and all his normal avenues had been shut off to him. That worried him.

He closed his eyes and searched for Cross. His brother had always appeared to him as a bright light in a dark sea of souls, but as he searched the complex where he was kept and even beyond, all he found was the darkness. He knew they had Cross, but he had no idea *where* they had him, but he never had trouble finding him before.

He'd always found his brother. Always.

Cross, where the hell are you, man?

Instead of an answer, the door to his room opened. He hadn't sensed anyone approaching, which showed him just how preoccupied he was. No one surprised Kale.

Tanya sauntered in and the door closed behind her. The deadbolt and electronic locks clicking into place. Locks were as much a part of Kale's world as isolation. The ceiling lights highlighted her high cheekbones, the full mouth. Such a beautiful monster.

Tanya approached him in two easy steps. "Kale," her voice soft, his name a purr. "I hate to see you so upset. You know you're special to me. When you're in pain, it hurts me as well." She moved closer to him and placed a soft hand on his face. Kale closed his eyes at the contact. The warm vanilla scent of her filled his head. "Talk to me Kale." Tanya's hand slid to his wrist as she pulled him to the bed. Kale sat next to her. She kept her hand in his, and leaned in so her face was close. "Come and tell Tanya what's wrong."

One finger traced the contours of his face, down his cheek, along his jaw, to rest at the hollow of his throat. He could feel the trail her touch had left on his skin as if it were fire, and he grabbed her hand to pull it away.

He didn't want too. He wanted to keep her hand on him. He wanted to feel something other than the cold and pain. He took a deep breath inhaling the scent of her and gathered his courage. He opened his eyes and tried to sound sincere. "No, not this time, Tanya."

She looked confused, hurt even. "Not this time, what Kale?"

"You know what."

"I can see you're upset. I care for you Kale. I know you find that difficult to believe sometimes, but it's the truth. All your life, all I've ever wanted is what was best for you. It hurts me to see you like this. I can help. That's why I'm here. I want to help you." She tilted her head to look at him as her free hand gently pushed the hair from his face.

She always sounded so sincere. Every word the truth, and exactly what Kale was desperate to hear, to believe. He hated that he needed her, that despite the fact that he knew she was using him, he wanted her.

God how he wanted her. How he wanted anyone.

He tried to pretend the isolation didn't matter. But it did. Kale craved what was denied to him. Simple human interaction. Even when he and Cross were little, he was the one who always did as Tanya asked, because it meant he got to see people, to talk to them. To pretend he was normal, if only for a little while.

Back then Cross had been his only companion and that had nearly been enough. But when they took Cross away and locked Kale in a little room it had almost driven him insane.

Maybe it had. Some days Kale wasn't sure. Tanya starved him of affection and then gave it to him in small doses to control him. Kale understood what she was doing. He could see it easily, but he was helpless to tell her no.

"You know I care for you. Haven't I always taken care of you?" Tanya pushed the hair from his face in a gesture that was both loving and terrifying. She wanted something from him. Something big. Kale could feel it.

"I can't."

"Kale," her voice was soft, believable. He always wanted to believe her.

His skin felt hot, it tingled where she had touched him. She was the only woman who had ever touched him. The only person for years, who had ever touched with him with something other than pain.

He wanted to pull her close. He wanted to push her away. He was so cold and her touch burned his skin. He shook with the need for her. He wanted to be warm if only for a little while. Tanya chased the cold away. She also froze his soul every time they were together.

Her hands slid down his neck and began to unbutton his shirt. Kale knew he should push her away. Tell her to get her hands off of him. But he had been alone for so long.

He tried to forget the way his body betrayed him. He took a deep breath and forced himself to remember Cross. "Where's my brother?"

Tanya tilted her head. "Kale, we've had this conversation many, many times. But I'm a patient person. I've told you, Cross is none of your concern. You do what you're told and your brother stays safe. What part of that is hard for you to understand?"

He pulled her hands off of him. He shivered from fear and false bravado. "The part where you brought him in. The part where you decided to change the rules. Cross isn't safe, not anymore." He didn't like the way his voice shook as he said the words. He wanted to brave, he wanted to be strong for his brother.

Tanya kissed him gently on his cheek and then moved so her lips lightly brushed over his. Kale breathed in the scent of her. She was like a drug to him. He needed more warmth, the cold was killing him. He let out a shaky breath, touched her hair and even as he hated his weakness, he kissed her back. His body hardening. The fire burning in his gut spread. He felt alive. But when did what he feel ever matter. He fought to remember what was so important only a moment ago. "I know you brought him in, I could feel him," Kale pull her closer.

Tanya let him. "And how exactly did you feel that, Kale?" she breathed into his ear. "You were in contact with your brother, weren't you?" Her voice had lost its seductive tone and was now accusatory. "What is my number one rule, Kale? The one rule you choose to break time and time again?"

Kale pushed away from her. He couldn't think clearly when she was near him like this. "No contact," Kale said.

"But you have contacted him, haven't you?" She closed the distance between them, her lips trailing down his throat. "I'm disappointed, Kale. But I can forgive you, all I need is for you to tell me the truth." She sucked his ear and little shivers of pure lust bubbled through him.

"You and Cross are up to something. I want you to tell me what. I want you to tell me exactly what you told him."

Panic washed over him. As loving and gentle Tanya could be, she could be just as cruel and hard. He had the scars to prove it. "No," he shook his head.

She looked disappointed at the answer. "Kale," she purred, as her fingers weaved through his hair. "We both know that's a word you are never to say to me. We both understand the consequences of that word. But I can forgive the indiscretion this once, if you'll do something for me. It's what you want anyway. I want you to contact Cross, for me, Kale." She wrapped her arms around his neck, and kissed him deeply, her body moving against his.

He was in hell. He was in heaven.

He turned with her in his arms and pushed her down on the small bed. She let him, but as he started to work the buttons on her blouse she placed a hand over his.

"Will you do that for me, Kale? I am concerned about Cross. He's lost—we need your help to assured that he is well. Isn't that what we both want?

"No tricks, I will allow you to break the rules this one time. Will you do that for me?" Her breath was sweet and warm on his skin. Maybe this time, she meant it. The concern in her eyes seemed genuine, as did her desire for him.

God, he wanted it to be real. He needed it to be real. His heart beat wildly against his chest, his need for her nearly overwhelming all else. He had to concentrate just to get the words out.

"Anything, I'll do anything." he said as his tongue tasted her neck. He straddled her as she undid the button of his jeans. She shoved his pants down past his thighs and then he sucked in a breath as her hand glided over him. Her hand gripped him too tightly, hurting him, but he didn't object. The pain was penance for his giving into her. He embraced the pain.

"Hell," he grunted, as his body took over and gave her what she demanded of him.

They had played at this game for far too long for him to object to it now. Tanya always got what she wanted from him and Kale – Kale got what he craved. He wanted to be stronger than he was, but the truth was he never would be and Tanya knew that.

"Find your brother for me, Kale. Can you do that?"

"I tried," His shaking hand slid up her thigh, pushing her skirt with it. "I can't find him." He stopped and suddenly realized what she was saying. "Wait. Are you telling me Cross got out?"

She stared up at him. "We need him back. He has been deceived. He's vulnerable right now and we know how to help him. He may have been drugged. He'd be helpless. You wouldn't want your brother helpless, would you?"

Cross needed to be safe.

She arched her body against him and images of his brother vanished. All that existed was the woman beneath him.

His hands found her naked breasts. Then his mouth.

"Would it be difficult if he was drugged?" Tanya breathed in his ear.

"Yes, his energy would be dampened." His heard his own voice husked with desire.

Tanya clasped his face in both her hands and his attention was suddenly riveted on her words, not her body. "Then you will look for him again? You'll tell me where he is? I don't want to hurt him, I only want to help him understand what is happening to him. You could be together again. Wouldn't you like that, to be with Cross again after all these years?"

Kale's head cleared a little. He could be with Cross again? "Yes," he whispered. "Yes I would like that."

"Then you will help me find him, won't you?"

"Yes. I'll help Cross."

I promise.

Tanya smiled and Kale took what she gave him. She helped him shed the rest of her clothes and wrapped her legs around his waist.

Kale knew what she was doing, but he was so alone.

He hated Tanya and he loved her. The woman had manipulated him on every possible level and it sickened him. She isolated him, made him need her, she made him love her. He was lost. This was hell and Tanya Santiago was his devil.

CHAPTER 14

Shadows and light. That's all Cross saw as he opened his eyes. Nothing new. He put a hand to his head to try and stop the pounding there and sat up. In that instance he remembered. His attack on Bernard, his panicked run, his confusion. And then the woman on the street. Before the uncertainty could build into fear and the fear into panic, a quiet voice startled him.

"Hey, you're awake."

The voice came from the corner of the room off to his left, it was female and Cross didn't recognize it. "Where am I? Who are you?" He turned toward its source and tried for intimidation.

"My name is Maizey and you are safe Cross Delancey." Ireland sang in every syllable of her words. She didn't sound very intimidated.

Cross rubbed the back of his neck, the source of the pain. "You'll forgive me if I choose not to believe just your word."

"You don't really have to now, do you?" Maizey moved from where she had been sitting and came closer.

He tensed slightly until he heard liquid being poured.

"Here," she placed a glass in his hand. "For the headache."

Cross eyed her suspiciously.

"It's just water, love," she laughed. "The sedative leaves you dehydrated. Come on, drink up. I have someone who has been waiting to meet you."

"And what if I want to stay right where I'm at?"

"Then I guess I'll have to bring him to you. I understand the nerves, but believe me, you have never been anywhere safer in your entire life. Go ahead, have a peek. I know you want to."

Cross understood what Maizey was saying. She was inviting him to have look inside her head. If she was trying to hide something from him, he would be able to tell. He hesitated only a moment before sending psychic energy in her direction.

He had never entered a more open mind. Most people have walls around their psyches. It was purely instinctive, not something done on a conscious level. Cross normally had to pick his way through several layers of protection before he found the truth of who a person was.

Maizey had no layers. No walls. She was refreshingly and candidly open. She had a vibrant aura about her.

Cross found the experience a bit unsettling. He had never met anyone who seemed so alive. The first thing he learned was that she had told him the truth. He was safe here, where ever here was. Not the Department, of that he was at least sure. He felt no threat from her or from the people he sensed around him.

The second thing he learned was the kicker. He pulled the seeking energy back inside and canted his head in her direction. He wasn't worried over his safety now, but he was, without a doubt, intrigued.

She let out a hearty chuckle. "Weren't expecting that, now were you? Come on, love, let's go meet Charlie." Maizey took Cross by one arm and gently guided him out of the room. He sensed the space he walked through was closed in.

"We're underground," he said. It wasn't a question, he knew it to be a fact.

"Safer that way. We have tunnels under every part of this island and most of the other boroughs. But our main division is here in Manhattan."

"Why?" he said.

"Why is it safer, or why underground?"

"Both."

"We are safe here," a deep voice filled with rich baritones and a pronounced Irish brogue answered Cross. He swiveled his head to the left and waited for the man to speak again. "From your Department of Paranormal Research. This place is a safe haven for people like us."

"Charlie?" Cross assumed.

"Indeed. And it is my pleasure to meet you at last, Cross Delancey."

Cross detected no threat from these people, and he sensed a lot of lives in the small area surrounding him. If Maizey was to be believed these people had saved him from Tanya, and wasn't that just ironic. Just a few days ago these people had been his job, his quarry. "And you definitely have me at a disadvantage. It was you that took me off the streets before Tanya could?"

"Not me specifically, but yes we made sure the Department did not get you back under its thumb."

"Let's start with why and work up from there."

"I have waited for this day for over twenty years," Charlie said. "Now that it's here, I find myself uncharacteristically at a loss for words."

"Okay, how about I start with some questions." Without waiting Cross turned to where Maizey still stood. "When I read you, I found that you're like me. You're a psychic."

"You flatter me. I am nowhere nearly as talented as you, but yes, I have the ability. I'm also telekinetic to a small degree, but mostly I can make people see whatever I want them to see, or whatever I don't want them to see."

"That was you. You made them lose me in that crowd." Cross thought he was beginning to understand now.

"Well I had to do something, love. You were like a lost little lamb out there. Ten seconds more and they would've been the ones to jab you with a needle. I can guarantee you wouldn't have woken up in as pleasant surroundings."

Cross's hand went to the tender spot at the back of his neck again. "Thank you, I think. So this place... All of you here..."

"Have some ability or another that would greatly interest that Department you worked for." Charlie said. "Most of us have hidden the truth of who we are our entire lives. Here we don't have to do that. Here we can be as free as anyone can be."

"How do you know me?" Cross said. "How did you know where I was, or where I would be?"

Charlie let out a sad heavy sigh. "We knew where you were because we have inside information."

"What? You mean you have a mole in the Department?" Cross considered that and then dismissed it. "No. No way. I would have known. That was my job. To figure out who deviated from the norm, who had aberrancies. I would have sensed it."

"But you didn't. That's how good my guy is," Charlie said. "Trust me, he was instrumental in giving you the time you needed to escape. But to answer your second question. I have known about both you and your brother since the moment you were born." Charlie sounded almost wistful when he spoke again. "You both look very much like my Maria."

Cross's breath caught in his chest. "Your Maria."

"My daughter, Cross. Maria Clarey, your mother, was my daughter."

CHAPTER 15

This one was going to be tricky, but Kale was reasonably sure he could pull it off. Tanya wanted him to find Cross. He knew he couldn't simply stick with the "'I can't find him'" line. There was no way she would buy it.

He had felt Cross in his head for days now, but he hadn't contacted him. Mostly because Tanya wanted him to. Just the fact that Kale knew his brother was alive sent relief surging through him.

Tanya was furious that her team had lost him. It took a great deal of effort just for Kale to keep from smiling about that. Cross always could take care of himself better than anyone Kale had ever known.

When she entered his room followed by Gabriel, Kale was shocked. He was seldom allowed to see or talk to anyone save Tanya. His isolation had been strictly enforced. If they needed to move him, he was always sedated first. Tanya always had him experiment with his powers through the walls of his room, never face to face. Not for years. For her to actually bring Gabriel to him, told Kale one thing. She was desperate. She wanted Cross back and no one was going to stop her.

Kale wasn't sure he could stop her. He only knew he had to try, because there was no way he was leading Tanya to Cross. No way in hell. Kale would pay for that disobedience. The price would be high, probably messy and undoubtedly painful.

"I assume you recognize your father," Tanya said.

Kale snorted. "My father. Yeah, whatever."

Gabriel looked older than Kale remembered him. Deep lines were etched around his eyes and mouth, but he still wore the same smug expression. Kale hated that expression. He understood Gabriel's psychic powers were strong. Big fucking deal. Kale was stronger, but he wasn't going to let Gabriel—or Tanya know it. Neither Tanya nor Gabriel understood exactly what Kale was capable of. He was counting on that.

"This is what's going to happen," Gabriel said. It was clear he wasn't pleased with being told what to do any more than Kale. At the end of the day Tanya owned him as much as she owned Kale. "I am going to link with you and you are going to find Cross."

Kale turned to Tanya. "I'm crushed. Don't you trust me, *darling*?"

Tanya stroked Kale's cheek with a crimson nail. "Not even a little. Gabriel will basically piggy-back your psychic energy. You are not to alert Cross to his presence, and don't tell me you can't keep his presence hidden. I know you can. I want you to find out who has him, where they have him, and I want you to tell me. Do you understand, Kale?"

"And if I say, no? If I just say screw you and decide not to help you find him, what then? What are you going to do to me? Hurt my brother?" Kale shook his head. He had been thinking about it since she left him spent, but with a clearer head. She didn't care what she did to him.

"Cross is, for the first time in his life, out of your control. He's safe. So if you can't hurt him, then who? Me? Are you going to beat me, torture me? Kill me?" Kale put a fist under his chin and pretended to ponder. "Do what you want to me. I really don't care anymore." That wasn't entirely true, but Kale was proud of his bravado.

Tanya kept the scary grin on her face and circled Kale as if appraising his worth. "Ah, Kale," she sighed. A disappointed parent trying to teach the wayward child a lesson. "I know you don't care what happens to you, and you're right, I can no longer threaten you with your brother's well-being. So what am to do?" She went to the door and rapped lightly. A girl was pushed through the opening. She couldn't be more than fifteen and she was clearly terrified as she looked around with wide, tear-filled eyes. Her hands were tied in front of her and Robert held her by one arm.

Tanya smoothed the girl's hair away from her face. The girl cringed at her touch.

"This is Sybil. Cross and his team were supposed to bring her and her brother in a few nights ago. Instead they managed to level an entire cemetery. While her brother is still out there, we did manage to find sweet Sybil."

Kale knew Tanya. He didn't need to sneak a peek in her head to know this was not going to end well. "Okay, I'm sorry."

He didn't want to look in the girl's eyes. It was as if she understood what was happening as well. "Look, I had to try, okay? Gabriel can go along for the ride if he wants, but I swear I'll find Cross, and I'll tell you exactly where he's at."

Tanya seemed disappointed. "Now, why couldn't I get that level of commitment from you before I had to go and threaten this sweet young thing?" She held a hand out to Robert who handed her his handgun. She held it to the girl's head.

Sybil squealed when the barrel touched her temple "Find your brother, Kale and let Gabriel in. If you lie I will kill her."

Kale held his hands up as if to stop her. "Okay, okay. Just chill." He flicked a nervous glance toward Gabriel. "Go, do your thing man, just stay in the background, I'll cover your presence. He'll never know you're there."

"He'd better not," Tanya said.

Kale felt Gabriel inside his head a moment later. This wasn't going to be easy. He closed his eyes to concentrate and then focused on Gabriel's energy inside his own mind.

Kale *pushed* Gabriel.

I'm doing what she wants, I'm looking for Cross.

It was a delicate thing to accomplish. Gabriel had seen him use his gift. He had been in Kale's head when he had *pushed* other people. Kale had no idea if he would see past the trick this time.

If he did, Kale knew he had killed the girl just as sure as if he'd pulled the trigger. He waited for a moment and *pushed* Gabriel again, this time a little harder.

I'm looking, I'm having difficulty tracking him down- too much pressure, I'm looking!

"He's looking," Gabriel told Tanya. "You have him a bit ruffled with the girl, but he's looking."

Kale smiled on the inside. It was working, now if he could just keep it up until he spoke to Cross. It was almost like splitting a piece of himself off and keeping it blind to what the other part was doing.

Cross! Where ever you are, please, man let me in.

Kale searched in the dark for Cross's energy and almost immediately found him. When Kale zeroed in on him, he was a little startled to find his brother had been looking for him. He took the energy offered to him by Cross, combined it with the ambient energy surrounding them, and materialized inside Cross's mind. That connection was there for him as it always had been.

But there was something different about Cross. Something that hadn't been there before, not for a very long time. Kale understood an instant later when Cross opened his mind to him. Kale's energy materialized in front of his brother. Cross looked good, rested, his mind felt at peace.

"You're okay?" The image of Kale sat next to Cross on the narrow cot. His brother was alone, but Kale could sense a lot of people nearby.

"I'm good, I was worried about you. I wasn't sure how to go about finding you. You were always the one to come to me."

"Where are you Cross? Where is this place?"

Cross ran a hand through his hair and shrugged. "I'm not really sure. I waited for your move, a distraction. When one didn't come, I took matters into my own hands and got out."

"I know," Kale looked sideways at Cross. "You pissed a lot of people off."

"I didn't get you in trouble did I? Tanya didn't hurt you?"

Kale narrowed his gaze at Cross. "I can handle Tanya." Kale suddenly understood what was different about his brother. "You know. Don't you?"

"Yeah, I know the truth. What I did when we were fourteen. What happened afterwards. What they did to me. What you did to keep me safe. What you've done all these years just to keep me safe. Kale…"

"My choice. It has always been my choice."

"I'm going to get you out."

"Tanya's looking for you. That's what I came to tell you. Don't worry about me. You stay clear of that bitch. If I don't contact you, it's because I can't. Do you understand?"

"Then I'll find you –"

"No, you're not listening to me. I didn't spend the last ten years keeping you safe just to see you wind up exactly where I am.

"Don't contact me, Gabriel will pick up on where you are. Stay as far away from this hell hole as you can. Run, Cross. Do what you wanted to do all those years ago, and just run. I got your back, man. I always have."

Kale felt Gabriel pressing him for information. Tanya wanted answers and Tanya wasn't good at being patient. He withdrew from Cross's mind. He didn't want to, but he knew he had to. He couldn't hold Gabriel back for much longer.

He also knew the lie he had to sell. The tears weren't hard to manufacture, and neither was the mental fatigue. Both were real, but not for the reasons he wanted Tanya and Gabriel to believe. He broke contact with Cross and stopped the push on Gabriel. The result left him unbalanced and he staggered. A moment later Gabriel ended the connection and Kale was alone inside his head.

He had fallen to the floor. With a hand on the bedframe, he righted himself. Tears leaked from his eyes as he pulled himself to sit back on his bed.

"What did he learn?" Tanya asked Gabriel. It was clear the information wasn't coming as fast as she wanted it. "Did you find him? Where's Cross?" she demanded of Kale.

He hadn't counted on using so much energy just to keep Gabriel out of his consciousness. He had planned on *pushing* her to believe him. Now he was going to have to make do with lying. "He's dead." Kale put venom and guilt, pain and anger behind the words. "You goddamn bitch. He's dead." He lunged for Tanya, but the fatigue was real enough. Controlling Gabriel's thoughts, while communicating with Cross, had tapped him out.

He fell to his knees and settled for leaning back against the bed and glaring up at her. It was a truth. In his mind, he would never see Cross again. He hoped to hell Gabriel didn't look too deeply at the words. He was too wiped to block him, or *push* him.

"What? How?" Tanya didn't sound happy. The hand holding the gun wavered as she took a step toward Kale.

"I don't know. I don't know. I only know he's dead."

She turned to Gabriel. "Is it true? Is Cross really dead?"

"His grief is real, but I couldn't get a clear read when I was in his head. He was blocking me. I'm not sure how, but I only saw what he wanted me to see."

Kale panicked. He stood, and wobbled until he could lean against the wall for support. "No, that's not true. He saw what I saw. I couldn't get a clear read on Cross because he was dead. Energy still surrounds the body for a few hours after death, so he hasn't been gone long. That's why I had a hard time finding him. That's why it seemed like I was blocking you. I swear I wasn't! I swear it." He was breathing too fast and sweating freely. He'd blown it. He underestimated Gabriel and he blew it. *Fuck!*

Gabriel shook his head. "He's lying. I'm not sure what he did, but I know he's lying."

Tanya kept her gaze locked directly on Kale as she put the gun up to the girl's head and pulled the trigger. Sybil's head erupted in a fine spray of pink mist. Gray mattered splattered the walls of Kale's room as her lifeless body dropped to the floor like a bag of wet laundry.

"No, no." Kale couldn't seem to turn away. The girl's eyes were open and stared up at him, accusing him, blaming him for her death.

"You killed her Kale. No one else, just you. You put your brother's life ahead of this girl's."

Kale slid down the wall to sit on the floor. A puddle of blood spread out from Sybil's head in a growing circle.

Tanya gave the revolver back to Robert. "Take care of this." She motioned to Sybil's body. "Then you get to have some fun. He can't *push* you. Not like this." She looked over her shoulder at Kale. "Just don't kill him. I'm not done with him yet."

Robert made eye contact with Kale and his mouth twitched. "Yes ma'am."

Kale squeezed his eyes shut. He had gambled and lost. Payback was coming and it had a hard on for Kale.

He had played with his guard's minds over the years. Pushing them, making them believe they were seeing things that weren't there. Creating the things he knew terrified them the most. It had been his only form of entertainment. They hated him, but they couldn't touch him, because Tanya said so.

Now she had given each and every one of them the permission for a little payback.

He heard Robert pull Sybil's body from his room and when he looked up he saw the swath of bright red. Her hair had painted the floor in blood.

A moment later three muscle-bond men joined Robert in his room. The door closed behind them with a final metal clang.

"You sure he can't pull any of that shit on us?" one of them said.

"Look at him. I don't think he could shove a six-year-old down the stairs right now," said Robert.

The first guy looked like a shark circling prey. "Sweet." He shook out a coil of rope.

They were right about one thing. Kale couldn't fight back if he wanted to, but that didn't mean he still couldn't screw with them a little.

The third man had grabbed both of Kale's wrists so Shark-guy could tie his hands together.

Kale grinned and waggled his brows. "Boo."

Shark-guy dropped the rope and double-timed it back to the door.

Kale winked. "Gotcha."

"You son-of-a-bitch," Shark-guy returned to where Kale still slumped next to the wall. He tied the rope too tight around his wrists, but Kale still grinned.

"You little fuck. Let's see how long it takes me to beat that cocky look off your face."

Kale saw the backhand blow coming and a moment later tasted blood. His brain buzzed as he felt them hoist him to his feet and loop the rope around a hook above his head on the wall.

His little cell had doubled as a hospital room for him more than once and the hook on the wall had been used to hold IV bags. Today it held Kale. His shoulders burned as they took his weight.

"Yeah, this is going to be fun," the first guy said. They all closed in on him and Kale closed his eyes. Maybe they would forget Tanya's instructions and just kill him. Maybe if they did him that small favor, he could finally find his freedom after all.

CHAPTER 16

" **M**y mother..." Cross couldn't finish the sentence. "You're my..."

"I'm your grandfather." Charlie clarified for him.

Cross needed to sit down. His knees buckled and someone helped eased him down to the ground.

"Quite a lot to take in all once," Charlie said.

"I don't ..." Cross shook his head. "I don't understand." He only had vague memories of his mother and he wasn't sure those could be trusted. "I don't remember her very well. They took my memories. They took me."

The enormity of what had been done to him suddenly hit Cross hard. He angled sightless eyes toward where he thought Charlie was. "I don't even know who I'm supposed to be anymore. What's real, what's fake, who's using me and who I can trust. I don't even know what or who I should be running from anymore." He was suddenly exhausted at trying to figure it all out. Too many secrets, too many lies, not enough truths.

A warm calloused hand touched his face. "That's what family is for Cross. To help you find your way through the maze of lies and deceit," Charlie said.

"What if you can't tell the difference?"

"They have hurt you so much, my boy. Just like they hurt my sweet Maria. She blamed herself for letting them have you and Kale. She was too good, too unspoiled, and they warped what she was until it broke. Until she broke." Charlie's voice was sad but resigned as if he had already grieved through a lifetime's worth of pain. "I can feel you teetering on the brink, Cross. I can help you. If you let me."

Cross had heard the words before, from Gabriel. He gave him a hard grin. "Everybody, suddenly, wants to help me, Charlie. What makes you any different?"

"I'm all for keeping that cynicism alive and kicking," Charlie said. "But what makes me different is I can actually help you see the truth."

Cross grunted. "That would be a great trick. I don't even know what the truth is anymore. How you could show it to me?"

"Well you got me there, I can't show you anything."

"You just said you were going to tell me the truth."

"No, what I said is that I could help you see the truth."

"I'm not in the mood for word games here, Charlie. Just tell me what the hell you want from me. You didn't save me from Tanya out of the goodness of your heart. You want something from me. What is it?"

Cross heard Charlie move to sit in front of him. "What I want Cross, is my daughter back. But Gabriel Delancey and Tanya Santiago took her from me. What I want is a world where people don't hunt each other for what they can take. A world where my grandsons are not treated like someone else's property. I want to live without the fear of being taken from my home in the middle of the night because I am not what everyone else considers normal." Charlie's voice had thickened with emotions.

"What I want, Cross are my grandsons, safe with me." That strong calloused hand touched his cheek. Charlie cupped his face. "I understand your reluctance to trust anyone ever again. I'm not asking you for that. My small talent is a simple one, but perhaps for you it might be the most important one.

"I can help you see past the lies and deceit, Cross. Past all the horrible things that have been done to your mind, I can strip it bare and allow you to see the naked truth. There will be no buffers, nothing to shield you from what you will learn. But when it is done, you will know, without a doubt, what is real and what it is they want you to believe."

Cross sucked in a breath. "You can do that?"

"Yes, I can do that, but the truth isn't always easy to accept. Sometimes it can do more harm than the lies."

Cross didn't even have to think about it. "Do it."

"You can't pick and choose what you see. I can't soften it."

"I get it, I can't move forward if I don't know who to trust. Do it."

He heard Charlie sigh. "I can't erase the damage caused by the bullet. But the things they hid from you, the things you thought were the truth, I can show you what is fact and what is fiction. First I need you to relax. Maizey."

Cross had nearly forgotten the girl was in the room with them. He felt her hand under his arm.

"Here, love." She led him to a low bed, or cot. "Just lie down and close your eyes."

"What exactly does he do?" Cross did as she asked and closed his eyes.

"He's already doing it," she said. "Open your eyes, Cross."

When he did he saw Maizey standing next to him. He turned and took in his surroundings. He stood in the middle of nothingness. A vast, white, featureless space surrounding him. He turned back to Maizey and realized he shouldn't be seeing anything at all. "Where are we? How am I seeing this? How am I seeing you?"

"You aren't really," she said. "This is your mind Cross. What you're seeing is your interpretation of reality."

"My reality is a fuzzy white nothing?" he motioned to her. "What about you, I don't know what you look like. Why am I seeing you?"

"Your reality is what you imagine it to be in your head. You hear my voice and in your mind you imagine what I look like. The nothing around us is there because you have yet to imagine what the world around you looks like. Once Charlie leads you into familiar territory that will change."

Cross thought he understood. She was right about one thing, Maizey looked exactly how he had imagined her. Long auburn hair, with freckles splashed across her cheeks and nose. Bright blue eyes that sparkled when she smiled. She looked exactly how she sounded. Beautiful with attitude. If this wasn't real, Cross couldn't say he minded very much.

"Why are you here with me? If this is my reality, my truths, why are you a part of it. I just met you."

"We have found that sometimes the truth can be, shall we say, unsettling. People can lose their way, reject what they are shown and then not know how to get back to where they started. I am here as an anchor. A lifeline if you need it, a guide if you want one. If you don't need me I will be in the shadows waiting to help you find your way out."

"You linked with me," Cross said. He could feel her in his mind, now that he knew to look for her. But her presence was amazingly subtle and unobtrusive. A whisper. A mere suggestion of a whisper. If she hadn't appeared to him he would never have known she was there at all.

Maizey nodded. "I hope you don't mind. It's safer this way." She closed her eyes briefly and then smiled as she opened them. "Charlie's ready." She motioned behind him and Cross turned to find his past.

He saw himself and Kale. They were six, maybe seven. Wires connected them both to monitors as men and women in white coats hovered around them. Kale and he lay side by side. His brother made faces, trying to get him to smile, but Cross knew he wasn't in the mood to smile. He was mad. He watched the little boy he used to be and he knew he was visiting a memory that had been taken from him. Tests and more tests.

Can you make the numbers on the monitor go up, Cross? Can you move the pencil on the table? Come on, try, you can do it.

Yeah, he could do it, but there was no way he was gonna, not for them. Especially not for her.

Tanya.

The tall blond woman sat at the edge of the bed and smiled at him. He remembered how much he'd hated that smile. How much he'd hated her. He could feel it seething through him now just remembering. How could he have forgotten how much he hated Tanya?

Small isolated things. The tree house built under the skylight in the indoor garden, a small attempt at normalcy. Kale and he looking up at the stars at night through the skylight, a promise made in blood and innocence, planning a future they both knew would never happen. The one thing that remained constant was his love for his brother and the anger. The anger and the hate he had at everyone. God, how he remembered that. How he felt that.

He remembered the punishments for disobedience. At first they were simple, but as Tanya realized withholding dinner was getting her nowhere, she became more creative. The beatings, leaving him tied and broken in his room, isolating him from Kale, from his mother. Tasers had been a favorite method of persuasion. One, as Cross remembered, that had almost broken him. For years he had managed to keep what he could do from them. But as shock after shock coursed through his twelve-year-old body he very nearly gave her what she wanted. He had managed to hold out- or rather pass out. He had known he had to get out or die in the attempt. If he didn't, when Tanya was finished with him, or when he convinced her he was of no use to them, she would have him killed. He'd known this because he had been in Tanya's mind. He understood what she had planned for both him and Kale. They were both to be rented out on military and private contracts. They were nothing more than a commodity to Tanya.

Cross hadn't fully understood what that meant back then, but his resolve to leave only hardened with the knowledge. It took some doing but he convinced Kale they needed to leave. Always the peacekeeper, Kale had tried to protect Cross from Tanya. He would show her anything she wanted, do anything she wanted if only she would leave Cross alone.

He can't do anything. I would know if he could! Cross had heard him tell Tanya that, more than once.

But Cross could do things. Things way cooler than peeking around inside someone's head. And Kale knew that.

Fourteen. They'd melted the locks on their room. Easy peezy. That was one trick Kale had never shared with Tanya- their ability to manipulate ambient energy and use it as a weapon. It was stronger when Cross and Kale linked together.

They were stronger together.

That was the one secret they both strived to keep from her.

"Nothing stops us." Cross had told Kale. "If we stay here, she'll kill us. We get out or we die. We die together."

It was a promise.

God, he could still feel the determination. He remembered feeling terrified as armed men shot at them.

They're trying to kill us! And then in the clarity of Charlie's truth, Cross looked again. The agents surrounding them held Tasers and big rifles with darts- CO2 guns. Tranquilizers.

Tanya had told him the truth. All those people. He had killed all of them. Not one of them was trying to kill him. They were only trying to stop him. How could he not have seen that?

His breath caught in his chest as another truth forced its way into his memory. He had known, and he hadn't cared! He could feel it all now. As clearly as if it were happening all over again. He remembered targeting the men, he remembered killing them. He'd felt nothing at their deaths. No wait, he did feel something – he'd felt vindicated.

He remembered Kale trying to stop him. But nothing was stopping him.

Except a bullet.

Cross went to his knees in his white-hazed reality and try to block the memories, but that wasn't an option, Charlie had warned him. "No more. Please, no more."

But the truth couldn't be stopped. Maizey appeared at his side and helped him up as the memories continued.

He felt hatred, intense hatred and it was directed toward one person. The only person he hated more than Tanya was Gabriel. They might have made it out if not for Gabriel. Images and feelings came at him hard and fast. Anger and fear and then a brief moment of blinding pain.

Waking up. Confusion, darkness. Understanding what they planned to do to him, and being helpless to stop it.

Cross squeezed his eyes closed at that revelation- he remembered being awake and blind, and listening to them discuss what they were about to do to him. My God, how he had fought them. He had tried to refuse Gabriel access to his mind, but he was too weak. Gabriel was too strong.

They took his memories. They took who he was and made him into what they wanted him to be.

Anger, shame and guilt overwhelmed him. Cross opened his eyes and found only the white nothingness once more. Where was he? What had they done to him? He didn't like this anymore, he wanted out. But more than that, he wanted to hurt someone, lash out at the injustice, at the rape of his youth, of his mind. But that rage had been at the core of the boy who had murdered twelve people without a second thought.

My God!

"Cross?"

He whirled toward the voice and found Maizey standing there. What was she doing there? He needed to hurt someone, he needed to let the anger out. God how he needed to let the anger out, but not at her. He gulped air but couldn't get enough in his lungs. Sweat ran down his face, everything spun around him.

Falling.

A hand under his arm steadied him.

"Let me take you home." An angel's voice with an Irish lilt. His blue-eyed angel with the red hair.

"Home," Cross considered the word. "I don't have one anymore."

Maizey smiled and his anger melted. "Yes you do, love. Come back with me."

Cross took her hand and the white nothingness faded into shadow and light.

Cross opened his eyes, the anger only a memory. The guilt very much alive. He took a breath and felt Maizey's hand still in his. "Did you see it too?"

"Aye, I did."

"I killed those people."

"I know. Not that they didn't deserve it."

"They were only trying to stop us and I killed them."

"And if they had managed to stop you, Tanya would have had them kill you and your brother when you were no longer of any use to her. I could see that. Don't you feel any guilt over their deaths, they weren't worth it. That is Tanya manipulating you again."

"Maybe I do belong inside a glass-walled room," Cross said.

"If I thought that was true for one minute I would never had brought you back here."

"I remember. I remember everything." He sat on the edge of the bed and waited until Maizey sat next to him. "All these years, Kale has stayed there to protect me, hasn't he?"

"Yes."

The voice that answered him wasn't Maizey's, and it wasn't Charlie. Cross recognized it easily enough, but that didn't explain why he was hearing it here. "Vic?"

"Surprise."

"You? You're the inside guy?"

"Imagine that. I pulled one over on a psychic," Vic rumbled out a laugh.

"How? I would've known."

"But you didn't, now did you?" Charlie said. "You promised Vic and Finn you wouldn't look in their heads. If there was one thing we were certain of, Cross, it was when you made a promise you kept it. You had no reason not to trust Vic, so why would you go back on your word?"

"Finn?" Cross felt like he was looking at his life from a completely different angle. Like a prism moving in the light, it showed you something different depending on how you look at it.

"He doesn't know. But you have to understand something, Cross, he fought for you."

"Sure right up to the moment he turned me in."

"He never turned you in. You did that all by yourself. He played along to keep an eye out for you. Right now he's suspended. Tanya pulled him from your case. He called me, wanted me to help find out anything I could about you. He wanted to help you, regardless of what it cost him. I just thought you should know that."

Cross considered that, but he wasn't ready to deal with his feelings toward Finn yet. Another thought pulled him to his feet. "I have to get Kale out of there. He's protected me all this time, and now it's my turn. I don't care what happens to me, but I have to get Kale out of there."

"Do you even realize where 'there' is?" Vic said. "Tanya has that boy's head so royally messed up, I don't even know if he wants out. No one sees him but her. No one talks to him but her. She has him so totally dependent on her, he doesn't know how to think for himself anymore."

Cross shook his head. "No, he's come to me. All these years I was never sure if he was real or imagined, but he always came to me. He warned me this was going to happen. He has always been watching over me, looking out for me. I refuse to believe Tanya owns him so completely."

"What do you mean, he's come to you?" Vic sounded confused and maybe even concerned. Cross wondered if he had just betrayed his brother, but then decided these people had saved him. For better or worse he had made the decision to trust them.

"Up here," Cross tapped the side of his head. "Ever since I woke up blind in the hospital all those years ago. He would appear to me in my mind." Cross considered that with his new-found truths. "He was trying to look out for me, protect me, all these years." He turned his head in Vic's direction. "It's my fault he is where he is. My fault Tanya has kept him the way she has. What the hell have I done to him?"

"Don't put that on yourself," Vic said. "You did what you had to do and so did Kale."

"He's my brother. I'll get him out of there if I have to do it on my own."

"No one said you had to do it on your own," Vic said. "I just said it wasn't going to be easy."

The hatred and the anger he remembered from the first time he tried to get them out flared to life inside of Cross. It felt good. He didn't want to forget how good it felt. He didn't ever want to forget that again. "Charlie, will you help me?"

"We've waited over ten years to get you back, both of you. I don't think there's anyone in these tunnels who wouldn't help you."

Cross had finally finished what he'd started when he was fourteen. He had gotten out. But the price had been too high. His sight and his brother.

Tanya had kept Kale like a pet. She'd twisted the truth and used him to perform for her. And Kale had let her to keep Cross safe. If Cross had known, he would have killed Tanya years ago. He knew now. "I am bringing Kale home." The tone of his voice left little to be argued with.

"We," Vic corrected. "We, are bringing Kale home." He clapped Cross lightly across the back. "Welcome to the Underground, Cross. Welcome to being one of the hunted."

CHAPTER 17

Finn was on his third beer. It was a particularly hoppy IPA that tasted smooth going down. Normally he would have appreciated that, but as he watched the sun set over the harbor, all he could think about was how messed up things were. Finn lived in a renovated 19th century firehouse in Battery Park. It was narrow but the open loft and exquisite views more than made up for the lack of floor space. The original wrought iron spiral staircase and fire pole had been preserved. The top of the front wall sported twenty foot arched windows looking out over the harbor. Finn loved sitting in his loft looking out over the water. He loved this hectic, noisy, dangerous city. This is where he normally found his center, his peace. But the last five days that peace eluded him at every turn, as did sleep.

Go someplace warm, Tanya had told him.

Screw that.

His head buzzed with the effects of the alcohol, but he wasn't nearly as numb as he wanted to be, or as he intended to be. He could still think coherently and that wouldn't do. He didn't want to think tonight, because when he did all he thought about was what a douche he was. He pulled on the beer, leaned back in his chair, planted his feet on the loft railing and thought about Cross. What the hell happened? Just a few days ago life had been good.

Now here he was suspended, alone, and cut so far out of the loop he didn't know how to get back.

When Coben and Tanya approached him about a special assignment, Finn had no problems saying yes. Fresh out of the academy and open to the possibilities the secret department offered him, Finn was eager to earn his stripes.

All the paperwork on Cross Delancey made the guy sound like a slightly less evil version of Hannibal Lector, minus the cannibalism. Between him and his brother, they had killed over a dozen special agents in less than twenty minutes with nothing but the energy of their minds. That was when they were fourteen.

He remembered the briefing Tanya had made him watch. A short taped session with Kale Delancey shortly after Cross had been shot...

The film had been in color, but the quality was poor. It showed an obviously upset young boy, maybe thirteen or fourteen years of age. Dark hair worn long and unkempt, bangs nearly hiding the dark eyes beneath. The boy was tall for his age, close to six feet already, but he was thin, all long legs and arms.

At first he was alone in the room. He couldn't sit still, he paced back and forth, tried to sit, then jumped up again, obviously agitated. Soon a door opened and a woman entered, a younger Tanya Santiago. The boy went directly to her. "Is Cross okay?" His eyes glimmered with unshed tears, and his voice went up an octave on the last word.

Tanya put a hand on his shoulder and led him to a chair at the table.

"Kale, we need to talk, okay?"

"I need to know how Cross is. He shot him, Gabriel --He shot him." Shock, tension and exhaustion were evident now as Kale all but fell into the chair.

"I know, Kale. Right now I need you to calm down and I need you to listen to me. Can you do that?"

"We just wanted out, can't you understand that? Cross and me, it's not right the way you keep us here. We just wanted out." There was no conviction behind the words. They were empty excuses made by a boy who knew that his punishment was at hand.

"You and Cross killed over a dozen of my agents. They had families. They were just doing their jobs. And you and Cross killed them because they got in your way."

Tears tracked down Kale's face as he shook his head. "They would have killed us. We felt that." Then one last shred of bravado made an appearance. "If I killed them, I could kill you too, you know. I want to know how Cross is and I want to see him, now."

Tanya smiled, like an indulgent parent considering her misbehaved, but much loved child. "You won't kill me, because I hold Cross's life in my hands."

"He's alive?" a small spark of hope flared in the boy's eyes, the defiance that had been there moments ago now gone.

"He's in a coma, but yes he's alive. If you want me to keep him that way I suggest you put away the attitude, and behave yourself. If Cross lives, you will never see him again. That's the first thing you need to understand. But his life will very much depend on what you do. If you step just a little out of line, he dies.

"Do you understand, Kale? If you do not do exactly what I tell you to do, he dies. This ill-conceived escape attempt has cost both of you. It may yet cost Cross his life, it has cost you more than that. I'm through coddling you."

"What do you want?" Kale said.

It had been apparent to Finn the boy was broken, but Tanya was nowhere near finished with him. She stood and rapped once on the locked door. A man was pushed through when it opened. He looked terrified.

"Who's that?" Kale said. The man obeyed Tanya's pointing hand and sat in the chair opposite Kale.

"It doesn't matter. I want you to *push* him. I want you to tell him to do something he wouldn't normally do."

"I won't hurt him. I already told you I wouldn't do that."

Tanya lovingly patted his face. "Yes you will, because if you don't, I will have them kill Cross. Right now, before we even know if he will survive the coma, I'll have them yank the tubes out that are keeping him alive and I will let him die."

"No," the man whimpered.

"I'm sorry," Kale said softly, but still loud enough for the microphones in the room to pick it up. His face hardened and stared intently at the man. Kale tilted his head to one side as if he were considering something interesting. "I think you should break your fingers, one by one."

The fear left the man's face as he stared back. "Really?" He spoke it like he wasn't sure it was the best idea.

Kale took a deep breath and his voice took on a confident tone that hadn't been there before. "Yes, definitely. I really think you need to."

The man considered the request for a mere moment and then nodded in agreement. "You know, I really think I need to break my fingers." He took his left index finger in his right hand and bent it back at a severe angle. The snap of his phalanges breaking under the pressure was clearly audible on the video. He didn't yell with the pain. He simply moved on to his next finger and repeated the process.

When all four of his fingers had been broken he looked at Kale quizzically. "What about the thumb? Technically it isn't a finger. Should I break that as well?"

Kale looked to Tanya begging her with his eyes to stop. She placed her hand on the man's shoulder, clearly pleased with what Kale had done. "I don't think that's necessary."

Kale looked relieved as he turned back to the man. "No, you don't have to do that."

"Did I do it right?" the man wanted to know. It was obvious he was concerned that he might have failed the task.

"You did fine," Tanya told him. "Why don't you go to medical to have your hand taken care of now." She rapped on the door and ushered the broken man outside. The door closed again and it was just her and Kale alone once more.

"You'll take care of Cross?" he said.

Tanya nodded. "I'm impressed. Tell me, was it difficult to get him to do that? I mean to override his basic sense of self-preservation. How did you do that?"

"I don't know how, I just know I can. It's easy, like breathing."

"What else could you have made him do?"

Kale lowered his head to the table. He seemed exhausted and it was clear he didn't like what he just made the man do. "I don't know," his words were mumbled as he spoke into his arm.

"Anything. I could have had him do anything." He looked up at her again, and his face was impossibly young and innocent.

The film froze there centered on Kale's face.

Finn had never forgotten the anguish in Kale Delancey's eyes as he was forced to hurt that man. Tanya had easily convinced him then that the boy was one of the most dangerous human beings on the planet.

Kale had been in custody ever since and, according to Tanya, not a threat. Cross, on the other hand, they assumed was manageable as long as he didn't remember his past. He had amazing abilities the department wanted to tap into.

Damaged by the bullet in the shooting, the kid had suffered brain damage resulting in his blindness and global amnesia of the event. The department, or rather Tanya and Gabriel had made the decision to exploit that. They'd wiped Cross's memories and reprogrammed him with a new life.

They told Cross who they wanted him to be and how they wanted him to behave. They told him his brother was dead. No brother, no family, the only memories he had were the ones the Department gave to him. His job working at the department was scripted. The post-trauma paranormal abilities he exhibited were for the most part harmless if not fascinating. He was controlled, and Finn had been put into place to keep him that way.

His babysitter.

The first time Finn had met Cross, he was disappointed. Where was the terrifying homicidal maniac the Department had brainwashed in order to control?

Cross was a quiet introvert who preferred to spend an evening home alone with his dog to going out drinking. Dark glasses hid more than just damaged eyes, to Finn they hid a damaged soul, one that Cross tried to hide from the world. At first Cross was hesitant to show the profiling abilities he was supposedly hired for. Until one case changed everything between Cross and Finn.

A kid they had been watching in Harlem. Loner, no friends, stayed out of trouble and off the grid, did everything he could to keep from being noticed, until he made a mistake. He popped a 24/7 gas station.

His name was Derone, he was sixteen years old and the claim was he could manipulate the elements. Finn had badged his way into the NYPD interrogation room where the cops had him detained.

One of the Department's techs had been monitoring the police frequencies. The local police often had run-ins with these kids long before the Department even knew they existed. Finn and Cross had been sent to run interference but the cops already had him in custody.

In the six months they had been working together, Cross had taken a back seat to Finn in every investigation, spoken only when he had to and never initiated any overtures of friendship. Other than an amazing ability to read people, Finn had yet to see anything remotely terrifying about Cross. But he dutifully wrote his monthly reports to Tanya and Coben.

Derone didn't look particularly dangerous to Finn as he sat down at the table and kicked back. "Derone, I know you're probably scared right now, but I'm not a cop. What I am is maybe a way out for you. These things you can do, they freak you out, right? That's why you do the drugs, so you don't have to deal with the things you don't know how to control."

Derone spoke for the first time. "You don't know dick,"

"Finn, we need to leave. Now." Cross, who had been standing next to the door, moved closer to Finn, his attention directly on the boy in front of him. Derone gave a crocodile smile to Cross.

The hairs on Finn's arms stood on end. He got that little ping, the feeling when someone had a gun pointed him.

"See, this boy has some sense to him," Derone said. He didn't moved but all his attention was on Cross.

Finn glanced from the kid shackled to the table to his partner.

A single bead of sweat ran from Cross's temple. His partner tilted his head to one side as if listening to something only he could hear. "Finn, get out of here."

It was a warning given nearly too late. The temperature in the room rose to that of a blast furnace in a matter of a few seconds. Finn watched in fascination as blisters formed on the back of his hands. The next thing he remembered was Cross stepping fast in front of him. Finn was never sure exactly what went down, but apparently one of those suppressed talents emerged.

Later Finn learned that Cross had slipped into Derone's subconscious. He had known the kid was about to fry both of them. In that single instant before Derone turned the interview room into a frying pan, Cross took all that lethal energy and contained it in a ball of white hot compressed energy. He pushed it, all of it, back inside the kid.

Cross had taken a portion of that energy and surrounded them with a protective bubble. Derone and everything in that room evaporated in a superheated firestorm. Cross emerged relatively unscathed. Finn suffered second and third degree burns on his arms and a concussion from when Cross had knocked him to the floor. He would've been dead if not for Cross. Derone was dead, the interview room was toast and Coben had a lot of explaining to do to the NYPD.

Everything changed after that day. Cross refused to talk about what he had done. It was as if it never happened. Tanya and Coben took a heated interest in Cross. They grilled him mercilessly. Cross answered all their questions as honestly and thoroughly as he could. When they realized they weren't going to get more from him, Finn was told to press his partner, to throw him into the deep end to see what other secrets he might be hiding.

But Finn took a different approach. Cross had outed himself to save his life. That was a debt Finn took seriously. Weeks later, after a quiet, uneventful night, Finn offered to drive Cross home. But instead Finn turned toward his loft. Cross picked up on the change in direction immediately.

"Ah, my apartment's two blocks back."

"Yeah, I know. I was wondering, maybe you might want to have a drink or three with me. I mean, if you want. You freaking saved my life man and I hardly know you. It's just, partners should know each other." Finn shrugged and realized Cross couldn't see him.

When his partner said nothing, Finn felt stupid about asking. "Yeah, okay, it was just a thought." He was about to turn around when Cross spoke up. "You got any decent scotch?"

Finn grunted. "My mother is Scottish and my father is Irish. What do you think?"

It was the first time Finn had been with Cross anywhere outside of work. It was as if he was meeting an entirely different person. When they got inside Finn's loft, Cross looked up toward the ceiling, twenty feet above them.

"Feels open in here."

Finn went to the bar and cracked open a fifth. "The views are killer. From the loft you can see clear across the harbor. It used to be a firehouse. They were going to tear it down and I bought it for a song. Did most of the work myself. Straight up or on the rocks?" Finn asked.

"Straight," Cross accepted the glass and Finn waited for his reaction. Cross sipped the whisky and then stopped and turned his head in Finn's direction. "Wow."

"Yeah, I know. My grand-da got this for me last time he was in Scotland. This, my friend, is eighteen-year-old Bunnahabhain single malt. Perfect balance of smoke and peat- in my not so humble opinion."

"If I knew you had this I would have insisted on saving your life a lot sooner."

Finn clinked glasses with him and Cross lifted his drink in solute, then sipped the scotch again. "So, why am I really here, Finn?"

"Really? Are you ever not suspicious? Seriously, I'm not allowed to invite my partner over for a drink? Does there have to be ulterior motives involved?"

Cross sipped again and seemed to consider that. "Which question do you want me to answer first?"

"Come on, I don't know about you, but this job takes up every aspect of my life. I have no friends outside the Department. If you thought I had ulterior motives, why'd you come?"

Cross leaned on the bar, and rolled his drink between his hands. "I'm sorry, but I get this weird nervous vibe from you every time we're together. Almost like you're afraid of me."

That put Finn on the defensive. "You promised me you wouldn't, you know, get in my head."

Cross raised his brows. "And I didn't. Jesus Finn I didn't have too. Hell, Coben could have picked up on the vibes you give out, and Coben is pretty much clueless. I don't know, maybe it's the psychic thing," He motioned to his eyes. "Or the blind thing. Sometimes I freak people out." He shrugged and finished the scotch. "I guess I expect it. I'm used to it."

"Really, you get that from me?" Finn had no idea he was that transparent. "No, man, it's not the psychic thing. Well, okay, maybe a little bit the psychic thing. It *is* kind of unnerving to have your own personal bullshit detector as a partner. I always feel I have to watch every word out of my mouth. It gets a little exhausting after a while, but no, that's not it."

"So, the blind thing then."

"Why the hell would that bother me." Finn was frustrated. How could he explain it to Cross when he couldn't even explain it to himself.

If Cross never took a look in his head than Finn knew he didn't realize what Finn's real job was. But that sure wasn't the reason for his edginess when he was around Cross. He stopped thinking about that when he realized Cross wasn't a threat.

"Okay, so maybe it was the glowing ball of death and destruction."

"Yeah, that was definitely a little unsettling, but I see weird every day, so again, no."

"Then what?"

"It's you, man. You know?" Finn sighed and filled both their glasses again. The scotch was tasting good and left a nice warm trail down his throat. It also gave him the courage to say what he wanted to say. "We're supposed to be partners, right? That means we're supposed to trust each other- with our lives.

"I don't even know you, not even a little. How am I supposed to trust someone I don't even know? You come into the office, you do the time, then you either grab a cab or occasionally let me or Vic drive you home. That's it. I know nothing about you personally. You don't say one word about what's going on in your head. It might have escaped your attention but I am not psychic. I actually need people to talk to me on occasion so I can understand what they're thinking."

"Well, you could've asked," Cross said.

Although he couldn't have seen the eye roll, Cross seemed to realize he'd earned it. "You are way obvious, Finn. I don't have to see to know half of what you want to say is written all over your face. You're an expressive guy, an extravert who gets his energy from external sources, people, places."

Cross sipped more of the scotch. "And for the last six months you have had to put up with me. I don't like people. I'm not big on talking or sharing my feelings, and you take that and turn it around to make it all about you. It isn't."

"I thought you said you weren't in my head." Finn didn't intend to sound defensive but it came out that way.

"I wasn't."

"Right. Then how'd you know all that?"

"Coben pays me good money to be a profiler. I happen to be very good at it and you're ridiculously easy to read."

Finn let out a long breath. "Now I feel like an ass."

"If the shoe fits and all that," Cross grinned. "But I could have opened up more. You're right, though, I guess I have 'trust issues'." He made quote marks with his fingers when he said it.

"You saved my life. I'm not sure if I thanked you for that," Finn said. "In some cultures that means you own me."

"I think we can forgo that," Cross took off the ever-present dark glasses and rubbed the bridge of his nose and then his eyes.

"Headache?"

Cross grinned. "Always, it's okay. It only bothers me at night. When it's quiet and there's nothing else to think about."

"I get that. Not the headache thing, but the too quiet at night thing."

"Night's suck."

"Yeah," Finn agreed. He wondered what kept Cross awake in the night. He wanted to ask but didn't feel he had the right.

He had never seen his partner without the glasses before. He looked disarmingly young and innocent without them. "Do you remember what is was like to see?" He realized how personal the question was and regretted it almost the moment it was out of his mouth. "And crap, I really didn't mean to ask that. I am an idiot."

Cross downed the last of the scotch and shrugged. "It's okay. Give me a refill and I'll tell you you're not an idiot."

Finn poured him another hit. He was feeling the alcohol and thought maybe Cross was a bit buzzed as well. "Yes, but will you mean it?"

"Ah, that would require a degree of drunken debauchery I'm not prepared for and one I'm sure you don't have enough scotch to reach."

"And you have a sense of humor, that's something I wouldn't have guessed."

Cross downed the shot fast and Finn topped him off. His partner was definitely feeling the scotch. Alcohol was a wonderful equalizer.

"There's a lot you probably wouldn't guess about me, but yes, I remember what it was like. Not a lot, but yeah some things."

Finn was seeing an amazing thing : Cross Delancey sharing a part of himself. There was no way in hell he was writing a report up on this. Coben and Tanya could go fuck themselves- or each other, for all Finn cared.

"What things?" Finn said.

"Colors, I think. I've been blind nearly as long as I could see so sometimes I'm not sure if what I remember is real or just my imagination. I see people as different amplitudes of energy. Not colors but in my head I always give them names. The higher the energy frequency, the hotter the color I give them." He shrugged. "Sounds stupid saying it out loud"

"Not at all. So what am I? What kind of energy am I?"

Cross raised his brows and the corner of his mouth lifted in an amused lilt. "You're easy. I see you as non-stop movement. Your energy is vibrant, but hot. You are how I remember red. Warm but unpredictable. Red can burn you if you're not careful."

Finn laughed softly. "That's kind of cool, I think."

"I don't remember much more. Faces of people I knew, places, it's all one big blur in my memory. But there is one thing I remember for a fact. Kale. I remember Kale clearly."

Finn almost choked on his drink. Coben and Tanya had told him they were never sure what Cross remembered about Kale. "Your brother?"

"Yeah. I know we were identical twins, but I never saw it, you know? Kale never cared how he looked. His hair was always too long, but yet he somehow always managed to pull off cool without any effort." Cross smiled warmly at the memory. "And he had this half-cocked grin thing going for him. I never could duplicate that grin."

Cross lowered his head and seemed lost in his past. "I miss that stupid grin. I miss my brother. I always felt as if half of me was lost without Kale." He shrugged and put the dark glasses on once more, hiding his eyes, and his memories at the same time.

Finn raised his glass. "A toast," he said. "To brothers," He waited for Cross to lift his own glass and then they clinked and downed the shot.

"I didn't know you had a brother," Cross said.

Finn filled their glasses again. "I don't. It seemed like such a perfect salute, I didn't want to kill the moment."

Cross nearly inhaled his scotch. "You're an ass."

"Well then, to asses."

Cross clinked glasses with Finn once more.

They finished that bottle of his grand-da's fine scotch that night and began a friendship that had spanned nearly a decade. Until Cross found out it was all a lie.

Except that it wasn't.

Not for Finn, not really. He never put everything in those reports to Coben and Tanya. Just enough to keep them happy. But in truth there hadn't been much more to report. The psychic thing and the one-time ability to channel ambient energy seemed to be Cross's only talents. He had honed them both over the years, but Finn had downplayed that as well.

In his own way, Finn tried to protect Cross as much as he could. He'd shielded him from Tanya and Coben every chance he got. Didn't matter though, Cross still believed Finn had lied to him, betrayed him. Sold him out.

Maybe he had. He hadn't told Cross the truth, was that the same as lying? Finn thought maybe it was.

What truly ate at him though was the look on Cross's face as Coben told him all Finn ever was, was his babysitter. That look of hurt and betrayal is what kept Finn awake at night. The truths they had shared, the secrets, the past. The doubts that clawed away at the back of his brain, Cross had told Finn all of these things. Not all at once. Cross did not trust easily, but Finn had worn him down. Finn had made Cross trust him.

It was fully dark now and the harbor lights filled his windows. It always amazed Finn how beautiful this city could be at night. The darkness could hide the ugly things that existed in the light. At night all Finn ever saw was the beauty. That was the illusion.

He wondered if Cross saw beauty in his darkness. Or if his friend understood that sometimes the illusion was all you ever got.

CHAPTER 18

His cell phone woke Finn. The buzzing aggravated the headache and his mouth tasted like he'd licked an ashtray. He grabbed the phone and put it to his ear. With his eyes still closed he put one hand to his temple to appease the pounding there. "What?" his voice was a whisper.

"Rough night?" Vic's voice was annoyingly chipper. Finn turned over to look at the clock, thinking he had missed something for work. Then he remembered he didn't have to worry about work.

"What do you want, Vic?"

"You weren't answering your door. I wanted to make sure you didn't die or anything."

"Wait. What? Where are you?" Finn sat up on the edge of the bed still holding his head. If he didn't it might fall off his shoulders.

"Standing outside your loft. I come bearing caffeine and sugar."

"You're here?" Finn tried to process that but all he got was caffeine. "Okay, uhh, hold on. Right there." He threw his phone into the tangle of covers, pulled on a pair of jeans and stumbled down the spiral staircase. Appalling sunlight stabbed at Finn's eyes and brain.

As promised Vic was waiting outside. "You better have coffee or I will have to kill you."

Vic held out a Starbucks Venti. "Double shot of espresso."

Finn cracked the lid and took a cautious sip. He leaned against the doorframe and sighed in ecstasy. "You can live." He turned around and walked back inside, knowing Vic would follow him.

He sat down cautiously at the bar. Vic propped one hip against the opposite side of the counter. "I was going to ask how the time off has been treating you, but I can see."

"Don't judge. There better be something in that bag that is mostly sugar."

Vic tossed him the bag and Finn caught it. Inside were two massive bear claws. "Oh, God. I knew there was a reason I kept you around."

Vic wandered around the loft picking up empties and dumping them in the trash. "I'm not sure a double shot is going to help."

"Shut it. I'll take some ibuprofen and down some water. I'll be fine."

"Uh huh. So what has you binge drinking, when I know for a fact that you are supposed to be somewhere warm and far away."

"Coben might have the power to take my badge and lock me out but he cannot tell me what to do on my own time." Finn downed four Motrin with the coffee.

"You sure about that?" Vic said. He motioned to the window overlooking the street. "Brown Honda, four or five spaces down."

Finn leaned forward just enough to see what Vic was talking about.

"Been there all night. Just changed shifts as I was pulling up."

"Watching me? Son-of-a-bitch. Why?" Finn rubbed a hand over his face.

"Cross got out."

Finn lowered the cup he was about to sip from, certain he misheard Vic. "What?"

"Cross is out, as in he is in the wind. The entire department at her disposal and Tanya could not hold one blind guy in a secured building. It would be fair to say she is pissed."

"Holy shit. Cross got out." Finn grunted out a laugh. "That's awesome. But why is she having me watched, I had nothing to do with it."

"Well as far as they know, Cross has no resources, no place to go for help. He is alone and blind in a city he doesn't know how to navigate without help."

"Again, why watch me? I'm the last person Cross would come to for help."

"Maybe. Maybe they think you might want to appease that guilt a little and try to find him." Vic seemed to coolly appraise Finn.

Finn didn't like that at all. "So, what? You're here to feel me out? What makes you think I care what happens to Cross one way or another?"

Vic pulled an empty out of the trash. "This does. How long have we known each other? In all that time how many times have I seen you get plastered? I'll tell you. Never. The Finn Doyle I know doesn't like to lose control."

"Bullshit."

"Truth. I've seen you put a few away, have a good time, nothing wrong with that at all. But this Finn? Sitting in the dark alone, drinking until you pass out? That's not the Finn I know. That's guilt, pure and simple."

Finn narrowed his eyes. "Then I guess you don't know me as well as you think. Thanks for the info and the pick-me-up, Vic, but you need to go now."

"So you can try to lose your tail and put out feelers for Cross? Tanya's got your ass, my friend. She's got your front door covered, your phone tapped and a GPS on your wheels. You're not going anywhere she won't know about ten seconds after you leave."

"If that's true then she knows you're here, too. How're you going to explain that you warned me about her guard dogs?" Finn was trying like hell to figure out Vic's angle but he kept coming up blank. "What's this all about Vic? Why are you here?"

Vic pursed his lips and silently regarded Finn for a long while. The man looked like he had something to say, so Finn let him have the time to figure it out. He wasn't going anywhere.

"What if I told you, that I knew where Cross was? What if I told you I could take you to him?"

Now Finn was confused. "Then I would tell you that if any of that was true and if Tanya does have my placed wired, you are in one shit-load of trouble."

Vic seemed to think about that. "Yeah, I don't think so. Maizey, why don't you introduce yourself to my good friend here."

"Hello, love."

Finn turned. A young woman with long red hair stood behind him. He hadn't heard anyone come in the door. He would've have heard that. He was pretty sure he would have heard that. "Who are you? How'd you get in?"

The woman stood next to Vic and gave Finn a wide grin. "I walked in through the front door, love."

"Vic, I am not amused. Tanya sent you. Take Red here and get the fuck out of my house." Finn couldn't come up with any other explanation. Vic was sent here to see if he would flip. To see if he would try and find Cross on his own. He would, but he sure as hell wasn't going to let Tanya or Coben in on that. And right now he wasn't letting Vic in on that either.

"God, I hope not," Vic looked smug. "No one saw us come into your loft Finn. No one is listening to us now. As far as Tanya or anyone who is listening is concerned, you're still passed out."

There wasn't enough caffeine or sugar in the world to appease the monsters pounding on the inside of Finn's head. All he wanted to do was go back to sleep and Vic and the chic he brought with him had worn out their welcome. "And as interesting as all that might be, I don't care. Get out and take her with you."

"He is so not a morning person," Vic said to Maizey. Suddenly the amused expression Vic had worn since Finn had let him in changed. "I'm not fucking with you Finn. I have never been more serious. But, knowing you like I do, I sense a little demonstration is in order. Maizey, if you would be so kind." Vic sat down at the bar.

"So, let me see, what would convince you?" Maizey circled around Finn, her brow creased in thought. "Well, it would seem you already realize that I might be a person of interest, as your

Department calls us, but you're still not quite sure if I'm friend or foe just yet."

"What part of get out are you having difficulty understanding?"

Maizey appeared amused. "You wear your anger like a shield, as you do your humor. You despise people getting too close to the truth of who you are, so you try to keep them at a comfortable distance. That is exactly why Cross scared you at first. Not the rumors of his instability, no you didn't believe that. What scared you was the fact that he is a psychic. He could worm his way through all those layers and walls you put up for everyone else. That's why you had him promise to stay out of your head."

Finn narrowed his eyes at the woman. "Yeah, I get it you're a psychic. Now get the fuck out of my head and get the fuck out of my house. Both of you." His voice was controlled fury. He tried to control the temper that boiled just beneath the surface. He hated this, the violation, the taking of what was his and his alone. The fact that she spoke the truth only fueled that anger. Maizey did not seem impressed.

"You also care very much for Cross." Maizey continued. She stood dangerously close to Finn, but didn't seem threatened by his words or his clenched fists held stiffly at his sides. "You were so young and so very eager to make a name for yourself when you graduated from Quantico. You believed every word they told you about us. The deviants. The misfits. We were dangerous and you, my dear Finnegan, were so altruistic. You wanted to protect the good people of this city from all the dangerous freaks."

Finn put a hand to his head as if that could stop her from prying. "Stop it."

"Then you saw Kale Delancey and you secretly wondered exactly what everyone was so afraid of. When you met Cross, he wasn't the monster they told you he was."

Finn collapsed on the nearest chair. "No, he wasn't." His voice was a whisper, his thoughts in chaos. "Please stop this."

Maizey knelt on one knee next him and took his hand. Finn, the anger gone, was now only numb. "He became your friend."

"Yes." He closed his eyes and decided he might deserve this private hell. "And I betrayed him."

"You faked the reports to Tanya and Coben. For years you tried to protect me. Didn't you?"

Finn's head snapped up at the familiar voice. Standing behind Maizey was Cross. It didn't occur to him to ask how he was there. "Guess I didn't try hard enough."

"I wanted to kill you back in medical. I thought you used me. You lied to me and I wanted to kill you for that alone."

"How are you here, Cross? Why are you here? Are you planning on killing me now?" Finn glanced from Cross to Vic to Maizey. His head hurt, he was dizzy and he had no more fight left in him. If Cross wanted to killed him, he didn't care at the moment.

"You can go from anger to self-pity quicker than anyone I know," Cross said. "No, I'm not here to kill you. I broke my promise." Cross tapped the side of Finn's head. "I had a look too and Maizey pretty much summed it up. I was the job until you got to know me, until you started to question things that were going on in the department. That's when you started faking the reports."

"Then why are you here?" Finn said to all three of them. "Did you feel a little psychological payback was in order? Mission accomplished. If you're not here to kill me, and you're satisfied I'm not going to turn you into Tanya, then I'm asking you one more time to get the fuck out of my house."

Vic merely laughed. A deep rumbling noise that was oddly disturbing in its total lack of humor. "Oh we're not nearly done here."

"What the hell do you want from me?" Finn said.

"I'm not who you think I am," Vic said.

"What, are you one them?" Finn said. "One of the freaks?"

"I'm just as ordinary as you. My job at the Department is just a front. I guess you could call me a spy. I belong to what we simply call the Underground. Not everyone out there with special talents is dangerous. Not one of them wants to end up in one of those glass-walled rooms. When they brought Cross in this last time, I knew exactly what they had planned." Vic looked like he just ate a bug at the thought. "I wasn't going to let that happen."

"You were on the monitors the day he got out. You helped him." Finn was beginning to understand. The understanding didn't make him like it any better.

Vic shrugged. "No one likes monitor duty so no one objected when I volunteered. When I saw Cross was making his move, I simply gave him the time he needed, and then made sure the lovely Maizey was waiting for him when he made it out."

Finn rubbed his still-aching head. "So one more time. Why are you here? Why tell me all this now?"

"We weren't sure we could trust you until Maizey and Cross had a look. Sorry."

Maizey winked at Finn.

"I owed you that, I guess," Finn grudgingly admitted. Didn't make him any less angry at the uninvited intrusion. "And what exactly did you learn? Are you going trust me, or kill me? Whichever it is I would appreciate if you would get on with it."

Maizey stood directly in front of him. "I don't usually look without permission, but we needed to know who's side you would be on if push came to shove.

"You're are a good man, Finn Doyle. You are a loyal friend. When it became clear to you that Cross was no longer an assignment, you did everything in your power to shield him from those who would do nothing but exploit him. You would have helped him if he asked it of you, but Cross felt betrayed by you and took fate into his own hands."

"We need your help," Vic said finally getting to the point.

"My help? You're the inside guy. What can I possibly help you with?"

"When Tanya and Coben put you on Cross's case all those years ago, she also brought you up to date on Kale, right?" Vic said.

Finn didn't like where this was heading. A cold slimy fist gripped his gut. "Yeah, and how does that help you?"

"She gave you his files. You know where she keeps him, the level of security she has on him."

"I need to get my brother out," Cross said. "And I need your help to do that."

CHAPTER 19

It was bad this time. Tanya had him beat before, but never like this. When they finished they left him hanging by his wrists. Kale lost track of time. The pain settled into the deep muscles of his shoulders and back. It couldn't hurt more if they had set him on fire. He couldn't feel his hands, but the blood flowing down his arms had long grown cold and sticky by the time they finally came to cut him down. Kale couldn't remember most of it, but he understood what they had done every time he moved. Every time he took a breath.

Someone had put him on his bed, but that was the only courtesy he was to receive. Both eyes were swollen, the right one completely, the left still had a small slit he could see out of. His nose was broken and clogged with dried blood, so he had to breathe out of his mouth. He tongued all his teeth, there were a few loose ones, but all were presented and accounted for, thank you very much.

Kale had no idea had much time had passed, he drifted in and out of consciousness. No one came to tend to his injuries. No one came to clean him up. No one came to give him water.

No one came.

Kale was alone, maybe that was the plan. They were just going to leave him in here until he died. Maybe they would leave his body here as well. He thought he might even be okay with that, because Cross had gotten out. He had kept his promise. His brother was safe. He only wished doing the right thing didn't hurt so badly.

Then his memory kicked in and he remembered the girl—Sybil. My God, Tanya had killed that poor girl. Tears leaked from his swollen eyes as Kale wished he would pass out again. He didn't want to think about the girl.

He didn't know how many more Sybils, Tanya could threaten him with, but he knew she would do anything to get what she wanted. He could push her, he knew that. He could tell her to let him go, he could tell her to walk him out of here and then forget about him. He almost had a dozen times over. But he couldn't. He didn't want her to forget about him. A part of him didn't even want to leave.

For ten years, this little, windowless room was all he had ever known. Tanya was the only person he knew, the only person he was allowed to see, to talk with, to touch. He could communicate with Cross telepathically but it wasn't the same. He knew nothing about the outside world. In truth the thought of going into the world outside his room terrified him. How could he leave? Where would he go?

Maybe he was as dangerous as Tanya told everyone he was. Maybe it was a good thing he was locked up.

Tanya loved him, Kale was sure of that. He failed her. That was why she punished him. He deserved it. He should never have tried to lie to her. Tanya knew everything. He was a fool. She was right, it was his fault that girl had died.

Kale squeezed his eyes closed and tried to hide inside himself. The heavy metal door of his room opened. Fear caused Kale to hold his breath. If they started in on him again, he was sure he would die. He let his pent up breath out and prepared for the pain.

A slight weight settled on his mattress. Even with his eyes closed, he knew who had come to him. Her energy was as familiar to him as his brother's. Dread and relief coursed through him. As much as he hated being alone, the thought of why she had come to him was terrifying.

"Look what you made me do, Kale," Tanya's voice was soft and held regret and sadness. She touched his face and he flinched at the contact.

"Can you see?" She lightly touched his swollen eyes. Kale nodded once and tried to curl away from her. He felt her leave the bed and thought she would leave him alone again. He searched for the darkness but couldn't find it. A warm wet cloth touched his face and he hissed as the water caused the wounds there to burn.

Tanya gently pulled him to his back, and he bit the inside of his cheek to keep from crying out. "Shh, be still. I'm just cleaning you up."

The warmth of the water and gentleness of her touch was deceiving, he understood that, but for now, all he could think about was someone cared enough not to let him die all alone. That thought nearly brought him to tears, but crying would hurt, so he kept his feelings in check.

"Why do you make me do these things to you, Kale?" The cloth moved over his eyes removing the dried blood. It hurt, but the warmth soothed him. Hurt by hurt, she methodically cleaned every wound she had ordered them to put on him. When she came to his wrists, he grimaced and let out a hiss. His vision was blurry but he could see the skin there was shredded. The wounds deep. He had fought hard.

"Do you think I like telling them to hurt you like this? Don't you think I knew how much they wanted to hurt you?" She wrapped his wrists in clean bandages and then leaned over and placed a soft kiss on his shattered lips.

"I need to hear it, Darling. I need to hear the words."

Kale turned his face away from her. She grabbed his chin and forced him to look at her. "Tell me. Tell Tanya and I'll make all the hurt go away," She held a bottle of water out to him. He was so thirsty.

Kale tried to grab it but she held it just out of his reach. "Tell me."

"I'm sorry." The words were barely audible but Tanya had heard him. She grinned and helped him drink. He gulped and the cold water spilled over his chest as he greedily swallowed. She pulled the water away.

"Why are you sorry Kale?"

God he hated this, but he had no pride left. He couldn't even remember what pride was anymore. He chose to stay. He chose to live this way. He was pathetic and he deserved anything and everything Tanya did to him.

"I lied to you." His lips split open again and blood ran down his chin. Tanya took the cloth and wiped it away.

"Will you help me find Cross? Or do I need to find another innocent child to convince you?"

"No!" he said the word loud and everything spasmed. He clamped his eyes closed and caught his breath. "No," he said quieter. "Don't do that. Please."

"You will help me?"

He nodded.

"Say it, Kale. I need to hear you say it."

"I'll help you find Cross, I'll help you bring him back."

My god, what have I become?

"That's my Kale. That's my darling. Now Tanya will make the pain go away."

Kale felt the sharp sting of a needle pierce his arm and then a few moments later, the hungry, demanding pain, fuzzed around the edges. If there was a God and if he chose to show Kale mercy, he prayed. He didn't think his prayers would be answered, he had learned long ago he was on his own. But there was always a chance, so he prayed that if betraying Cross was his only choice, then maybe this God would be kind enough to see that he never woke up.

****

They were eight or nine, Kale couldn't remember. Tanya had locked them in their quarters after punishing Cross for not cooperating. Nothing new there. It killed Kale every time.

"Why can't you just do what she wants?" Kale cried as Cross curled up on his bed. His face was bloody, from falling when they used the Tasers on him. Kale could tell by the careful way he moved it hurt more than Cross let on.

"Because she doesn't own me," Cross said.

"I don't understand you, all you have to do is show her what you can do. What's so bad about that?"

Cross turned to look at him sitting on the floor next the bed. "Because it won't stop there. What happened when you showed her what you could do, huh? Yeah, she wanted you to use it- on people. She wanted you to use it to make people do stuff." Kale looked at his feet. Cross was right, but he couldn't stand to see his brother hurt like this.

"If they think I can't do anything, maybe they'll leave me alone."

"Or maybe they'll kill you before you convince them. Please, Cross," Kale was crying harder now. "Please, I couldn't take it if they killed you. You're all I have. I don't want to be alone."

"Then why don't you push her? Why don't you push Tanya and tell her to leave us alone, tell her to just let us out of here."

Kale backed away from the bed as if Cross were a snake ready to strike. "I can't," He shook his head denying even the possibility. "I can't do that, Cross."

Cross grimaced as he turned to face the wall. "Yes you can. You just don't want to. There's a difference."

Cross didn't understand. Kale couldn't push Tanya. Tanya was nice when you did what she wanted. Why couldn't Cross just do what she wanted? Kale knew his brother was hiding his talents, and that was one thing he absolutely would not tell Tanya. He had sworn to Cross he would keep that secret and Kale kept his promises. Cross always talked about the day they got out of here, out of the Department. Kale didn't like to upset his brother, but he understood something Cross never would. They were never leaving this place. This small facility was home and it always would be. Kale saw no point in antagonizing the people who had the power to hurt you. He didn't understand why Cross did.

He would never understand that.

Kale!

Someone calling his name. The scene behind him faded. He wasn't a child anymore and he was the one who had taken the brunt of Tanya's fury this time.

Kale?

Go away.

He didn't like this dream anymore.

"Kale."

Kale opened his eyes, at least the one that wasn't completely swollen shut. Cross squatted on the floor by his bed. For a moment he thought Cross was still part of his dream, then he understood. Cross had a found a way to come to him. Not physically, but the way Kale had appeared to Cross over the years. Manifested energy.

"Not too shabby," Kale smiled and then winced as the healing cuts split again on his lip.

"What has she done to you?" Cross looked appalled.

"You can't come here to me anymore, Cross." Kale tried to sit up but his broken body decided that probably wasn't a good idea. He clutched his side and made do with turning so he could see his brother better.

"She did this to you because of me, didn't she? She did this because I got out and now she wants you to help her get me back."

Kale saw the anger flash across his brother's face. "I'm sorry. I'm so sorry, Cross. I tried, but she killed her. She killed that poor girl right there."

Cross looked where Kale pointed. He knew Cross could see the blood that still stained the floor, Kale could see it too. He could feel Cross inside his head. Getting answers to questions was quicker this way. Kale didn't object, it was something they used to do all the time as kids.

"Sybil? Sybil King? She killed her? Why?" Kale could feel the anger radiating from Cross. He needed to make this better, but he didn't know how.

"It was my fault. This is all my fault. I lied to her – told her you were dead. I hoped she would just leave you alone if she thought you were dead. She told me what would happen if I lied, but I did it anyway. I thought I could lie to her. That girl died because of me."

Cross shook his head. "You listen to me. Tanya killed Sybil, she is the only one who is responsible for that. Do you understand me?"

Kale didn't understand. "I tried Cross. I always seem to try and I always fail. I'm sorry. She's going to make me look for you again. If I don't do what she tells me, she'll kill someone else." Kale looked away. He was ashamed of what he had become. "I wish I could have been more like you. I wish I could have been stronger, braver. You were always the strong one Cross. You were always braver than me. I'm glad you got out."

"Stop that. Stop saying good bye to me. We aren't done here. All our lives you were the one who tried to protect me, Kale. Now it's my turn."

Kale shook his head. He didn't like the look on Cross's face. He knew that look. That was look he put on when all hell was about to break lose. Kale was pretty sure he didn't have it in him to confront hell at the moment. "Let it alone, Cross. You have no idea what she is capable of. Stay safe, stay hidden."

"Yeah, I don't think so. Tanya Santiago is responsible for our mother's death, she kept us isolated and imprisoned, used us, beat us and experimented on us. She took my memories and gave me a lie as a life. You, she manipulated on every imaginable level. She kept us from a family we never knew we had, Kale." Cross's face grew serious. "I'm not afraid of Tanya. Not even a little."

Kale wasn't impressed. Cross didn't know the Tanya he knew. "You should be."

Cross turned Kale's face toward him, his eyes gentle but his voice determined. "You listen to me. I got your back. I'm coming to get you out of here and when I do we are finishing what we started ten years ago. We are both getting out of here. I promise you that."

Kale wanted to believe him.

"Do you understand me? I'm coming for you, don't you ever doubt that. Don't you for one second forget that. Stay strong Kale. You aren't alone."

Then Cross was gone.

You aren't alone.

Kale turned to face the wall. His body screamed in protest. He sure felt alone.

CHAPTER 20

G abriel sat on his sofa in his quarters. Niko, Cross's dog curled up next to him sleeping. He pet her silky ears and opened his eyes. The dog soothed him. Gabriel knew what Tanya had done to Kale. He didn't approve, but then no one ever asked for or cared about his approval when it came to Cross or Kale. Gabriel told them they could not be controlled. Tanya told him Kale was not a problem, and Cross would be in hand soon enough.

Gabriel had told Coben and Tanya if they wanted to still study Kale, they needed to kill Cross. That's what he told them when Cross was in a coma after the boy tried to escape, after he had tried to kill his own son. That's what he told them when Cross was brought in a few days ago. Cross was dangerous, but no one wanted to listen to him.

Now Cross was gone and Kale was groundless. A child who worshiped at the shrine of Tanya's lies. Beating him half to death wasn't going to garner Kale's cooperation, all that was going to do was elicit Cross's wrath. The loyalty his sons had for each other was boundless. The only thing Tanya did right concerning Kale and Cross was keeping them apart. Now that Cross knew Kale was alive nothing would keep him from his brother. Nothing.

Gabriel knew that boy. He had been in his head many times when he was younger. Cross hated the intrusion and learned how to block him, but Gabriel knew how to enter undetected. He knew, when Cross was young, he had been holding back from Tanya. The raw power Gabriel sensed seething just beneath the surface was terrifying.

He had tried to tell Tanya. "Cross is gasoline just waiting for a match. You have no idea what you're dealing with."

Tanya waved off his concern. "I'll break him darling. Just wait."

Gabriel was still waiting.

He knew either Cross or Kale would try to get in touch with the other. Without Tanya's permission or knowledge, Gabriel had set up a series of energy markers inside Kale's room. Psychic trip wires. If anyone manipulated energy inside Kale's room, Gabriel would know about it. Tanya might be confident in her ability to control his sons, but Gabriel always was a believer that forewarned was forearmed. Cross's mental barriers were completely removed, it was only a matter of time until he understood the enormity of what had been done to him. Cross was not known for his forgiving nature.

A little over an hour ago. Gabriel's tripwires alerted him. With Niko still resting her head on his lap, Gabriel found Kale and opened the smallest of psychic cracks into his son's subconscious. If he stayed there without interfering or probing, whoever was manipulating that energy shouldn't know he was there. Just like a fly on the wall.

Gabriel could never see anything when he entered someone's mind, it was all a mental impression. But he was amazed at what he picked up. Kale was dreaming when Gabriel first entered his mind. Besides the nearly overwhelming pain he could almost physically feel from Kale's injuries, Gabriel could sense the mental cracks as well.

Kale's sanity balanced on a table of air. If Tanya's plan was to break Kale, then he would have to say she succeeded. A part of Gabriel hated Tanya for that. That was the part that wanted to save Kale. The caring surprised him. Gabriel had prided himself on being merely part of an experiment as far as Kale and Cross were concerned. He never claimed to want to be a father to them. Maybe because he knew it would never be allowed. Convincing himself he didn't care hurt less than admitting his feelings. But having Tanya break one son to get to the other found Gabriel at odds with how he thought he felt about everything.

Kale's dream was interrupted by the energy that brought Gabriel here. It didn't surprise him in the least when he recognized Cross's familiar signature. What he felt, however, was much stronger than any energy vibe he ever got off of Cross in the past. Gabriel wasn't sure what, but something had changed. The anger that had prompted a fourteen-year-old to go on an unprecedented killing spree was present combined with a new found knowledge that Gabriel found terrifying.

This Cross wasn't confused. This Cross wasn't undecided. This Cross had an agenda and was very motivated.

Gabriel stayed in the furthest recesses of Kale's mind. Cross was distracted by his brother's pain and his own anger. When he was certain that Cross had left and Kale was sleeping, he backed out.

He opened his eyes and found Niko staring at him. "Well, now what am I supposed to do with that?" he asked the dog. "Tanya would love to know Cross is out for a little post traumatic revenge." Niko perked her ears at Cross's name. "What do you think, Niko? I still think your master is dangerous. But do I let Tanya try to bring him in or do I keep this little gem all to myself." Gabriel considered his own question. He knew the answer. He'd wanted Cross dead for ten years. Now he might have the chance to do what should have been done all those years ago. Or he could try something altogether different.

He could help his sons.

"Tanya and Coben are not going to like this. But they refuse to see Cross for the danger he is. They think he can be tamed, they think he can be controlled. They tried, I'll give them credit, they did try, but this sleeping dragon has just opened his eyes. Cross is awake and he is hungry for blood."

Niko cocked her head as if she were considering an answer when a light rap on the door had her jumping from Gabriel's lap. She growled softly in her throat as if she knew who waited on the other side of the door. Maybe she did. Gabriel sensed Tanya's presence and tried to figure out what she was doing at his quarters.

"Come in, Tanya. The door's not locked."

Niko's growl grew as she hid behind Gabriel.

Tanya wrinkled her face in disgust as she looked at the dog. "You still have that thing here."

Gabriel soothed Niko with a touch. "I like her company. What do you want?"

Tanya looked from the dog to Gabriel. Her dark eyes, while always hard, and suspicious seemed to consider Gabriel as if he were a new species she was sure was poisonous. "I need to ask you a question."

"Then ask." He didn't like this. Tanya wasn't here for a social visit. Tanya didn't do social. He could have looked in her head, but it was difficult to read someone and talk to them at the same time. She would know what he was trying to do.

She stepped further into his quarters, her finger trailing along the surfaces of the furniture as if looking for dust. "You know what I've had done to Kale." It wasn't a question. He didn't treat it as one.

"Of course." She didn't ask how he felt about what she had done, so he kept that to himself.

She stared at him for a moment before continuing as if she was trying to read him. "I need to know, whose side you're on."

Now he was totally confused. "I get a choice?" He tried to make light of the subject until he understood what she was after.

"At the end of the day Gabriel, when you have to choose a side, I need to know are you going to stand with us, or are you going to side with the freaks?"

"Maybe if you told me exactly what you're talking about I could answer that."

Tanya observed him. "I think this department has been quite lenient with you, wouldn't you say? We have allowed you a great deal of latitude, you can come and go as you please. You've helped us on any number of cases and we appreciate all of that."

"But?" Gabriel knew where she was going now.

"But," Tanya continued. "You're not the only psychic I have at my disposal. You might be the most talented psychic I've ever known, but I do have backups."

"And your back up detected my presence when Cross contacted Kale." There was no sense in denying the truth. But he had to wonder why Tanya had someone watching Kale. He also wondered how he could have missed that.

"Why didn't you tell me what you were going to do? That worries me Gabriel."

"How do you know I wasn't going to report what I found out to you? It only just happened, Tanya."

"Don't insult my intelligence. You would have told me."

"Or not. Maybe the real question is why you thought it was necessary to find another psychic. I've helped in all manner of things over the years. Why would this be any different?"

"Because this time it involves your sons."

"You had Kale beaten to bait Cross in." He thought about that and chastised himself for not thinking about it sooner.

Tanya dipped her head in acknowledgement. "And when he comes, I need to know, whose side will you be on?"

"You've made a mistake Tanya."

"I don't think so."

"That arrogance is going to be your undoing. This all started with such altruistic notions, do you remember? We wanted to save lives, maybe even eliminate war. We wanted to improve the human condition."

Tanya laughed, the sound like bells in the winds, delicate and beautiful. Gabriel knew better. He understood the monster behind the beauty. "Hitler claimed much the same thing when he employed psychics. Please Gabriel, don't tell me you actually believe the hype we've spun for funding. The *people* we keep here are not interested in saving humanity. They most certainly don't care about improving the human condition. Most of them are trying their level best to take humanity down an evolutionary trail we could never come back from. This is Darwinian mentality at its purist. We cut off the serpent's head before the serpent can do the same to us."

"Sounds a lot like a sister organization from a few years ago. Its leader claimed much the same thing. To better humanity at the expense of innocent lives."

"You mean *The Program?*" Tanya scoffed. "The General and his experiments were never sanctioned by our government."

"Neither is this Department. Technically."

"John McKinley was insane. There is a difference between what that man did and what we do."

Gabriel didn't think so, but he also didn't feel like arguing. "So you want to know which side of the evolutionary scale I sit on, is that it?"

"Something like that. What you can do? I can use that, I can respect that. But the things Cross and Kale can do? The things that the other people we have contained here can do? They need to be handled carefully. They need to understand their place. They cannot be allowed out in the general populace."

Gabriel gave Tanya nothing. "Do you understand what you've done? Because I'm not sure you do."

"If you're talking about Cross, I know exactly what I'm doing. He isn't a threat. The energy levels he displayed when he contacted Kale were not much more than his norm. We can control that. We can control him."

"Then you're an idiot. You've nearly pushed Kale over the edge, beat him almost to death and for what? To bring Cross to your door? You have a selective memory Tanya. Cross isn't fourteen anymore."

Tanya stepped back. "And I think I have my answer. It's a shame, really. You were such a helpful freak. Stay out of my way Gabriel and perhaps you can still be of use." Tanya turned and walked out the door. The locked clicked loudly into place a moment later.

CHAPTER 21

Cross pulled out of Kale's mind. His breath came in fast gulps and sweat dripped from his face, rolled down his chest, his back. He had never manifested energy like that before. It took more out of him than he realized. Or maybe it was simply the emotional toll seeing Kale had taken on him. In all the times Kale had appeared to him over the years his brother had appeared to him as a fourteen-year-old boy – the last memory Cross had of him. This was different. For the first time in nearly ten years, Cross looked upon his adult brother.

The things Tanya had done to him made him want to hurt someone – badly. The man Cross saw was thin, it was obvious Kale had not been treated kindly over the years and recent abuse had been more than evident. Kale had been beaten terribly. His face bloody, bruised and swollen. By the way he tried not to move, his ribs were hurting. Bloody bandages encircled his wrists and fresh blood dripped from split lips. This changed everything. His plans went from figuring out how to get Kale out, to saving his life.

"Cross?"

Finn's voice brought him back to the present.

Finn's loft.

Maizey and Vic sat near him. Cross squeezed his eyes tight trying to purge the image of Kale broken and bleeding, out of his head, but then decided that he wanted the image to stay. That image would motivate him and right now Cross was very motivated.

When he thought he could speak, he turned in Finn's direction. "Kale tried to help me. He warned me about Tanya, that she would stop at nothing to bring me back. He told me to run." Cross lowered his head. He kept his voice low and even because if he didn't he would scream. "Tanya somehow found out that that he helped me."

Finn seemed to understand. "What did they do to him?"

Cross raised his head again and glanced in Finn's direction. "They beat him, Finn. They beat him so hard he could barely move. That's what my brother did to keep me safe. That is all he's done since he was fourteen. They took my memories and scripted my life, but at least I *had* a life." The anger could not be contained any longer. Neither could the guilt at what had become of Kale. Tears leaked from beneath the dark glasses. "I wasn't linked with him very long, he was so weak. He couldn't hide anything from me this time. Did you know, Finn? Did you know she keeps him in a small room? Like a pet." Cross's voice waivered. He took a moment. When he spoke again his voice was calmer, but the emotions were still as raw. "Since he was fourteen, that's all he's known. While I went to school, dated girls, had friends, all Kale has ever known is that one room and Tanya. Did you know Finn?"

"No, I swear. Tanya told everyone he was unstable and unpredictable. She said she was the only one who could control him. I had no idea what that meant." Finn sounded sincere.

"And you never thought to find out for yourself? You never once thought to tell me he was still *alive*?" Cross leaned forward with his head in hands. "My God, what the hell did you people do to us?" Cross didn't know which emotion to embrace, disgust, nearly overwhelming guilt or the anger that he now knew had always fueled him. All he could see in his mind was Kale, broken and bleeding because of him. And his brother was still trying to protect him

Run!

No way.

Not a chance.

"Listen to me." Finn's voice was quiet but intense. "You came here because you wanted my help. I don't know what I can do to get Kale out of there, but I'm in."

"I won't let him die there," Cross said. "Don't tell you're in unless you understand what that means. You saw the tapes of our escape attempt when we were fourteen? You saw what we did?"

"Yes."

I'm not fourteen anymore. What I could do back then?" Cross felt the power stirring to life inside him. He desperately wanted to show them exactly what he was capable of. "That was nothing. I'm not afraid of doing what I have too."

"I get that. When I tell you I'm in, I'm telling you I'm all in."

"I would do this alone if I had to, but it would be better if I didn't."

"You don't have to do it alone," Maizey put a hand on his shoulder. "There are hundreds of us down in those tunnels. Some are too scared, or too young but there are more than enough to amass a respectable force against Tanya and her department."

"Thank you." He had meant it when he said he would do it alone. But help was good. It was very good. "When we tried to walk out of there all those years ago, I had no plan. Just arrogance. My powers are stronger than they were then, but I'm also smarter. We need a plan. I want Kale out of there in one piece. Risking his life is not an option."

"Understood," Vic said. "Why don't we introduce Finn to the underground and we can figure out that plan. Maizey is impressive, but she can't keep the smoke screen up indefinitely."

Finn looked a bit unnerved. "It's not that I don't believe you, but we just walk right out of here? No one will see us?"

Maizey said. "Have a little faith Finnegan."

"Faith. I'll get right on that."

It took everything for Cross not to go to Kale now, but he wouldn't be helping his brother if he went in with only his anger as a shield. He had to wait, and so did Kale.

I'm coming man. Hold tight.

CHAPTER 22

Vic and Maizey led them to a homeless shelter not far from Finn's loft. With Maizey still shielding them in case they had company, Vic walked to the back room and entered a closet and pushed the back wall. The wall slid away and a hidden spiral staircase emerged. Without a word, they followed Vic down into the dark. A back door to the tunnels.

Finn looked down at the impenetrable black. "Have faith," he whispered and started down one step at a time. About two minutes in light began to leak up from below. After being submersed in total darkness the dim lighting made him squint. The only person who seemed comfortable traversing the stairs without light, was Cross.

"How do you do this all the time?" Finn whispered. His voice was unnaturally loud in the confined space. "It's terrifying."

He heard Cross laugh. "It's amazing what you get used to when you don't have a choice."

"Almost there," Vic said from ahead. The light grew brighter and as they reached the bottom, a soft yellow glow showed Finn the underground. The stairwell opened into a long tunnel that Finn recognized as a subway. A very old, abandoned subway tunnel. Golden arches spanned the ceiling in beautiful mosaic patterns. No rails just concrete and dirt for a floor. Graffiti lined the walls along with tables, chairs. Sleeping bags were strewn about. Small children played in the shadows as their parents or guardians watched them. The adults looked up and gathered the children to them in fear as they entered.

As they recognized Vic and Maizey they visibly relaxed and let the children resume their play.

Tunnels led out of the room at various intervals. "What is this place?" Finn said.

"Exactly what it looks like," Vic said. "There are dozens of abandoned subway lines all around the city. Most people have no idea what is right below their feet. Some entrances have been completely hidden, others destroyed. This was once the City Hall Line. It's been abandoned since 1945. People thinks it's haunted and we try to encourage that belief."

"Wow. How many live down here?"

"Two hundred more or less. They come and go as they wish as long as they are sure they aren't being followed. Most have ways to keep their passage undetected," Vic explained.

A stab of guilt hit Finn. "We did this," he said. "The Department. We forced these people to live like this."

"Most of the ones we brought into the Department were rogues, Finn. They were dangerous. Those are the ones who don't care who they hurt. I have no guilt in handing them over to Tanya and Coben," Vic said. "But sometimes the innocent ones get caught in the net."

"I had no idea. There are so many. I didn't know." Finn watched a little girl around two or three. She tossed a ball in the air and then kept in there with an invisible force. Finn could see the air shimmer around her as she manipulated the ball. He didn't know what she was doing, but it was kind of cool. It was also kind of terrifying.

"You!" A man came from one of the tunnels and immediately focused on Finn. He pointed a meaty finger at him. "You're the cocksucker who brought my boy to that place!" The man ran straight at Finn with a clear agenda. It happened so fast no one had time to react. The man was on Finn in a moment. He tried to dodge the punch but the guy was fast. A fist made exquisite contact with his jaw. Finn went down and the man followed him raining punches to his face and body. Every time Finn thought he could evade the assault, the guy was right there. Finn never got in one punch of his own.

"Will! Calm down." Vic was on the guy trying to pull him off.

The assault stopped and Finn glanced up. Vic had the guy's arms pinned behind him. The guy was fighting to get free.

Cross put a hand under Finn's arm and helped him back to his feet. The room spun a little but he stayed on his feet. He wiped blood from his face with the back of one hand.

"What is he doing here, Vic? You tell me that. What's this little prick doing in a place we all thought of as safe?" Will looked like he wanted to take Finn apart piece by piece.

"He's here to help," an older man said. He wasn't a big man. His voice was soft, but it was clear the amount of respect he commanded. "I'm sorry, Will, I should have prepared all of you that Vic was bringing him here. I promise you Mr. Doyle was fed false information when he did the things he did for the department, as was my grandson."

Finn raised his brow at that. *Cross's grandfather?*

"I'm sorry for the less than warm welcome Mr. Doyle. But I'm afraid most of the people down here have not have favorable experiences with the Department of Paranormal Research. My name is Charlie. Let me see what I can do about those injuries."

"It's okay, he clocked me good, but nothing worth complaining about."

Charlie held his hands up in acceptance. "Let me know if you change your mind. You might want to get some ice on that eye. It's already starting to close."

Finn resisted the temptation to touch his swelling eye.

Will looked resigned, but not so much that he wasn't ready to give Finn another go. "How is he supposed to help? He's the reason most of us live down here in the dark."

Cross stepped in front of Finn. "He has information I need to get my brother out of there. He promised he would help. Trust me, if he doesn't, if he looks for one second like he's going to flip, I have no problem putting him down." Cross's voice was soft. He held his head at an odd angle as he spoke, as if the words hurt him to speak them.

Finn wasn't sure if Cross was serious or not.

"Yeah, and why should we be trusting you any better?" Will took a step toward Cross. "No offense Charlie, I understand he's family, but until just a few days ago we were hiding from this one too."

"He didn't know any better, Wills. He does now," Charlie said.

"Oh, I see, so because he knows 'better' now, all is forgiven. All the people, all the *children* these two have handed over to that place, we're just supposed to forget about that. We're supposed to trust them with our lives now?" Will, approached Finn and Cross. "I don't know about anyone else here, but my trust needs to be earned, not given." Will had about two inches on Finn and stood in his face glaring down at him. His eyes all hard dark slits. Finn held his ground. The guy had gotten the better of him once. It wouldn't happened again.

"Back off, man," Finn warned him.

Will stayed where he was.

"It won't be so easy next time," Finn said.

Will gave Finn a nasty sneer. "Next time nobody's going to pull me off you."

"Yeah, we are all sincerely impressed by the manly display of testosterone. Can we please dial it down a notch or three," Maizey shouldered her way through the crowd that had been forming a circle around Will, Finn and Cross. She stepped between Will and Finn and shoved Will back with a hand on his chest. "We get it, Will. You don't like them, you don't trust them. Too fooking bad, love. Trust or no, these boys just might be our only way to finally shut the Department down for good, or at the very least give us a way to fight back." She put a hand through Cross's arm. "So unless you have a better idea, go hate them in private – and quietly. You're giving me a headache."

Will didn't seem very happy about getting dressed down by Maizey in public, but he took a step back. Maizey did not seem impressed or intimidated. Finn was liking this girl just fine.

"If we're finished getting to know each other," Charlie said. "I want to discuss strategy and pick Finn's brain. I need to know how the compound is laid out, security, weapons. I'm sure Cross has questions about Kale."

"And as important as all that is," Maizey snugged Cross's arm to her. "I think you all failed to notice this boy is about ready to drop." All eyes were suddenly focused on Cross. Finn noticed he swayed slightly under Maizey's firm grip. His legs bowed a little and his one hand held his head as if it were too heavy to hold up on its own. "I'm afraid he's not used to tapping into the kind of energy he needed to manifest in front of Kale like he did." A thin trickle of blood ran from Cross's nose.

Finn was at Cross's side in an instant, trying to see behind the reflective lenses. "Jesus, this is what happened before, when he collapsed outside the department. Cross, you okay?"

Cross didn't answer. "Is he all right?" Finn turned to Charlie who in turn looked to Maizey.

"He just over did it, Love. Help me get him somewhere quiet where he can rest. I'll take care of him."

Finn took his partner's other arm and followed Maizey. "When you're done Finn," Charlie said. "Find your way back here. While Cross rests we need to talk."

Finn nodded and then turned to tend to Cross.

CHAPTER 23

Maizey led Cross down a series of tunnels and turns. Finn helped to keep him on his feet, but Maizey sensed the overwhelming fatigue crashing down on him. They stopped outside a small cave-like room that, with the help of soft drapes, pillows and lighting was warm and inviting.

"Put him here." Maizey pulled back the covers on a small cot and Finn helped Cross onto it. She pulled his shoes off and tried for a convincing grin. "He'll be all right, Finnegan. Think you can find your way back? Charlie will be waiting on you."

Finn seemed hesitant to leave Cross. Maizey stood and faced him. "I'm not going to hurt him, love. I understand how hard this must be for you. He's been your responsibility all these years and now you have to share him."

"I hate psychics."

Maizey laughed. "I know. Go on now with you. I'll take care of your Cross for you."

Finn paused only a moment turning and walking back into the tunnels.

"He's worried." Cross's voice was soft, his faced pinched and tired.

"Aye, I feel that too. I also know what you're feeling now as well. Come love, let me help." Maizey sat on the edge of the bed and took Cross's dark glasses off. Behind them his eyes were closed. A bright red smear of blood trickled from his nose and trailed down his chin. She took a cloth to wipe it clean when he stopped her.

"It's okay," he said. "Just tired. Talking to Kale, I wasn't expecting it to take so much out of me."

Maizey pushed his hand down and wiped the blood away. "If that's all it was, love, I would have let you stay where you dropped. You forget, I can get inside your head too."

"And I really wish you wouldn't."

"Stop being stubborn. What were you planning on doing back there? Falling on your face? You were barely holding it together."

Cross leaned back into the pillows and sighed. "I hate psychics." His voice held humor even as his face sagged in exhaustion.

"I know, now, shut up and let me take care of you." She moved off the bed to get fresh water and rinse the rag. "Now while you lay there and try to be quiet I'll answer the questions you don't have to ask. See, there are some advantages to being psychic."

Cross opened his mouth to say something when she stopped him. "Shh, lay there, be still and listen. You might have learned the truth about who you are and what you are capable of but that doesn't mean you know how to use that power surging through you just yet. You're a little out of practice. What you did to make contact with your brother was the equivalent to that of a beginner runner doing a marathon. Right now you're paying the price for that, understand?"

Cross gave her a small nod. Maizey came back to sit on the bed and placed a warm wet rag on his eyes. The scent of lavender and vanilla filled the room, Cross exhaled and the tension seemed to drain from his body. Maizey placed her hands on either side of Cross's head and closed her eyes to focus. Maizey didn't need to dig too deep to know Cross suffered far more than physical pain. The emotional turmoil of discovering what had been done to him, of understanding what his brother had sacrificed for him all these years, ate away at him. He tried to keep everything folded up and buried deep inside of him. But no one had given him a chance to take a breath the last few days let alone compartmentalize his feelings. Maizey could feel the cracks breaking at the surface of the calm he projected. She also knew he wasn't going to be able to keep the pretense up for much longer.

If Cross lost it, she feared the uncontrolled anger he had let loose when he was younger would look like a minor incident in comparison. She didn't want to help Cross because she felt sorry for him. She did, but that was beside the point. If Cross didn't learn to control the volatile mix of power and emotions boiling through him, he might end up destroying them all.

Her fingers gently caressed the side of Cross's head and she felt him sink deeper into a relaxed state. "I know you're hurting love, I can help with that." She kept her voice soft and mellow.

Cross tensed slightly under her hands. "Gabriel told me the same thing not too long ago. That didn't work out so well, so thanks, but no." He took her hands and held them between his own.

"I'm not Gabriel. I have nothing to hide from you."

"Everyone has something to hide, Maizey. No one shows their true selves, everyone tells just enough of the truth to get what they want."

"Fair enough. What if I showed you the truth of who I am, would that convince you? I would let you in, so you wouldn't have to exert yourself, no need to go poking around in my head, I'll lay it all out there for you, the ugly, naked truth. You would know if I was lying to you. If I did that for you, then would you trust me enough to help you?"

"What makes you think I need your help?"

Maizey sighed. "Because Cross, what you fail to understand is terrifyingly clear to me. You have no idea how to handle the powers inside of you. Some of them, you don't even realize are there. If you don't let me help, you are going to let that anger you try so very hard to hide, rule you. If you do, none of us are getting out of this alive. The only person who will survive is Kale. If you're dead, who will save your brother then? Who will care what happens to him when no one alive will he even know he exists? He will belong to Tanya, body and soul until the day he dies." Maizey meant every word, she had seen it all come to pass as one possible future.

"So if laying myself bare before you is what it takes for you to trust me, then I will show you anything."

Cross let her hands go. "I wish I could say I could trust you without doing that –"

"But you can't," Maizey finished for him. "I get that. You have been lied to and manipulated your entire life, let me show you there are people out there who are worthy of your trust." Maizey took his hands and placed them on either side of her head. Cross instinctively understood what to do. She opened her mind to him. For a psychic to do that would be the same as standing naked in front of a crowd. The barriers she kept in place fell, the half-truths we all are comfortable with, dissolved. Maizey allowed Cross Delancey into the most private parts of her soul. Sex wouldn't have been as intimate as what she and Cross were about to share.

A little girl of six or seven just learning she was different. A mother dead in child birth, a father who never forgave that child for the one thing she could never change, her existence. The forced isolation, the days of no one talking to her. A mean man who fed her and clothed her but starved her emotionally. Being punished for what came naturally to her. Beaten to make her stop what she didn't know how to control. Growing up, a teenager who knew the things inside of her were bad, they were wrong. Ashamed for who, and what she was, but hating the man who was her father, for keeping her this way. Resentment kept her soul company. It fed on her misery and nursed her hatred.

Anger made her strong, so she let that anger take her over. Ambushing her father as he came to feed her was easy. The door unlocked and she pulled him inside, the anger a force within her – she was so strong. She didn't realize he was dead until she saw the blood. He wasn't supposed to die, she only wanted –out!

Stupid drunk, stupid daddy. Fell and hit his head. The fire was an accident, the candles that lit her small room fell with him. The cheap worn carpet went up with a whoosh! And suddenly the curtains were an angry hungry flame that ate everything in its path. She stood there until it was almost too late and then the way to the door was blocked. The flames searching for her. Finding her.

The fire had tasted her but she survived. Charlie had found out about her through his information network. He had watched her and now he had saved her.

The little girl who had grown into a beautiful teenager had grown into a woman because Charlie took her in. Her beauty had been a price she was more than glad to pay. As she looked at the melted ruin of her face and arms, she often thought what price can one place on freedom?

She didn't want the scars on her body to matter, they were nothing compared to the scars on her soul, but they did, they kept her as much a prisoner as her father. Then she learned something about herself that changed everything. She might not have any control over the way she looked, but she could control how others saw her. It wasn't hard. Maizey picked a mask and that is the face she showed to the world. Not many knew her secret, the way the scars still burned and stretched when she moved, when she talked. The ugliness that went far deeper than her skin.

The shame.

Then learning what Charlie had planned. She could make a difference instead of wishing she was something she wasn't. Learning how to love herself. Learning to forgive her father and then learning to forgive herself.

Understanding she was willing to do anything to keep others from going through what had been her life.

Maizey surfaced from the memories. She had given Cross the chance to see her as she truly was. He didn't need sight to see her, he only needed Maizey to allow him inside, and she had. With her illusion removed, she took his hands and guided them over the taught ridges and valleys that was her face.

"This is who I really am, Cross." She watched his face closely, looking for the telltale signs of shock or disgust. She waited for the hands beneath hers to jerk back as he understood what he touched was not the beautiful girl she had shown to him in his head. "You wanted truth, this is my truth. This is who I am behind the magic. If what I showed you was a lie then I'm sorry. Sometimes we deceive ourselves so much it becomes difficult to know where the lie stops and the truth starts. I guess the lie has become comfortable to me over the years. The lie is how I see myself." She didn't cry now. She was glad of that. Showing him her truth was one thing but showing him the shame she felt by way of tears was something else altogether. She still had some pride left to her.

"That truth is yours now," she said. "You can do what you want with it." She suddenly felt very small. Her truth wasn't noble or self-sacrificing. It was ugly and selfish and for all her psychic prowess, she couldn't begin to think of what Cross would think of her now. Cross moved his hands from her cheeks to her eyes, where lids were pulled tight with scar tissue, to her misshaped nose and down to the nearly lipless mouth. He moved his head as if he were seeing her with his eyes and not his hands. Shame washed over her. She wished, for all her truths, that she could be beautiful for him. She wanted to be beautiful for him.

His one hand cupped her face as the other smoothed her hair. He held her gently as if she might break if he touched her wrong.

"I have spent nearly my entire life in the dark. I stopped judging what I couldn't see a long time ago. What I consider beautiful is what most people don't even know how to look for. Would you like to know how I see you Maizey?"

She nodded, not trusting her voice to speak. He still held her face in his hand and felt the movement. "I see you as a bright powerful force, all crazy yellows and reds. You are energy and movement. You are warmth and caring. You feel like home to me." He brought both hands back to hold her face.

Wanted or not, tears burned tracks down her face at his words. She knew he felt them as he held her and wiped them away with a thumb. "But mostly what I see when I *look* at you is hope. I see hope, Maizey. And hope is the most beautiful thing there is." Cross leaned in and kissed her ruined mouth and for one still moment, he made her feel beautiful.

CHAPTER 24

A calmness settled over Cross as he released Maizey. He wondered if it was something she had done to him to make him feel this way. If it was, he couldn't say he objected.

"Now you know," she said.

He felt the truth in Maizey's words, in the past she'd shared with him. She was no threat to him. Shame washed over him for a moment.

"Now I know," he agreed.

"Will you let me help you?"

"This will help me free Kale?"

"Yes."

"Then, yes," Cross said. "I believe you. Do what you have too, show me what you need too, but understand one thing before you do."

"And what would that be, love?"

Cross reached a hand out and found her face once more. He let his fingers move lightly over her features. She had put the illusion back on. "I understand what drives you now, and you know the same of me."

"Aye, I do."

"Then you understand that Kale comes first. Whatever it takes, my life or anyone else's, Kale comes first. He's sacrificed too much of himself for me already."

Maizey took his hand and held it for a moment before kissing the palm and letting it go. "I know. And that is exactly why you need to learn what I have to teach you."

"As long as we're clear."

"As glass, Love. Are you ready to learn exactly what has all those people in that department of yours scared shitless at the thought of losing you?"

Cross grinned and spread his hands giving her the go ahead.

"Well then," Maizey took a breath. "Let's start with what you do know. The psychic ability is a given, I am confident you know what you're doing when it comes to delving into other's psyches. As for the ability to manifest energy, you obviously knew how to do this before they messed with you, before you were injured, do you remember how you did that?"

Cross almost said no, when one thing, one single incident came front and center. "There was one time. Finn and I brought this kid in- real unstable abilities and sociopathic tendencies on top of that. Short story he was about to kill Finn. I interceded."

"How?"

He thought about how to explain it to her and realized he couldn't even explain it to himself. "I don't know. I knew I had to do something. All I remember is being angry. This little shit was about to kill my partner and I was going to have a front row seat. I wanted to hurt him, I remember that. The rest," Cross raised his shoulders in a helpless gesture. "I didn't do anything. It just happened."

"You did it, the power's always been there. It's part of who you are. I felt that much, but because of what they did to you, it's been pushed so far into the background, you forgot about it, but when you needed it, your reflexes took over. All we need to do is coax it back out into your conscious life."

She was right, he could feel that power simmering inside of him. He always could, like a caged animal still and quiet waiting for the time to pounce. Cross simply needed to let it out of the cage. He closed his eyes and pictured Kale bloodied and beaten in his cell, he thought of the life his brother must have had and what had been done to both of them. He felt familiar anger begin to bubble through him and then, yes, he found that caged beast and cracked the door open.

Energy flowed through him. It was like taking a breath, natural, instinctual and easy. He opened his eyes and the room was brighter. He followed the glow and realized he held a glowing ball of pure energy between his hands. It pulsed and waited for him to do something with it. It also scared the crap out of him. "Well shit, now what do I do?"

Maizey laughed not at all worried at what she was witnessing. It was as if previously homicidal men manifested power in her presence every day. "What do you want to do with it?" she asked.

"I don't know," he admitted. "I don't want to hurt anyone."

"Then don't. This power, this energy comes from you, Cross. It's yours to command. You can use it as a weapon, or you could simply let it go."

"Let it go?" Cross wasn't sure he completely understood.

"Let is dissipate back into the singular elements from which you collected it."

"I can do that?"

"You can do that, love. Just let it go," she said again.

Cross wasn't so sure, but he trusted Maizey. He opened his hands and gently released the energy there. Through his shadowy vision he saw the brightness he had been holding expand until it covered the ceiling above them and then it separated. Cross saw this as brilliant glowing specks. Then the specks faded and rained down on both of them. Cross feared for Maizey's safety but to his complete and utter surprise she laughed.

"It's beautiful," she said. "Like falling stars."

"I didn't hurt you?" Cross said, a smile on his face.

"No, Love," Cross felt her touch his face. "You did it and that's only the beginning, but first would you like to learn how you can see again?"

Cross brought his head up and stared at where he knew she sat. "What?"

"It's not like you used to see, but would you like to know how to use that power to see when you want?"

Cross's heart rate bumped up and his breathing quickened. "You can do that?"

"No but you can."

"How? I'm blind Maizey, no amount of energy can fix that."

"It won't be sight, not like before, but it might be something you can use to get by with. A sort of sight is better than none, right?"

"How do you know I can do this?"

"Well, from what I can gather from looking around the nooks and crannies of your subconscious, this is how it works. When you lost your sight, it took a while, but you began to rely on other cues, your hearing, touch, you remembered details of the physical world so you could navigate, right?"

"Yes." He still didn't understand, but he was definitely intrigued.

"Okay, that was how you adapted physically, but what you never realized was your other abilities adapted as well. You just learned you always had the ability to manipulate energy, but that too adapted to your loss of sight."

Cross thought he understood what she was getting at. "The first time I tried to get out."

"Yes, you saw the threat and turned it against the person trying to hurt you. Without your sight you didn't know how to do that. Thanks to Coben and Tanya you forgot you even knew how."

"But my body remembered." Cross said. It was starting to make sense.

"And it adapted. Now as you gather the energy around you, your mind can stream it back out. Energy can't be destroyed, but it can be transferred. So my best comparison would be radar. You ping energy out, it bounces off objects around you and they become visible to you. Does that sound right?"

Yes," Cross was excited now. "You think I can do that?"

"It's all about control, Cross. Right now when you gather energy to do anything, you go for broke. In essence, you're using a sledge hammer to crack open an egg. You need to only take what you need. I can't tell you how much or how little, but I think once you realize what to do it will come naturally to you now that you understand. Want to give it a try?"

Cross exhaled and tried to relax. Nerves crawled like ants along the inside of his skin as he attempted to focus. He used his hands to gather the energy around him, he tried to keep it under control but it was difficult. The now familiar tingle danced between his hands as he kept the power whirling quietly. "Okay, now what?"

"Now, instead of expending it out, absorb it inside of you."

"What? You're kidding."

"Trust me, love. It won't hurt you. This is what you were born to do."

Cross considered that. "I don't know how." The energy between his hands buzzed like angry bees waiting to be set free.

Maizey sounded infinitely patient. "Yes you do, trust your instincts. Charlie removed anything that could have blocked you, now all you have to do is stretch yourself. You can do this Cross."

Sweat beaded on his head. He was breathing fast and he wasn't nearly as confident as Maizey gave him credit for.

Trust yourself.

Cross took a breath and let it out fast. He wanted to take that ball of seething energy and compress it, make it smaller until it slipped right into him. So that's exactly what he did. He molded and squeezed and pressed and as he did he felt heat, but it didn't burn. The more he pushed, the warmer he felt—on the inside. It was a good feeling, satisfying like eating after along fast. His palms touched each other and Cross understood that he no longer held the ball of energy, it was now *inside* of him.

Maizey was right, this felt right, natural. He didn't think he needed the sledge hammer to see, so he opened a very small doorway in his mind and let the energy trickle out in a slow steady stream and as he did, the world around him lit up in a blue-electric pulse. He laughed as he realized what he had done. Actually it was more like a giggle, Cross didn't care. He had done it.

He turned to see Maizey sitting beside him. "I see you."

Maizey smiled and Cross was sure he had never seen anything more beautiful. "There you go, love. Now you can't keep this up 24/7, but I think you'll find it doesn't take much to 'keep the lights on'."

"No, this is like breathing. Now that I know how, I don't even have to think about it." He stood and turned in a circle. "I can see."

"You can, but remember what I said about running that marathon? After a while you'll be able to do this without payback, but you need to work those mental muscles out a little bit at a time."

"I'm almost afraid if I stop I won't be able to do it again," Cross said. It was the truth. He didn't trust himself to call up his sight again, but he did trust Maizey. He let the rest of the energy out slowly, as he did he took in every detail of the room he was in, the colors, the fabrics, but mostly he watched Maizey and as the last of energy left him, like a breath exhaled, his sight dimmed and being in the shadows again was all the darker for having been shown the light.

He was standing in the middle of the room when his knees buckled. He had no center, nothing to reference up from down. Cross was standing one moment and the next he was spinning. Maizey caught him before he hit the ground, or floated away, he couldn't tell which.

"And that would be the marathon," she said as she brought him gently down to his knees.

"Ah, right," his hand went to his head to try and stop the spinning. A queasy rolling gripped him. Maizey half dragged him back to the bed, Cross tried to help, but his brain stopped taking requests.

"This gets easier, right?" he hoped.

A light kiss on his head and a blanket was thrown over him. He curled into its warmth and tried to will his world to be still.

"Infinitely. I promise, but for now just sleep."

"Don't leave," his words slurred and an uneasiness gripped his heart at the thought of waking up alone in the dark. He held a hand out and felt her fingers, cool and slender, wrap around his.

"I'm right here, love. I'll be right here when you open your eyes. Trust me."

Cross squeezed her hand and let sleep suck him under.

Trust me.

Those words followed him down as he realized he had done just that.

Chapter 25

The plan was full of holes, both Vic and Finn knew it, but it was the best that any of them could come up with. It could work. It probably wouldn't get them killed. Maybe.

"Tanya took my badge," Finn reminded Vic.

"I am aware of that."

"I can't come with you."

"You can if Maizey hides you."

Finn paced in circles and rubbed his head. "What makes you think she hasn't moved Kale?"

"Because whenever she moves that boy, she puts the entire building on lockdown and doubles security. She hasn't done that. But she has sequestered herself down in the tombs for the last few days. Something is up."

The tombs. Two floors beneath the streets of Manhattan was a place very few people knew existed let alone have ever seen. That is where the most dangerous freaks were kept. Restricted entry. Excruciatingly tight security. Motion and heat sensors every few yards. If alarms sounded it was never a drill and the guards there were instructed to shoot to kill. No exceptions. Tanya was Lord and Master of the tombs and as far as Finn knew there was one and only one occupant locked down there alone in the dark.

Shut away from humanity, sunlight, and all contact, save Tanya was where Kale Delancey existed. To say he lived would be an unfair exaggeration.

"I was only ever down there the one time. Tanya wanted to convince me that Kale was the least dangerous brother. Took me twenty minutes to get through security. I never even saw him face to face. She took me to the control room and I watched a live feed."

"What did you see?" Vic said. Finn knew he was curious. Everyone who worked for the paranormal department had heard about Kale Delancey, but almost no one saw him. He was an urban legend. Except Finn knew he was real, he had seen the man. He had no idea how rare that was until years later.

"I saw Cross," Finn said. "If Cross had been kept a prisoner for the last ten years. I don't know what I was expecting, but he was just one man, sitting there staring at nothing. I felt sorry for him, not afraid of him."

"Said the man about the caged lion right before the lion ate him," Vic said. "Look, as far as I know, they still think I'm the faithful employee. I'm due back tonight, I'm on night shift. Thought it might be easier to get to Kale then."

"This is suicide, you realize that, right?" Finn said.

"Relax, man. I don't do suicide. This is the best I have right now but feel free to chime in if you think of something better."

Finn sat down opposite Vic and spread his hands giving him the go ahead. Vic reached behind him and pulled rolled paper from a cardboard tube. They looked like schematics. "This is the complex. All the upper levels here," Vic pointed to the two different levels shown on the paper. He pulled another paper from behind the first and placed it on top. "And this shows the two underground levels. Kale, as far as anyone knows, is in the bottom most level."

Finn leaned in and studied the schematics. "Where did you get these?"

"I'm not the only one at the department with a hidden agenda. Suffice it to say, we have more inside help than just me."

"Like who?" Finn was beginning to feel like everybody was keeping secrets from him.

"You don't need to know right now, when you do I'll tell you."

"Screw that Vic. I'm putting my life on the line here. I think I should at least know who I'm trusting that life too." Finn was liking this less and less.

"And if Tanya finds out who gave me these, she will have no problem killing him, or torturing him for information about who he's working with. I think we all have something at stake here, Finn so don't play the *life at stake card* with me. Everyone here has played that card more times than I can count. Just trust me, these are accurate."

"I don't like not knowing all the facts, Vic. I feel like my ass is hanging out in the wind here. Everyone wants me to trust them and I'm not sure I can do that."

Vic's eyes darkened as he hardened his face. "Then walk. You don't want to help us get Kale out of there, I can show you the door right now. How's that for trust?"

"All these people here. They live this way because of the Department that, until recently, you worked for. They trusted you because I vouched for you. There are families here, Finn. They trust the lives of their children on my word that you are not going to bring Coben and Tanya and half the department down here to scoop them up like they're unpapered *pollos* crossing the border."

Vic walked around the desk to stand in front of Finn. "I get the uncertainty. I understand it, but I don't have time to wait around for you to get comfortable with trusting us. You are either in or you are out."

Finn stared back into Vic's very black, very angry eyes. He felt like an ass. Even Cross, who had more reason than anyone not to trust him, had decided Finn was worth the risk. He didn't want to die. But sometimes dying for the right thing was better than staying alive for the wrong ones.

"I'm in," he said. He held Vic's gaze a moment longer. Vic seemed to consider his decision then gave him one brief nod.

"All right. Then let's see what we can come up with to get Kale out of that place and still be alive at the end of the day."

Pulling the schematics closer to him, Finn studied the drawings. "Alive works for me."

CHAPTER 26

Tanya and Coben were in the control room watching a live feed of Kale. He curled into himself on the thin mattress. She had ordered all his bedding removed. Leaving Kale only the bare mattress and the clothes on his back. The temperature in his room had been turned down to a chilly fifty-five.

"If you kill him, we'll have nothing to barter for Cross's cooperation," Coben said.

"I don't intend to kill him," Tanya said. "I simply want him miserable."

Coben watched Kale shiver. "I would say you succeeded. You said he'll do what you want. Isn't this a bit much?"

Tanya swallowed her disgust. For the life of her she couldn't understand why Coben was in a position of power. He didn't have it in him to do what was necessary to get the job done. "Think about it. We know Cross and Kale have been communicating telepathically. Possibly for years. We also know they would do anything for each other, so it's reasonable to believe that Cross knows what I've done to Kale. He is going to come for him. And when he does he's mine."

"I understand that, I approve of that, but why make Kale miserable?"

Tanya bit down the fury that bubbled through her. How dare he question how she handle Kale? She pushed down what she wanted to say and put a pretty smile on her face. "Because Coben, Kale is dangerous. My hold on him is tenuous. I want him incapable of pushing anyone. He requires energy to *push*. If he is hurt, feverish and uncomfortable, he can't control, influence or push anyone.

"I want him miserable, Coben, because he's not as dangerous that way. That is, unless you can think of a better way to control him."

"You could sedate him."

"And where would be the motivation for Cross to come and save him? I need him hurt Coben, so Cross will risk anything to save him. If Kale were simply sleeping, there would be no urgency. Without urgency, Cross would be careful.

"I don't want him careful, I want him reckless."

Coben looked back at the monitors once more. He didn't look much happier, but he did appear resigned. "Don't kill him. I have government contractors willing to pay a lot to use that talent of his. I need him alive, Tanya. Alive and willing to do whatever you tell him to do. Is that clear?"

"Don't worry Coben. You'll be able to whore him out soon enough. And if you're lucky we'll be able to offer his brother as an added bonus."

Coben considered that, then grunted. Without another word he left the control room.

Tanya glared after him. She glanced down at Kale for a moment and then pushed a button on the console.

"Yo," her chief of security answered.

"Robert, how is Kale doing?"

"Hurting."

Tanya considered. As much as she hated to give Coben credit, he did have a point. Kale was of no use to her dead. "Give him some water, clean him up and give him something for the fever."

"Yes, ma'am." No hesitations, no questions, Robert would do as he was told. That's how it should be. Coben should take notes from her security team. "Robert?"

"Yes?"

"There's no need to be gentle, am I clear?"

"Absolutely."

"Don't do any additional damage, take care of him, but no hand holding."

"Understood." Robert ended the conversation.

Why are you doing this, Coben had asked her.

Because I can.

****

Kale was so cold. He shivered and pain spasmed in his chest and he couldn't breathe. Cross needed help. Kale could hear his brother calling for him. He tried to find Cross, but he was in a maze. Every turn he took ended in a dead end. Cross kept calling.

"I'm coming, man!" Why couldn't he find him? One more turn, one more hallway and then... There! He saw Cross at the end of a long tunnel. He tried to run, but he hurt too badly. He forced himself to keep moving.

As he got closer, he realized it wasn't Cross who waited for him at the end of that tunnel.

Sybil King stood there. Her hair was matted to her head with blood. She grinned at Kale with crimson stained teeth. "You can't get out," she said. "You're going to die here and when you do, I'll be waiting for you."

Sybil laughed and Kale shivered with more than just the cold.

Kale opened his eyes and pain greeted him. He was sweating, and yet he shivered from the fever that ravaged his body. His arms were being lifted and as his vision cleared he recognized Robert peeling the filthy bandages from his left wrist.

He grimaced as scabs and skin were pulled off with the gauze. The wounds smelled horrible and an awful yellow fluid mixed with the blood. Kale tried to pull his hands away but Robert grasped them firmly.

"Take it easy, Kale. Just getting you cleaned up. Thirsty?" Robert held out a bottle of water and Kale grabbed it with his still bandaged right hand. He gulped and spilled more water than he swallowed. He didn't care. He was so thirsty.

Robert held out some pills to him. "Here, you're burning up. This'll help."

Kale downed them with what was left of the water. He eyed Robert suspiciously. He had never been like this. He had never helped him. He had certainly never been alone with him before.

"Why?" Kale said.

Robert took Kale's other wrist and ripped the stiff bandage off causing more blood and pus to roll down Kale's arm.

He hissed with the pain and grimaced.

"Because I do what I'm told," Robert said. "Maybe if you did that, you wouldn't be where you are now." He scrubbed the wounds on Kale's wrist. Kale pulled his arm back and held it against his chest. "Stop. Please, it hurts."

"Like I give a fuck." Robert reached for his arm again.

Kale was too tired to fight him. Then he remembered his dream. Sybil King with her blood matted hair waiting for him.

He squeezed his eyes closed and understood that was to be his end. That reality was as clear to him as the pain Robert caused him. He glanced behind Robert to the door of his room. It was open.

That door was never left open.

Maybe it had been laziness on Robert's part, or maybe he was afraid to be locked in a room alone with Kale. Or maybe Robert was confident that Kale was too weak to cause him any trouble.

Kale remembered Cross calling for him in the dream, He thought he remembered Cross coming to him earlier, but he wasn't sure if the memory was part of his delirium or just another dream. But one thing he knew for certain. If Cross knew what Tanya had done to him, his brother would come. Tanya was counting on that. He shook his head. "Not gonna happen."

"What?" Robert didn't even bother looking at him as he asked the question. "What're you talking about?"

Kale saw one chance. Maybe they would catch him. Maybe he didn't have the strength. He didn't care. He didn't fucking care anymore. He had to try.

He pulled his arm away from Robert and waited until Robert looked at him. "Stop." It wasn't a hard push. Barely more than a nudge but Robert stopped what he was doing. His face blanked and he looked at Kale for further instructions.

Kale's bruised mouth pulled up into a small smile. He tried to sit up. "Help me." Robert helped him sit.

The room spun a little but Kale ignored it. He was never going to get a second chance at this. "Tell me where Tanya is."

"At the main house."

"I don't know what that means. Explain."

"She's not in this complex today. That's why I'm here."

"She's not in this building?"

"No."

"Okay, Robert. Listen carefully. You are going to take me from this building."

"I can do that." Robert told him. Kale was reasonably sure he could make everyone around them forget they even saw him with Robert. It wasn't hard to push him, but Kale knew it would probably get more difficult the longer the push went on. If he was well, this would be a piece of cake, but pushing someone was a delicate matter. It required a great deal of concentration.

Like a well-trained athlete, Kale had practiced this his entire life, Tanya had seen to that. *Pushing* was like breathing to him. Except that right now, Kale was feverish and in pain. Getting Robert to guide him out of the complex was going to take every bit of concentration he had.

He had no idea how to get out, no idea of where to go or what to do once he was out. But out was infinitely better than in. He would worry about what to do if he actually managed to pull this off. He would have preferred to *push* Robert into taking him somewhere safe, but he didn't think he could keep it up that long. He was shaking now with the simple effort of keeping Robert's attention on him.

"Go." Kale stood and swayed. His head swam and his concentration wavered for a moment. When his vision cleared Robert was shaking his head and looking confused. Kale *pushed* him again, a little harder.

"Help me, take me to a back door. Someplace no one will see me."

Robert blinked, his face compliant once more. He put an arm under Kale's to support him. Together they walked out of the little room that, for the last ten years had been Kale's world.

He tried not to think about that. If he thought about that he wouldn't be able to concentrate enough to push Robert.

They passed no one in the hallways but Kale noticed the cameras and other devices on the ceiling. "How are we being watched?"

"Thermal sensors, Motion detectors, security cameras."

"Are they all on?"

"Just the cameras now. I was with you so the thermal and motion detectors weren't needed."

"Tell them to turn the cameras off."

Robert took the phone from his belt and pushed a button. "Turn the cameras off on this level." He looked at Kale. "They want to know why."

Kale took a breath. *Pushing* Robert was getting harder every minute, but he was committed now. He could collapse later. He held out a hand for the phone. "How many levels need cleared for me to get out?" He asked Robert.

"Two."

Kale put the phone to his ear and *pushed* the person on the other end. "Shut down the cameras and everything that would alert anyone to anything not normal for..." He looked to Robert for help.

"Sub levels one and two."

"Sub levels one and two," Kale repeated. "Oh, and you won't remember this conversation." Kale handed Robert the phone. "Go. Fast."

They met four more people as Robert guided Kale up and out. Kale *pushed* them each in turn. But he was slipping. He hoped wherever Robert was taking him, it was close.

After what seemed like a few dozen eternities. Robert stopped in front of an emergency exit. It took Kale a moment to understand. "Here?"

"Yes."

"This is out?"

"Yes, there is a stairway that leads up to street level."

"And where will I be exactly when I go up there?"

Robert's face creased in thought. "Back alley. I think."

"Perfect. You've done well Robert. Now I want you to do one more thing for me."

"Yes?" Robert waited for his final instructions.

"I want you to go back to my room and lock yourself in. Stay there until someone comes to get you. You will not remember any of this. I did not push you. You don't know what happened to me. Understand?"

"Sure."

Kale closed his eyes briefly and swallowed. Adrenaline helped but without Robert's support he wondered just how far he would get without falling flat on his face. Without waiting to find out, with one hand bracing hurt ribs Kale pushed open the door and staggered up into the light.

CHAPTER 27

Utah Case didn't hate her job. Seriously, there were way crappier ways to make a living. Being a barista in the slightly upscale Blue Bean coffee house wasn't bad. The hours sucked and people were rude and obnoxious. But hey, she was in New York. She had made it. So she could definitely put up with whatever life threw at her until she figured out what to do with the very expensive degree her parents had made sure she got.

Twenty-six-years old and she still didn't know what she wanted to be when she grew up. Did that make her pathetic?

She had already turned all the stools over and locked up inside. As she went out into the alley to empty the trash, she checked to make sure she had her pepper spray. It was getting dark and that's when all the wack-a-doodles came out. She turned to go back in when she noticed the security chain dangling around the light pole she had chained her bike to that morning. No bike now.

"Fuck!" she pulled the chain loose and flung it against the dumpster. It made an impressive loud *thwack* as it hit the metal.

That's when she saw a foot sticking out from the side of the dumpster jerk out of sight. She unclipped the pepper spray and held it loosely in her hand as she cautiously peered around the dumpster.

The foot was bare and bloody, the sole shredded. The she heard a low moan. The moan is what did her in. She was getting ready to back off and just let EMS handle the guy when she heard the moan. It was sad and pitiful and Utah couldn't walk away now. *Patron saint of impossible causes* – that's what her mother called her. Maybe she was just stupid.

"Shit." Mad at herself for even looking, she edged closer, pepper spray held in front of her, finger on the trigger.

"Dude, hey, you okay?" Utah stepped closer to get a full view of whoever the foot belonged to. "Holy shit,"

The guy curled up next to the dumpster looked like he had been on the losing end of a MMA cage fight. His eyes were swollen and bruised. His lips scabbed with dried blood. Fresh blood ran shiny and red from his nose and ears. Both wrists were circled with horrible oozing wounds. He shivered as if freezing.

She squatted down next to him. "Hey, hang on, okay? I'm going to get you some help." She pulled out her phone.

The man's eyes opened, just tiny slits, but he was in there. "No." The hand that caught hers was hot and slick with sweat.

She shook her head. He was obviously delirious. "Dude you so need help."

"They'll find me."

Oh, crap. "They? Like in the police?"

He shook his head. "Tanya. Please help me."

"Me?" Utah almost laughed. "Man, I can't even make rent and still buy groceries most months. Seriously, I have no idea how to help you. Let me call 911, man. You look like you're about ready to kick it. If this Tanya did this to you, the cops will get her."

"You don't understand." The guy opened his eyes wider and pulled himself up until he was slumped against the dumpster. He coughed and squeezed his eyes tight, as if he was hurting bad. When he opened them again his eyes were glassy but he seemed more focused. "They're looking for me."

"Why? Dude, what did you do? Why do they want you?"

He closed his eyes again but this time he looked like he was concentrating like mad. He took one hand and scooped at the air as if he was gathering imaginary balls and holding them.

Utah was ready to chalk him up as one of the crazies. She was backing away from the guy and had pressed 911 into the phone, but before she could hit send, a glowing ball of moving light flowed between the guy's hands.

He held it there as it pulsed and sparkled. Then he took it and threw it up above them. The light dissolved into a million points of beautiful light that looked to Utah like dazzling fireflies. It rained down on them like a cool shower. Utah held her hands out as the sparks of light danced briefly on her skin. Then the light faded and the alley was in darkness once more. Utah looked in open mouth wonder at the man sitting next to the dumpster.

"That's why," he said. More blood flowed from his nose and he gave a small grunt as his head slumped against his shoulders and his eyes closed.

Utah was afraid he might be dead. She cautiously crept up to him and placed a shaking finger on his neck. A fast bump bump bump ran under her fingers. She pulled her hand back and ran it over her hair. "Oh shitohshitohshit." She walked in rapid circles and tried to calm down.

"Okay, think, Utah, think!" She hit the side of her head as if that might jar an idea out of hiding. She should just call 911. The dude had to be crazy. But that thing, the light thing, what the hell was that? The only thing she could think to do was the last thing she wanted to do. She called her brother.

As she waited for him to answer she looked at the unconscious guy. "Dude, I swear if you're crazy I'm going to kill you." On the fifth ring, right before she was getting ready to hang up, her brother answered.

"Utah, hey."

"Yeah, hey Jude. How's it going and stuff?" *How's it going and stuff- brilliant.* "Umm. Listen, I really hate to bother you, but, yeah- someone stole my bike and I can't get hold of the roommate – not that he would come get me anyway, but you know how weirded out I am with the subway, uhhh..."

"Someone stole your bike?"

"Uh, yeah. Came out back and there it was, well I mean there it wasn't, just the chain all cut, and yeah, no bike. I mean maybe I shouldn't have called. I don't know what I was thinking, I'll walk, it's cool."

"Where are you?"

She exhaled. "Work, in the back alley. That's where I keep my bike. Kept- kept my bike."

"You can't walk all the way to Harlem this time of night." Jude sighed. "All right. Stay where you are. I can be there in ten minutes."

"Thanks man. You're a life saver, seriously." Utah ended the call and squatted down next to the guy again. She touched his forehead with the back of hand like her mom used to do when she was sick. His skin was hot, like blister-inducing hot. "Okay, weird light dude, I don't know if you can hear me, but I didn't call 911. But you might wish I did. I just lied to my brother to get him here and he is not going to like this one little bit."

Utah sat down next to the guy and tried to figure out what the hell she was going to tell Jude when he got here. Her brother was a lot older. He was the favorite child, the golden boy. Jude could do no wrong in their parent's eyes and Utah was the big oops. The *-I–thought-I-was-in-menopause-oh-crap-I'm-pregnant-*kid.

He never tried to make her feel like a failure, but he couldn't help it. The guy had an entire alphabet behind his name – MD, PHD – he taught at Columbia, she never was sure what exactly but he was pretty important. She was doing okay most of the time as long as she didn't stop to compare herself to Jude.

She kicked at the guy's leg, suddenly pissed at him. "You sure as hell better not die before he gets here."

A few minutes later Jude's Mercedes SUV turned into the alley. She had her bike stolen and he came to save her in a freaking Mercedes. Families. Sometimes they were they easiest people to hate, and the hardest to love. Maybe because you knew that no matter what you threw at them they would always take it and still be there when you really needed them.

Jude got out of the car searching the alley through the glare of the headlights. "Utah?"

"Over here." She stood to the side of the dumpster and waited for him. "Promise you won't be mad."

"Mad? What are you talking about? Why would I be mad about your bike getting ripped off?"

"Not about the bike. Jude, he needs help." Utah squatted next to the guy as her brother came around the side of the dumpster.

His eyes went wide when he saw the guy. He hesitated for maybe a second before bending down. He felt for a pulse and lifted the guy's eyelids. "Jesus, what the hell happened to him? Do you know him?"

"Haven't a clue and no. I came out to empty the garbage, saw the bike was gone and found him. Looks like he got hit by a bus."

"Looks like he got hit by something, Jesus." Jude took his phone out.

Utah put her hand on it before he could make the call. "No," she shook her head.

"No, what?" he looked at her suspiciously. "What's going on, Utah? Why don't you want me to call for help? Why'd you call me instead of 911?"

"He was scared, told me someone was looking for him. Jude he was so scared."

"I bet he was. You're unbelievable." He took his phone back.

"Wait, Jude, please. Okay I know I mess everything up, I work in a job I'm over qualified for and mom and dad are constantly disappointed in me. I get that, but this isn't about me.

"Look at him! He didn't want me calling for help because he knew whoever was looking for him would find him if I did. Do you want whoever did this to find him? You're a doctor. Didn't you take an oath or something? Please, I didn't know what else to do. Will you help me help him?" She decided to keep the glowing ball of light thing to herself for now.

He stared at her, his face completely neutral. Utah hated it when he did that. She could never tell what he was thinking. Just when she thought he was going to leave, or worse, call for help, he pulled the guy upright. "Help me get him to the car."

Utah went to the guy's other side. "Thank you Jude, Thank you!"

They dragged him the few feet to the SUV and laid him on the back seat. Jude closed the door and looked at Utah over the roof. "Don't thank me. You're going to detail the inside of my car and get out every drop of blood this guy bleeds on it." He got in the driver's side and waited for her.

"Oh absolutely, you bet." She got in and Jude backed out of the alley and sped off toward his apartment.

CHAPTER 28

Robert sat in Coben's office with his head in his hands. He tried to block out Tanya's rant. He'd already been chewed a new one and then some. Something more than humiliation consumed him. He was mortified, ashamed and fucking pissed off. He swore if he ever saw Kale Delancey again he wasn't going to wait for the guy to try and push him, he was putting a bullet in his brain. He didn't give a fuck how valuable the psycho was. This was personal. He didn't remember anything, but it was more than obvious what had happened.

"You just walked him to the door? Then you went back and sat in his room for three hours until someone noticed something was wrong!" This time it was Coben who was stating the obvious. Robert lifted his head and stared at him.

"He *pushed* me Coben. Something Tanya assured me he was incapable of doing." He shot Tanya a sideways glance. Anger was beginning to replace his humiliation. "It's not like I simply decided to let him go, for God's sake." He turned to Tanya. "You knew better than anyone what Kale was capable of and you sent me in there by myself. So don't try to pin this all on me. You gave me orders. I followed them while you had lunch with the upper echelon. So maybe instead of trying to figure out who to blame we should be trying to figure out how to find him."

Tanya and Coben both surprised him by looking embarrassed. Coben cleared his throat. "No one is trying to blame anyone, Robert. You're correct. Kale is weak and injured. He has never been outside before and he has no resources. He can't go far. Are you up to getting a team together?"

"Yeah, I can do that."

"Then do it. You have the authority to do whatever is necessary to find Kale and bring him back."

Robert stood. "My pleasure." He was turning to leave when Tanya stopped him.

"Robert, I want him back here alive. Is that understood? You sedate him and bring back – alive."

He clenched his fists and answered with his back still to her. "I understand." He left the room and mentally prepared a list of agents he wanted with him for the hunt.

She wanted her little pet back alive. He knew why. Everyone knew. Perverted bitch, she got off on the freak. True, she seemed to be the only who could control him, but still, it was sick. She wanted him alive? Yeah, well, accidents happened. Didn't they?

****

Finn answered his phone on the second ring. His watch informed him it was five in the morning, but without windows or daylight it was hard to tell. He missed the light. He'd been underground for only a day, but it was a day too long. He pushed the claustrophobia down, checked the caller ID and answered.

"Vic? What's up?"

"Kale got out."

"Say again?"

"You heard me the first time. I don't know details. But this place is a nut house right now. Apparently Kale's security screwed up big time. He was supposed to be compromised, in other words-safe."

"What did he do?"

"He *pushed* them. Guess Tanya didn't think he could. Look I don't know anything more than that. I don't know where he went, or if they have any leads on him, but it's been about twelve hours and that boy is in the wind. Word is he is not in great shape so he couldn't have gone far."

"Holy shit."

"Yeah. Gotta go. I'll try to come in later today, but it's tight here. Might be better if I stay away."

"I hear you. Stay cool. Thanks for the heads up." Finn sat there with the phone in his hand trying to understand, what this meant. He needed to tell Cross, but he had to do so carefully. He knew his partner. Cross was going to act first and think later. That wasn't what they needed. They needed information. Kale getting out changed everything. This was no longer a rescue mission

One of Finn's best attributes, as one of his instructors at Quantico had told him, was to see *beyond the static*. In other words he had the capability to see the next three steps in the equation. It made him an excellent chess player and an even better agent. He sat up, fully awake now and thought about what Vic's news meant. Their goal up to this point had been to rescue Kale. All of them had been willing to do whatever it took to see that goal accomplished.

Kale just changed all that. He'd taken matters into his own hands and rescued himself. Now all they had to do was find him. Before Tanya did.

Considering the psychic connection Cross shared with his brother, finding Kale shouldn't be terribly difficult. They simply had to find Kale before Tanya did. That was step one. Step two was the hard part. Tanya wasn't used to losing. And she had lost both Cross and Kale. That meant they were all officially righteous targets.

Tanya was going to use every man, every weapon, and every trick at her disposal to get them back and exact revenge on anyone she thought responsible. That would include Finn and everyone in the Underground.

Tanya had an organized team trained for situations just like this. Finn had a group of paranormal misfits who would rather kill him than help him. Go team. He had to do the impossible with only the improbable for help.

He needed to bring Kale in to safety which right now meant into the Underground. Then what? If either Cross or Kale stayed here, Tanya would find them. It wasn't a question of if, but when. And when she found them, every man, woman and child in these tunnels would end up in the crossfire or worse, in a glass-walled room. Or dead.

"So we don't let that happen."

Finn jumped at the voice. He had been so absorbed in his thoughts he hadn't heard Cross come in. The large common room was, for now empty of everyone save Finn and Cross. "Shit," he pressed his hand on his chest. "Don't freaking do that."

"Which part? Scare you, or get in your head?" Cross walked confidently to the table where Finn sat.

"Both." As he watched Cross take a seat, it hit him. "Hey, don't take this the wrong way, but aren't you blind?"

A sly grin spread across Cross's face. "Yeah."

"Then explain how you just walked in liked you own the place."

"Pretty sweet, huh? Maizey showed me."

"Showed you what?" Finn moved a hand in front of Cross's face. He caught it and stared at Finn. Stared directly at him.

"How to use the energy around me to see. Sort of." He let Finn's hand go. "It would seem when I lost my sight, my paranormal abilities adapted, only with Gabriel's mind-fuck I never knew it."

"You can see?"

"Not like before, not like I used to, but yeah. I can see. It's kind of beautiful. I absorb the energy around me. When I let it out again, it pings off objects around me. Everything shows up in glowing blue and white. Like electrons dancing on the edges of light."

"Sort of like radar?"

Cross appeared to think about that. "More like a lateral line. You know, like how a shark finds prey?"

"That's pretty freaking cool."

"Infinitely better than not being able to see, but it does have its limits. I can't keep it up for very long. It takes energy to use energy. I get tapped out after a while."

Finn grinned. "So you're just showing off now?"

"That and I was curious. I wanted to see what you looked like."

"And now you're jealous, right? Cause now you know I'm a chick magnet."

"Yeah, sure." Cross lowered his head and laughed. "Actually you look exactly how I imagined you. Except you didn't have blue hair." When he raised his head he looked directly at Finn. "Now that the party trick is over, I do have a suggestion."

"About Tanya. And I thought you promised you wouldn't look in my head."

"You really want to go there Finn? As far as I'm concerned anything or anyone that gets me out of this mess alive is fair game. Any promises I made to you before I understood what happened to me are null and void. If you have a problem about that, I gotta say I really don't care."

The expression on Cross's face as he spoke concerned Finn. Not because Cross looked pissed off, but because he looked utterly empty. Finn would have preferred pissed.

"Fair enough. So what's your suggestion?"

The empty look gave way to something else. Finn couldn't decide what it was, but he was certain about one thing. Cross was teetering. This was not the collected, methodical man he had worked with for the last decade. This was someone he didn't recognize.

"First," Cross said, "I would say I agree with you. We need to find Kale. I've been trying to contact him, with no luck. If he's in worse shape than the last time I contacted him, it's no wonder. I'll work on it."

"Okay, and then once we find him, what do we do then? We can't put these people in danger. They gave us refuge and if we stay we'll repay them by bringing a war to their doorstep."

"I agree."

"So what do we do?" Finn said.

Cross suddenly resembled the homicidal fourteen-year old Finn had seen pictures of. "We bring the fucking war to Tanya." Complete and total hatred laced through every syllable.

"You're kind of freaking me out a little here, partner," Finn said. Cross looked like he wanted to hurt someone- anyone, very badly and Finn was the only person in range. The hairs on his arms stood up. He wasn't cold, he was scared.

"I'm not your partner, not anymore."

"Who the hell are you then? Because I'll tell you something. You sure as hell don't resemble the Cross Delancey I knew a few days ago."

"That's because I'm not. That Cross was never supposed to exist. He was created by Tanya and my father. He died when I learned the truth."

"And this Cross? How does this Cross differ from the one I knew?" Finn eyed Cross with more than a little concern.

"This Cross is never letting anyone take anything from him again. This Cross is strong and doesn't give a fuck. He'll do what has to be done." No empty look this time. Anger was the mood of the moment.

"And what needs to be done, Cross?"

"Tanya and anyone who helped her put Kale in that room for ten years, who decided taking my life from me and let me live a lie, they need to pay. Whatever it takes to accomplish that is what needs to be done, Finn." Without another word, Cross turned away from him and walked out of the empty room.

For the first time, Finn almost felt sorry for Tanya. He didn't think she knew exactly what she unleashed when she showed Cross the truth.

CHAPTER 29

Kale opened his eyes and immediately understood two things. He wasn't in his own bed and he wasn't alone. He didn't know if that was a good thing and decided to err on the side of fear. He sat up quickly, or at least he gave it his best shot. Pain was a vice gripping his ribs and stealing his breath. He grimaced as his arm braced his chest. He didn't even come close to sitting up.

"Hey, hey, take it easy. You're safe."

A few blinks brought everything into focus. A man he had never seen before sat next to the bed and next to him was a young woman. She was vaguely familiar, like someone he remembered from a dream.

Then it all came back to him. *Pushing* Robert. Stumbling through to the outside. Wandering aimlessly before collapsing next to the green garbage bin in the alley. A girl. The same one sitting next to him now. He'd been sure she would call someone and he would be back inside when he woke up. She hadn't.

He was out.

He was out!

What the hell did he do with that?

He had never been so terrified in his entire life. Turning to get a better look at the girl, he said, "Thank you,"

She smiled and he was certain he had never seen anything as beautiful in his whole life. She had short spiky blonde hair streaked through with purple. Her eyes were an incredible clear blue. They hypnotized him.

"I thought you were dead," she said.

"Not far from it," the man said. "What's your name?"

Kale watched him adjust the IV attached to his arm. "You a doctor?" he said instead of answering.

"Yes." He laid the back of his hand on Kale's forehead. "What happened to you? Utah said someone was after you? Care to explain that?"

"Not really." He looked at the girl again. "Utah?"

"Dude, you scared the crap out of me. I mean I went to take the garbage out and you know, found my bike gone and then damn, there you were looking like, wow, bad dude. You didn't want me calling EMS and I didn't know what else to do so I called Jude."

Kale's eyes flicked to the man next him. "Jude?"

The guy gave him a quick nod. "And your name?"

He couldn't think how it would hurt to tell them. "Kale, my name is Kale."

Jude didn't look happy. "Okay, Kale. Let me explain something to you. I didn't take you to the hospital against my better judgment and because I have a soft spot for my baby sister. That doesn't mean I don't think you shouldn't be in one. As far as I can tell, someone, pretty much beat the crap out of you, fairly recently. If I start from the top and work my way down, you have a serious concussion, your nose is broken, you have two very impressive shiners, not a clue if there is any eye damage. Ribs? Without x-rays hard to tell but I would bet more than one are broken. Your midsection is a patchwork of bruises and you're pissing blood so let's put a little internal damage on that list.

Your wrists? Jesus, I don't even know if I want to ask. It sure as hell looks like you were restrained and not in a nice way. The wounds are severely infected and I am fresh out of antibiotics. You have a fever and, until I started the IV were pretty dehydrated. All I'm doing is putting a Band-Aid on one big fucking problem."

Jude stood, and Kale could see the frustration in his face.

"So, do you want to rethink that request about not going to the hospital? Because I'm telling you pal, there's not a whole lot more I can do for you here."

Kale braced one arm across his ribs and tried to sit up, Jude pushed a pillow behind him. He grimaced as he moved but managed to keep the groan to himself. "Where am I?"

"My apartment. Manhattan, a few miles from where Utah found you. No one saw us bring you here."

"How long have I been here?"

"Since last night. Twelve, fourteen hours."

Kale didn't want to get these people involved, not with Tanya. Jude was right, he needed help. It was a very big world and he had no idea how to navigate it. He needed Cross. So like it or not, these people had just adopted him. He only hoped he was up to protecting them if it came to that. Knowing Tanya he had no doubt it would come to that. Twelve hours and he still hadn't been found, meant that Tanya had no clue to his whereabouts.

Yet.

That was good. He wondered how Utah and Jude were going to take what he was about to tell them.

He held his wrists up. "Rope," he said. "And yeah, they weren't very nice about it. After they tied me, they hung me by my wrists. All that weight bites pretty deep. That's when the real fun started."

"Holy fuck," Utah said.

"I don't remember much of it, but when they were finished they left me hanging there for a few hours, until Tanya finally had them cut me down."

"You mentioned her before. Who is she?" Utah said.

"Complicated answer," Kale wiped a hand over his face. Every now and then his vision would blur or double. "How prepared are you for a story you probably won't believe?"

"The ball of light," Utah sounded like she was talking to herself.

"The what?" Jude turned to look at her.

Kale grinned. He had forgotten what he had shown her. A simple manifestation. A party trick. It had taken barely any effort and had obviously impressed the hell out of her. He wondered if he should do something more impressive to convince her brother he wasn't crazy. "Yeah, the ball of light."

"I thought I imagined it. I didn't, did I?"

Kale shook his head.

"Mind telling me what you're talking about?" Jude was looking at Kale like he was an escaped psych patient again.

"Okay, this is the 'You aren't going to believe me' part," Kale took a deep breath and jumped off the cliff he had been standing on. "My name is Kale Delancey. My twin brother, Cross and I were born and raised in what we called the Department. Officially it's called the Department for Paranormal Research."

Jude raised his brows. "Paranormal?"

"See that's where all the 'You don't believe me' part starts coming into play. Hang on. It gets way better. So Cross and me, we have these, abilities. Talents, if you will. The Department is very interested in learning how we do what we do. Tanya runs the place. She is, shall I say, quite protective of me.

"When Cross and I were fourteen, he convinced me we should try to escape. That didn't end well. They shot Cross. When he didn't die, Tanya and Coben- he runs the place with her- decided Cross was way too dangerous to bring back the way he was, so they wiped his memories and reprogrammed him. For the last ten years, he believed I was dead and his life was anything but what it had been.

"Except last week Cross started remembering his real past. So Tanya brought him in. The short version is Cross escaped and I wouldn't help Tanya find him." He motioned to bruised and beaten body. "She was just a tad disappointed in my decision."

Jude's face turned a violent shade of red. He looked like he was about to rupture something he might need later. "Wait a minute," he said to Utah. "It's gotta be the head injury. Or the fever. He's delusional."

"Show him," Utah said.

Kale let out a quick breath. "This is really a lot more impressive when I'm stronger." He scooped the ambient energy surrounding them and formed the glowing ball of light between his hands. He wanted to do more, but he was tired.

"Technically this is called psi energy. I take energy from whatever surrounds me and use myself as a conduit." Kale let the ball of light grow. The look on Jude's face was pretty hysterical. It always hit the scientific ones the hardest. "Like I said, this isn't very impressive, but I'm not exactly working at my best here. I can do pretty much anything I want with it, this will have to do for now." He gestured the light up and left it drift to the ceiling, and then made a small flick of his wrist. As it had in the alley, the energy dissipated into a million tiny sparkles that rained down on them. Kale closed his eyes and rested his head back. He really was feeling pretty crappy, but the day he couldn't do that- would be the day they buried him.

"See?" Utah sounded like a proud parent. "The light thing."

"How did you do that?" Jude said.

Kale shrugged. "How do you know how to breathe? I just do it. That's one of the reasons Tanya wants me back."

"What else can you do?" Utah said.

Kale was feeling lightheaded. "I can *push* people." He closed his eyes wanting very much to go back to sleep.

"What's that?"

"Utah, he needs to rest, let him be."

Kale suddenly remembered Cross. "*Pushing* is how I got out. That's my big thing. It's why Tanya wants me back. It's also why she thinks I'm dangerous." Kale attempted a laugh. He didn't feel very dangerous.

"Back up for one minute. You said you and your brother tried to get out when you were fourteen. How long have you been there? How long has this Tanya had you?"

"All my life, man. All my life." Kale slid down inside the warm covers, but before he stopped resisting and slid into oblivion, he made one final request. "I need to find my brother. I need to find Cross."

"Cross, is he like you? Can he do things, like the light?" Utah said.

With his eyes still closed, Kale smiled. "Cross makes me look like a bad street magician." His voiced slurred a little and he fought off the oblivion. "I need to find Cross." He tried to sit up.

Jude kept him in place with one hand. "How far do you think you're going to get like this? Come on, you have my word, I won't tell a soul you're here. You know Utah is tight. So rest. Let me take care of you. When you're better, we will all look for your brother together, okay?"

Kale was sure he had heard him wrong. "You'll help me?"

"Yeah, now sleep." Kale felt Jude's hand slide over his eyes, closing them. He couldn't stop the slow slide into sleep this time.

Jude rested his arms on his knees, his hands clasped. He stared at Kale Delancey for what felt like a long time. Utah disturbed the silence.

"Are you okay?"

"I don't know." It was an honest answer.

"Are you really going to help him?" Utah sounded like she thought he might go back on his word.

He didn't like that. He turned to face her. "I told him I would. I have never gone back on my word before and I don't intend to start now."

"But?" Utah knew him far too well.

He didn't like that either. Jude wiped a hand over his face and continued to stare at Kale Delancey. "But, what are we supposed to do with him, Utah? The guy is hurt and sick. This isn't a hospital, I don't have the things he needs here."

"You found the IV. Maybe you can find some antibiotics. You can help him, I know you can."

"He needs more than good intentions. I happened to have a liter of saline for a class I was giving to my pre-med class on starting IVs. That was luck."

"So write a prescription. You're a doctor, so you can do that, right?"

Jude stood and looked to the ceiling, briefly trying to rein in his frustration. "Ever the eternal optimist." His little sister never changed. "Yeah, I can do that."

"So write one for me. It might not be exactly what he needs, but it's better than nothing, right?"

Jude just stared at her. "Well, yeah. Why didn't I think of that?"

Utah stretched and yawned. "Sometimes the smarter you are, the more difficult it is to see the simple solutions."

Jude grunted out a laugh. "Apparently. Hang on, let me find the number I need to call this in." It didn't take long, to call in a prescription for an antibiotic in Utah's name at a local pharmacy.

"I'll pick it up. Are you going to be okay alone with him?"

"Why wouldn't I be? I can handle him." Jude paced around the apartment. Not being in control never suited him well.

Utah seemed to sense his mood. "Okay, what is it?" She sat at the bar in his kitchen and looked totally at ease. Like she found half-dead, men on the run and hiding from subversive organizations every day.

"What is it? Seriously?"

"It's the glowing ball of light thing. Isn't it?" She nodded as if answering her own question. "It freaked me out at first, too."

"And yet you failed to share that little piece of information with me when I brought him home." He nailed her with a looked that he hoped told her how unbelievably blasé she was being about this whole thing.

"I knew you wouldn't have believed me. I mean, really, Jude, you saw him do it and you still don't believe it, do you?"

"I don't know what to believe. I really don't. Maybe it was an illusion. Granted a hell of a good illusion, but it had to be just an illusion."

"Why does it have to be? He called it psi energy. I mean I don't have a dual degree, but I've heard of psi energy. It's a real thing." Utah opened his fridge and pulled out a carton of orange juice that she started to drink from. He snatched the carton out of her hand, poured the juice into a cup and handed it to her.

"Psi energy is something that strange people on the internet believe is real. Like some people like to believe in Hogwarts."

"He's not crazy, Jude."

"It's a theory, Utah. That's all it is. It isn't real."

"I don't know, it sure as hell looked real to me." She put the glass of juice down and leaned forward.

Jude knew that look. His sister had the clueless thing down to a science but he was one of the few people who knew just how brilliant she truly was. Utah wasn't comfortable with it, so she downplayed it – *like totally.* She wasn't downplaying now.

"Look, I know you Jude. You require all these facts and logic for you to confirm that something has merit."

"It helps."

"Yeah, but it isn't everything. Are you going to try and tell me that we, as a species, know everything there is to know? You always told me seeing is believing. Well you just saw what that man did and you still don't believe him. The problem is, you can't put all your facts in a neat little algorithm, so you simply dismiss what is right in front of you. I think it actually physically hurts you to stretch yourself into the realm of *what if.*"

"That's not true. As a scientist I ask myself, 'what if' all the time."

"Yes, but the answer only satisfies you if you can prove it."

"What's wrong with a little proof?"

Utah walked around the bar and squatted next to where Jude sat. "Facts and logic aren't everything. Five hundred years ago we were convinced the earth was the center of the universe. Three hundred years ago we were burning women at the stake for being witches. Two hundred years ago we thought it was a fine idea to enslave our fellow human because they were a different color. A hundred years ago people were dying from diseases that don't even exist today. Twenty-four hours ago you were convinced that using your own body as a conduit for manipulating energy was just a preposterous theory." Utah took Jude's hand. "We are highly fallible creatures, Jude, prone to misconceptions, misdirection and prejudices. Facts and logic only go so far. When they fail, sometimes all we have to go on is faith."

Jude held her hand and gave her a tired smile. "Says the agnostic."

"Doesn't mean I don't believe in anything. We both saw what he did, Jude. If we choose to believe in that, that we choose to believe the rest of his story."

Jude took a deep breath and glanced over at his sleeping patient. "Is it really that easy for you?"

She raised her shoulders. "Right now, you're wishing you never picked up the phone when I called you, or that you had called 911 when I did. The *facts,* Jude, are that you didn't. You brought him here and you agreed to help him. He can't not exist now, just because it's uncomfortable for you."

"So in other words we do the right thing even if it doesn't make any sense."

She stood and kissed him on the head. "Exactly."

"I hope this Kale Delancey understands just how lucky he is, that he collapsed in your alley."

"If he doesn't, he soon will. I'm going to go get his medicine. You try not to let him die before I get back." She took some money from his wallet on the table, blew him a kiss and walked out the door.

Jude watched her go and then turned back to the still sleeping Kale. "I'm not supposed to let you die, so how about you help me out and keep breathing." He propped his feet up on the bed, closed his eyes and waited for his sister to come home.

CHAPTER 30

They needed supplies. Maizey was the logical choice to leave the tunnels to get them. In a pinch she could be anyone, or no one at all. She didn't mind, in fact she volunteered. She understood the necessity of living the way they did, but she couldn't say she liked it. Knowing there was all that rock, and dirt and buildings just above her head made her a little bit claustrophobic. She could handle it but she didn't mind leaving when she had the chance.

Armed with a pocket full of cash and a list, Maizey headed off to the nearest CVS for medical supplies. She was also searching for any clues to Kale's where abouts. Since he and Cross were identical twins, it would stand to reason that their energy would read the same if not very similar. So as Maizey walked the streets of Manhattan, she *searched* for Kale. She looked for a person's unique energy signature like a dog homed in on a scent cone. But instead of a scent, Maizey sought the unique trails of energy people left in their wake.

If Kale was anything like his brother, he should have left an extremely vibrant trail. She cast out her psychic feelers, but all she got was the chaotic rush of the people nearby. Flat dull auras, nothing remotely interesting and the psychic noise was giving her a headache. She lowered the intensity of her search as she walked into the CVS and grabbed a basket. She had started filling it from her list when a girl entered the store. She had short blond hair streaked with purple. The psychic energy surrounding her nearly overwhelmed Maizey, even at the subdued level she was receiving. But the energy she sensed from the girl was not her own. It was cast off and a very recent cast off.

Maizey closed her eyes and let the energy envelop her. This girl had recently been exposed to an incredibly powerful psychic and its signature was familiar. She opened her eyes and smiled.

She had just found a trail of bread crumbs leading directly to Kale Delancey.

Part of her was elated, the other part was worried. If Maizey could detect Kale's energy this easily, she was sure Tanya had people at her disposal who could do the same. She needed to get this girl off the streets. Better yet, she needed her to get to Kale.

Maizey kept an eye on the girl. She was in line to pick up a prescription. Maizey paid the cashier and left the store. Once outside she bought a hot dog from a corner vender and ate it while waiting on a bench.

The girl left the store a few minutes later and headed, at a leisurely pace toward the Upper East Side. Maizey could have followed her with her eyes closed. That's how strongly Kale's energy permeated her.

She finished her hotdog and then started to gradually close the distance between them until she was directly behind the girl. Sending out a delicate tendril of psychic energy, she confirmed two things. The first, was that she had definitely been exposed to Kale. The second was that she had no idea Maizey was following her. She learned quite a few other things about the girl as well. The girl had a strong, open mind. All of her feelings were right on the surface. Maizey read her as easily as words on a page. She learned the girl had helped Kale, and she was returning there now. As the girl slowed to cross the street, Maizey stood next to her. Just another face in the crowd.

"Utah?"

She spun around and Maizey saw surprise and fear in her eyes, but only for a moment. She was good at concealing her true feelings. "I'm sorry, do I know you?"

Maizey smiled and shook her head. "No, but I think we have a mutual friend."

"How do you know that? How do you know me?" All attitude and suspicion.

Maizey liked this girl. Subtlety wasn't going to work so she decided to just go for it. "Kale Delancey." Utah's pupils dilated, she sucked in a quick breath, and she backed away.

Maizey didn't have to get inside her head to know Utah was trying to decide if she should deny the name or just run. She pressed a little deeper into the girl's thoughts and understood the source of her fear. Kale had shared a lot with her.

"I'm not Tanya. I'm a friend."

Utah blinked twice. "You know about Tanya?" She still wasn't sure which way to jump.

"I know a lot of things. I know your name is Utah Case, I know you found Kale yesterday, I know your brother is hiding him in his brownstone about a block and a half from here, and I know right now you're trying to protect him. Please believe me. So am I."

Utah let out a breath and her body language softened in a heartbeat. "Are you like him?"

"I don't think there is anyone quite like Kale, but yes, I am, in my own way."

"That's how you knew all that? Who I am, about my brother?"

Maizey nodded. "We've been searching for Kale. I'm glad you found him before Tanya."

Utah bit her lip and Maizey knew she was struggling with trusting her completely. Desperation seemed to have made the decision for her. "He's hurt and he's sick, really sick," she held up the bag from the pharmacy. "This is medicine for Kale, but he needs more than just antibiotics. Jude, my brother, he's a doctor but he can't do much for him at his place. Can you help him?"

"I can, but I need you to trust me. Think you can do that?"

****

Utah was excited and nervous. But mostly excited. She had to remind herself to simply breathe and try to act normal. That was hysterical. Act normal. Her notion of what was normal had been flipped on its head in the last few hours. She took a deep breath.

She didn't even have the key out of the lock when Jude pulled the door open and yanked her inside.

"Jesus, where the hell have you been? I kept having these visions of you being kidnapped by the people looking for him." Jude snatched the bag of pills from her.

"Sorry. I would've called but my cell died."

"Why can't you ever remember to charge it?"

"Jude, we need to talk." Utah said as he disappeared into the kitchen, apparently to get something for Kale to wash the pills down with. As he did, Maizey appeared where there had been nothing, and next to her, Kale's brother. She jumped a little at their sudden appearance. Knowing Maizey had concealed herself and Cross was one thing. Actually witnessing them become visible was another.

They were supposed to wait until she told Jude they were there, but she guessed Cross was impatient. She couldn't blame him. If it had been Jude lying there, she wouldn't have waited either.

Jude came back from the kitchen. He was opening the bottle of pills and had yet to notice Maizey or Cross. "He's really feverish, I don't even know if I can wake him up enough to make him swallow these." He glanced up and froze.

"Jude, these people can help him."

"What have you done?"

Maizey had knelt at Kale's side. She stood now and faced Jude. "She did the right thing. So did you. I'm Maizey. This is Kale's brother, Cross. We're here to help."

Jude had yet to move. Utah watched his expression change as he tried to come to terms with what was happening. "You said yourself, he needs more help than we can give him."

Jude looked at Utah for the first time since entering the room. "How do you know they're not the bad guys?"

"They convinced me."

"Look we can explain everything later," Cross said. "Right now, Kale is what matters."

Utah knew the guy was blind, but he sure as hell looked like he was seeing his brother. He looked like he was seeing everything.

He knelt next to the bed and took off the dark glasses. Without them the resemblance between him and Kale was startling. Cross closed his eyes and held Kale's hand.

Utah quietly moved next to Maizey and whispered. "What's he doing?"

"He's trying to find Kale."

Utah must have looked as confused as she felt.

Maizey explained. "We can't move him like this. Cross is trying to bring Kale's consciousness back to the surface. Once he does that he can help him feel better for a short while."

"So you really can help him?" Utah still didn't understand completely but she was content to watch. Jude looked like he was ready for an epic meltdown. But he was quietly, if not suspiciously watching.

"Yes, then we can help him."

****

The first thing Cross saw when he walked through the door was Kale. Not through a veil of manifested energy, but through his newly acquired sight. Maizey had asked him to wait until Utah had a chance to prepare her brother for them, but he couldn't. She'd also warned him to use his sight sparingly. He understood, but he had been practicing. He could *turn on the lights* for hours at a time without it draining him now. When he walked through the door he sensed Kale's presence and couldn't wait another moment.

Lying on a sofa in the corner of the room, Kale lit up in Cross's visual spectrum like a beacon. Cross let Maizey guide him to the bed. He could have managed it on his own, but his feet didn't seem to want to move. For the first time in ten years Cross was physically in the same place as his brother.

He reached out and touched Kale's hand. The skin was dry and so hot. "You're real," Cross whispered. "I should never have doubted you." He glanced up to Maizey. Kale was in far worse shape than he realized.

Maizey met his eyes and he heard a brief whisper in his head.

Do you need me to help? She was asking if he needed her help to wake Kale up. He shook his head and took off his glasses. They interfered with his blue and white spectrum vision. He closed his eyes and let his consciousness flow into his brother.

The first thing he felt was the pain. He grimaced as he tried to get a handle on that. Cross had forgotten when he shared a consciousness, he shared everything, joy, sorrow and pain.

Kale's pain was huge. Broken bones, bruised flesh and the perhaps the worst of it, a massive infection that had spread from the deep wounds in his wrists. He pushed past all of that and moved deeper into Kale's mind. Where would his brother go in his memories for comfort.

A shared memory came to him. Yes, he knew where to look for Kale.

Cross pictured the place in his mind, and suddenly the tree house appeared before him. It looked like a dream, incomplete, but with enough form to give it substance. Cross looked down at himself and smiled as he saw his fourteen-year-old self. He climbed the rickety ladder and soon he was sitting next to his brother. "I found you."

Kale glanced up with that stupid half-cocked grin. "How'd you know to look for me here?"

"It was one of the few places we ever had any real privacy. It's where you always ran to when you were hurting. You're kind of hurting now, Kale."

Kale grimaced his agreement. "Yeah, but I got out." His tone was one of pride.

"I know."

"Tanya did a number on me though, man. I think I might be dying."

"Not if I can help it. That's why I'm here, Kale. Do you remember when we got sick as kids? Remember that bad reaction I had to something they injected me with? They were all worried. Do you remember what we did?"

Kale's eyes widen as he did remember. "We shared it."

"We shared it," Cross agreed.

Kale considered that, but he looked worried. "It's too much, Cross. I can't share this with you. It would hurt you, too."

"I can handle it. Listen, I told you I would come for you and I did. You already did the hard part. You got out. Now I need you to trust me to do the rest, okay?"

Kale still didn't look sure. Cross clutched his brother's arm, the one with the scar. He turned it over. "I would die for you, too Kale. But not today. Okay?"

Kale looked at the scar and then he looked over at Cross. "Okay." He sounded exhausted.

Cross gave him a quick nod. "Let me take what I can and then you follow me out, understand?"

Kale nodded back.

Out. Cross wanted to share the pain and the hurt so that Kale could wake up. So they could travel. Finn should have everything they needed by the time Kale was ready. But time was not their friend. Tanya and Coben were out there looking for both of them. They needed to move fast, but first he needed to help his brother. This time it was his turn to save Kale.

He began, slowly at first, to syphon the worst of the pain to his own body. It wasn't real no matter how it felt. Cross wasn't actually hurt. He was only fooling Kale's body into thinking it wasn't as injured and as in pain as it truly was.

He was sharing the shock and the pain. When Kale was stronger, he would give it back. The tricky part was, while his mind knew the difference in what was real and what wasn't, his body didn't.

He seized up as the worst of the pain knifed into his system. Having dealt with his own pain all too often, he knew how to keep it at a manageable level. But this pain was almost more than he could handle, it shadowed his new vision and threatened his balance.

He sensed Maizey at his side. "You okay?"

"I'm good," he said. If he thought about it too long, Kale's pain would surface, but for now it swam in lazy circles beneath the surface of his consciousness. He couldn't keep it there for long, but hopefully he wouldn't have too.

"Kale?"

"Here, man. Good to see you, Cross. I mean really see you." His brother's voice, his *real* voice, was quiet but he was there. He was awake. More than that. He was *alive.*

Overcome with raw emotion, Cross held out a hand and felt Kale take it. They hadn't been close enough to touch in a long time.

Such a simple thing, to touch his brother's hand. He had thought he would never have the chance to do it again. Cross held on tight.

"You good?" he asked Kale. He wanted to say so much more, but the words wouldn't come. He felt Kale's presence in his head. His brother understood.

"A little shaky, but yeah, I'm good."

"What the hell just happened?" Jude's voice. "What did you just do to him?"

"He made it possible for Kale to travel," Maizey said.

"Travel? He's in no shape to travel. Where do you want to take him?"

"Jude, I know this is a lot. But hey, if you can handle the glowing ball of light thing, you can handle this." Utah said.

"Maizey," Cross said. "Will you explain what's going on to the good Doctor? It might save some time."

"Jude?"

"Just start talking," Jude said.

"Actually, this will be easier."

Jude took a step back, let out a short gasp and then fell silent. Maizey had just entered his mind. She would calm him and show him exactly what had happened and what they needed to ask of him. She would show him the truth in a way he could accept. It was an invasion, but they were precious short on time.

"Hmm, Finn is outside." Kale said.

Cross raised his brows. "Right on time for a change." Then he sensed something else.

"I feel it too," Maizey said.

"What?" Utah said.

A moment later Maizey's cell phone rang.

As she answered it, Cross said. "We have company."

CHAPTER 31

Tanya paced her office, trying to see through the anger. She needed to control the rage boiling beneath the surface. In a space of two days she had lost not one but both Delancey brothers.

Cross, she could almost understand. He probably couldn't remember a time when he had belonged to the Department. Even if the truth was something other than what he remembered, his outrage and escape while not acceptable, was understandable. Even predictable.

Kale, on the other hand, was a personal betrayal. Tanya had prided herself on being able to control Kale. He had never seriously denied her anything in the past. Of course he'd put up mock protests but in the end, Tanya always got what she wanted. Always.

She should have realized without Cross as leverage, Kale would be unpredictable. She thought the girl's death had him sufficiently terrified. He always seemed so afraid of his powers, Tanya had honestly never thought he would use them to escape.

But he had.

Now both of them were in the wind. They both should have been scooped up within hours of their escape. But forty-eight hours later and they were both still missing. Which told Tanya they'd had help.

Cross had to have had assistance in leaving the complex.

She considered every possibility and every time she came up with the same conclusion. There was a five minute loop on the surveillance video. Five missing minutes. A lot could happen in five minutes. Cross had probably only needed three to get out. The loop gave Vic a plausible excuse for why he hadn't realized Cross was gone sooner. Tanya found the excuse shaky, but Vic had never been even a blip on her radar before. She let it slide until she looked closer at the man.

Tanya wanted to hear it again from the man himself. She planned to confront Vic with what she suspected, and see his reaction.

A knock on her door interrupted her thoughts. "Come."

Robert opened the door and Vic followed him in. Tanya waited as Vic made himself comfortable in the chair opposite her. Robert stood at the door, hands clasped in front of him, his side arm visible at his hip.

Vic seemed entirely too at ease. "Any news on Kale?"

Tanya tried to read his body language, but he gave her nothing. He leaned back in the chair, one ankle crossed over a knee, his arms casually resting on the chair arms.

"No, nothing. I was wondering if you might have heard anything from Cross."

"Nada. But I'm hardly the first person he would've come to for help. What about Finn? I know you told him to take a vay-cay but do you honestly think he's going to do that?"

"No, I don't. Which is why I've had him under surveillance since Cross escaped. But you know that, don't you Vic?"

"Well, I assumed you would, but I didn't know it for a fact until now."

Tanya deliberately placed her hands on the desk and slowly stood. She walked around the desk to face Vic, leaned back with her arms crossed. "You're a smart guy, Vic. That's probably why you have the job you do. But for the sake of expediency and to cut through all the bullshit would you mind if I just cut to the chase?"

Vic chuckled. "As if you need my permission."

"For the life of me, I couldn't figure out how someone like Cross, and by someone I mean, blind, could get out of a secure building on his own. I get him taking down the guard. That was a pretty sweet move. But it should have been stopped there. The room was monitored, cameras following Cross's every move. Live feed. But, you know that part because you were the guy watching the monitors."

"That's never been a secret. You saw the feed. Someone messed with the system, and there was a five minute loop."

"And who would have known how to do that?" Tanya said.

"Well, that's obvious, don't you think?" Vic never once changed his self-satisfied expression. He still appeared relaxed and confident.

"Indulge me."

"Cross had inside help."

Tanya choked out a laugh. "Do you think?" She paced slowly in front of the desk, keeping her eyes focused on Vic. She was done playing. "You set the loop, Vic. You silenced the alarms and you made damn sure Cross got outside before anyone even knew what was happening.

"I was an idiot not to see it sooner. Gabriel checked the discs, there was no trace of psychic manipulation on them. It was manually looped. You said so yourself, you were the only one who had access for the time in question. I have to admit it though, you got me. I did not see that one coming." Tanya stopped pacing.

Vic put his hands up in a, *what can I say,* gesture.

"You're not going to deny it?" Tanya wanted to smack the cocky grin off his face.

"Would you believe me if I did?"

"Not for a second."

"Then I suppose it would be a wasted effort, wouldn't it?"

Tanya fought the urge to have Robert shoot the arrogant bastard. Everything she had put into place ten years ago had fallen apart because of this man.

Cross had slipped through her fingers, and now Kale had somehow managed to get out of the most secure building in the entire East Coast. She took one quick step toward Vic and pulled her hand back. She swung her arm back to slap him hard across the face.

He caught her wrist and then bent it back. The pain was intense. He used her own forward momentum against her. He had her on her knees in a moment.

Before she could utter one word, or even make a sound, she heard the soft *snick* of the slide on a Glock.

Vic let her go.

She looked up and saw the barrel of Robert's Glock kiss the side of Vic's head. His hands rose out to his side.

Tanya stood and smoothed down her skirt. "Thank you Robert." She wanted him to pull the trigger. She wanted that badly. Tanya closed her eyes for a moment and fought to rein back the need to hurt Vic. "You're lucky I need you."

She turned as if to leave, but then spun quickly. No open hand this time. Tanya closed her fist and hit the bastard in the face as hard as she could.

Vic's head snapped to the side and blood spurted from his nose. But he was still smiling, showing teeth stained red by the blood.

"You're not going to get them back, you know. Either of them."

Tanya took a moment to compose herself. "I wouldn't be so sure about that, Vic. I have the entire power of this Department behind me, plus I have rooms and rooms full of freaks, with all sorts of wonderful abilities, who would do just about anything for a little freedom. Maybe even turn on one of their own." She watched with intense satisfaction as Vic's grin faltered the tiniest bit.

"Get him the fuck out of here," she told Robert.

Robert cuffed Vic's wrists. "Where do you want him?"

"Put him in the deepest, darkest hole you can find."

Vic's laughter as Robert pushed him out of the room infuriated her.

She was no closer to finding Cross or Kale, but now she had someone who knew where they might be. Vic Harris might think he was tough, but even the strongest man could be broken. Tanya had yet to meet a man she couldn't break.

CHAPTER 32

J enner Coben was not happy. "I don't like this. I don't like it at all." He sat behind his desk and read Tanya's report. Gabriel stood by the door while Tanya sat on the other side of the desk.

"This doesn't exactly thrill me either. We can work with it but we need to move quickly. Every moment Cross and Kale are out there is dangerous."

"Dangerous to who? Do you really think they'll put the public at risk?" Coben said.

"Kale? Not in the condition he's in. But Cross?" Tanya gave a small laugh. "Coben, we gave him every reason in the world to unleash that anger he's buried for ten years. Now you tell me if you think he's going to be judicious about who he unleashes it on. The sooner we have him back the lower the body count will be."

Coben sighed and shook his head. "Might as well get this over with, but I'm warning you Tanya, this man was one of my agents. He's not one of your play things, like Kale. If you hurt him there better be a damn good reason for it."

Tanya held his gaze for a moment too long, but Coben refused to look away. She finally broke the eye contact and walked to the door. She opened it and spoke to the guard Coben knew was there. "Bring him in."

A moment later Robert brought Vic into Coben's office. He hands were cuffed in front of him. His one eye swollen, and dried blood was on his face. Coben narrowed his eyes at Tanya. "You told me he was fine. This doesn't look fine to me."

"Oh, please, Coben. Robert barely touched him."

"Vic, are you all right?" Coben said.

Vic grinned. "I'm touched Coben."

"All right, let's get this over with." Coben continued. "I'm disappointed in you Victor. I can't tell you how disappointed. I trusted you and this is how that trust is repaid?"

Vic laughed. "Gee, Dad. I'm really sorry." Robert punched Vic hard in the kidney. Vic grunted and doubled over but the smile never left his face.

Coben stood pushing his chair back. "Was that necessary?" he said to Robert. " It doesn't need to be this way, Vic. That's why I wanted to talk to you. I know you to be a reasonable man. Answer our questions and I promise you won't be harmed."

Vic straightened up as much as he could. "You're clueless aren't you Coben. It doesn't matter what you promise me here in your nice neat office. The moment Tanya and her pet dog here get me alone I guarantee you they will see a need for violence."

Coben threw a look in Tanya's direction. "We'll see about that," Coben returned his attention back to Vic. "First I want to hear it directly from you. You helped Cross leave? You silenced the alarms and doctored the monitor feed?"

"That I did."

Coben wiped a hand over his face. He thought maybe it had been a mistake. All Vic had to do was deny it and he would have cut him free. But now he was tied in. Vic openly admitted his involvement in front of not only him but Tanya and Gabriel. He asked the one question he desperately wanted an answer too. "Why? Why do this Vic?"

"Why?" Vic sounded incredulous. "You can stand there, look at me and then ask me that? Coben I don't think you're a bad guy, but I do think you need to be a bit more informed on what happens in your own department."

"What are you talking about, I know exactly what happens in every aspect of my department."

"Oh, then you're aware that the black widow over there," Vic gave a nod to Tanya, "Takes great pleasure in torturing your new acquirements. Jesus, she kept Kale in a cage for ten years, and when Cross proved to be too much for her to handle, she altered his memory, all because he objected to being owned. These are people Coben, they have rights."

"These people are dangerous. You certainly had no objections in doing your part in caging them. Why all the moral outrage all of a sudden?"

"Yeah, some of them deserve to be here, but you cast a net and didn't even care who got caught in it. Some of the ones I brought in, I also let go if I could- erased their records. You have no right to do the things you do."

"The government gives me the right." Coben moved around his desk to stand in front of Vic. "It's you who are misinformed Vic. This department exists for one reason. To protect the public. Do have any idea the plans we have in motion? The things Kale is capable of doing? He could save millions of lives if his talent is used in the right way."

The cocky grin left Vic's face for the first time since entering the office. Coben liked that. "What are you talking about?" Vic said.

"You know what Kale can do? Pushing people." When Vic nodded, Coben continued. "Then think about this Vic, how many good men do we lose every year in military conflicts? How many people do you know personally who've been killed in combat?"

"How could Kale help with that?" Vic was trying to figure it out, but Coben could see he wasn't having any luck.

"Imagine this, Vic. The United States in in the midst of a conflict. Before things escalate, we bring Kale with us to peace talks, or negotiations, or anywhere he can have access to the people who have the power of opposing governments. Kale pushes those key people, he tells them to do exactly what our government wants them to do. We can stop a war before one shot is fired. Think of the lives that can be saved."

Vic looked horrified. "Imagine this Coben, what if the people with the power want to do away with, let's say a foreign political leader they deem dangerous. What if they have Kale tell this person to put a gun in his mouth." Vic shook his head. "You're not God and Kale isn't a weapon."

"Yes, he is darling," Tanya spoke for the first time since Vic entered the room. "He's my weapon and I want him back. Enough explaining. I want you to tell me where Cross is. If we find Cross, we find Kale."

"What makes you think I know where either of them are? I just opened the door."

"Well I think that's where I come in," Gabriel pushed off the wall he had been leaning against. "I don't have to explain myself here, do I Vic? You know all I have to do is look inside your head and I can find out everything you know about Cross and Kale. You also know that if you fight me when I do this, it can cause damage to your mind."

"You're going to do it anyway, why all the drama?" Vic stilled grinned, but Coben thought it faltered just a bit.

"I've known you for over ten years Vic," Gabriel said. "I respect you, but at the end of the day I do as I'm told just like everyone else. I would rather not turn your mind into pudding. You know I can find out what I need. You also know that you could simply tell them what they want to know."

Vic raised his shoulders. "I don't know where they are."

Gabriel lowered his head as he approached Vic. He looked to Coben. "You sure you want to play it this way?"

"Just do it," Coben said.

Gabriel met Vic's eyes again. "I am sorry my friend." Coben watched as Gabriel closed his eyes and in the next moment, Vic's face creased in pain.

This was not going to end well.

CHAPTER 33

We have company.

As soon as the words were out, Jude's apartment door exploded in a fiery burst.

Cross felt the heat a moment before the door shattered. "Get down!" He instinctively took what energy he could from the explosion and formed a shield around them all. The shock wave forced him down and back, until his feet slid on the smooth wooden floor.

His shield held, but he hoped to hell it didn't have to hold for long. He was still carrying most of Kale's injuries and pretty much running on fumes. The energy for his shield came from the fire that now burned all around them. Whoever was attacking them realized what he was doing, and was compensating for it.

His shield buckled and shrank a little around the edges. Everyone huddled closer.

"Oh, shit." Cross grunted with the effort of keeping them from frying as the building burned around them. He went down to one knee to pull more strength from the energy around him.

Danny King stepped through the ruined doorway. "You! This is all your fault. You should've have just left us alone. It's your fault they took Syb!" Danny said.

Cross had no idea how Danny King had found him or what had happened to his sister. He did know they were all going to die soon if he didn't do something and do it quickly. He tried to syphon power from Danny but failed.

Then a sudden surge of energy hit him. He felt a hand on his arm and his brother's familiar aura inside his head.

Power surged through Cross's hands. Together they were close to unstoppable. Keeping the shield in place, Cross stood. He took the fire pouring from Danny and funneled it into a swirling mass of seething energy. Cross manipulated it as if it were a lit match. With an effort of pure will, he took control of the fire. He compressed it until it was nothing more than a single flame, and in one movement, smothered it.

Now the danger came from the building burning around them.

"What happened to Danny?" Cross said.

"Down. When you took control he collapsed," Maizey said. "It's getting hot in here, Cross.

"Get us out of here, Maizey. Kale and I can keep the shield up for a while longer."

"Everybody grab hands, stay tight, and follow me," Maizey took Cross's hand and lead them to the door. Even with the shield up, smoke choked him and made his eyes water. "Get Danny," he told Maizey.

"He just tried to fry us!" Jude protested.

"Just get him."

Cross heard Jude drag Danny into the protective shield and heave him over a shoulder.

"Stairs," Maizey warned. Sirens were in the distance and getting closer. They needed to get out of here. Stumbling, coughing, clinging to the railing they inched down the stairs.

"Are we clear?" Cross yelled when they eventually reached the bottom.

"We're good," Maizey said.

Cross dropped the shield. When he did, Kale broke contact and the power that had been tripping through him dissolved into a bone-weary exhaustion. He hurt everywhere as his world spun around him. He could only imagine how Kale must feel. When he fell to his knees and felt hands on him, it didn't occur to him to object.

"Finn?" He hoped.

"Yeah, man. Jesus I won't ask what happened. I got a pretty good idea. I couldn't stop him."

"It's okay." The sirens were nearly on top of them. Other people were in the street to watch the fire or see what was happening. "We need to disappear."

"I got wheels," He heaved Cross to his feet. The world wobbled a bit but his knees held. Cross felt for Kale and helped him stand.

Finn led them both into a van of some sort and everyone else clambered aboard. "Jesus, Danny King? Really Cross? The guy just tried to barbeque you."

The air was heavy with smoke and heat even inside the van. "I can handle him, just go!"

Finn obviously realized the time for arguments was not now. He put the van in gear and peeled out just as the first fire truck pulled up. "What if someone saw us?" Finn said.

"Go it covered," Maizey said. "I had all of us and the van concealed. No one saw anything but a very nice building on fire."

The girl had some serious skills. If Cross didn't feel like he was about to pass out he was sure he would've been impressed.

"Crap. It was rent controlled too," Jude said.

"I'm sorry, man," Kale's voice was quiet and sounded weak.

A low moan came from the floor near Cross's feet. Danny was starting to wake up.

"I got this," Kale said.

"You're barely hanging on as it is," Utah said. "Let someone else take care of him."

"Well unless there's someone else who can *push* him, I'm it. Don't worry this doesn't take a lot out of me." But before Kale had the chance, Danny slumped against the wall once more. Unconscious or passed out.

Utah sighed in obvious relief. "Thank God. See, now you don't have too. Just relax, okay?"

Cross was relieved. He didn't have it in him for round two with Danny. In an enclosed metal box. He shuddered inwardly just thinking about how that might have played out. "Where are we going, Finn?"

"Back to the tunnels. Right now it's the safest place for us. Kale needs attention and you have looked better."

"I've felt worse." Maybe. "What about him? Danny. He's not going to wake up in a good mood."

"I got him," Maizey said.

Cross looked in her direction. "What do you mean, 'you got him'?"

"I pushed him, told him to go to sleep for a couple hours and when he woke up not to be so angry."

"You *pushed* him? You mean Kale pushed him." Cross was confused.

"Wasn't me," Kale said.

"One of my best kept secrets," Maizey said.

"You can push." Cross wanted to curl up into a ball and go to sleep for about a week and all he'd done was fight off a flaming ball of death. Maizey had pushed Danny while camouflaging the van and six people. "Damn."

The next moment he was on his back feeling more than a little nauseous. He couldn't remember going down, but apparently impressing Maizey with his fortitude wasn't in the cards for the day.

He closed his eyes and wondered if she'd pushed him too. Didn't really matter. Either way everyone was going to have to figure out how to survive without him for the immediate future.

CHAPTER 34

Tanya sat behind the tinted windows of the Cadillac escalade, secure in the fact that she could not be seen. Vic had been a bust. It turned out he really didn't know where Cross had gone.

Gabriel had been thorough but he had concluded the man knew nothing. It was a pity, Vic's body had survived Gabriel's less than delicate mental inquisition. Tanya would have to decide what to do with the rest of him.

Right now she was depending on the young Asian sitting next to her to find the Delancey twins. He was trying his best not to appear nervous but his constant hand wringing and fidgeting told her different. His name was Woo, and he had a talent for seeing in a non-visual part of the spectrum. He could see the auras people with special abilities gave off.

People like Cross and Kale Delancey. They didn't even have to use their abilities. All they had to do was to have been in a place for more than a few minutes. Their presence would leave a psychic signature, a shedding of energy that permeated everything they came into contact with. It was, according to Woo, like looking for a shadow, or a scent left behind.

As far as Tanya knew. Woo was one of a kind. She had promised him improved living quarters, perhaps one of the secured apartments Cross had escaped from. But only if he led her to the Delancey brothers.

The trail Woo followed led to a burnt out brownstone on the Upper East Side. The area was still taped off and trucks surrounded the building. The fire that had hollowed it out, smoldered and firemen with hoses fought to douse it for good.

"They were here," Woo said. "Both of them and not too long ago. Their presence is very strong here. Exceptionally strong." Woo took a breath. "This fire was caused by a person with abilities. A battle of wills was fought here. Fire against fire- or against something as potent as fire. A lot of power."

"Can you track them?" Tanya said.

Woo snickered. "Yes. Someone concealed them, but she can't hide them from me. I could see this trail with my eyes closed. So much power. Wow!"

"Concealed how?"

"From the visual spectrum. But whoever did this didn't plan on concealing them from the magical spectrum."

"There's no such thing as magic," Tanya said.

Woo shrugged. "Magic, abilities, power. It's all just semantics. Whatever you want me to call it, I see them. I can track them."

"Just give Robert directions."

"I did good, right? You'll take me out of that room? I mean, I can't go back there. It's been years. Please." Woo sounded desperate and unsure of himself. Tanya knew he was neither. This was all a game to him.

"I don't have Cross or Kale back yet. When I do, then we'll talk about an upgrade in your accommodations."

Woo picked at his cuticles. Tanya noticed they were raw and bloody around the ragged edges. Someone was going to pay for making her spend time with him. He was a pathetic sociopath and borderline schizophrenic.

Cross and Finn had brought him in about three years ago. Woo had been hunting down his own kind- people with abilities and systematically killing them. He had tracked them with their own auras. When asked why, he told Tanya it was the only way to keep his head from exploding.

Woo heard voices, lots of freaky little voices telling him to do horrible things.

They'd tried hundreds of drugs over the years they had him. But the normal psych meds had no effect on him. He was unbalanced and dangerous, but right now he was Tanya's best chance to find one or both of the Delancey brothers. But there was no way in hell Woo was buying any time out of his cage. Tanya might be desperate but she wasn't stupid. She would use Woo like she used everyone – to achieve a goal. He meant nothing to her.

Woo directed Robert out of Manhattan and into Harlem. "They're weak now, very weak, but their auras are truly spectacular." Woo sighed. He looked as if he had just been watching porn.

He looked directly at Tanya. "Such power. I've never felt anything like this. You can't take this one." He giggled. "She'll destroy you."

Who he was talking about, Cross? Kale? More likely no one, just another voice is the chaos. "I'll take my chances. Just find them."

Woo nodded eagerly. "Find them." He told Robert to take another turn, then suddenly he sucked in a breath like he was in pain. His expression went from amused and confidant to furious in a heartbeat. "No... Nonono! How could she do that? No one has ever done that to me before."

"What happened," Tanya said.

"She found me. No one ever finds me!"

"What does that mean?"

"It means she found me! How else do I need to fucking say it? She realized I was tracking her and she blocked me." Woo hit the seat in front of him. "Bitch, no one gets away from me. No one!" Apparently Woo forgot he was hunting for Tanya and not himself. He grew more agitated and began kicking the seat, Tanya glanced at Robert who pulled the SUV over and calmly reached around and shot the Taser probes against Woo's thigh.

Woo went rigid and then went limp. When he lay stunned, Robert uncapped a needle and injected a sedative.

Only when Woo was unconscious did Tanya move.

She put her head in her hands for just a moment. "Do we know who the burned building belongs too?

"A professor at Columbia, some doctor by the name of Jude Case," Robert said.

"Get Woo back into a secured cell. Then I want everything there is on this Dr. Case. Family members, friends, anything. What do Cross or Kale have to do with him? I need information Robert, and I need it now. All we know is they were headed for Harlem. Set up patrols throughout the borough. They cannot just fucking disappear.

"Find them. Do you understand?"

"I understand."

Tanya tried not to scream in frustration. Was Cross Delancey worth all of this? Perhaps when she got them back, she would kill Cross in front of Kale, just to teach him a lesson. Any future escape attempts would lead to immediate consequences to one of his fellow freaks. Any disobedience would be dealt with in the same manner. If he pushed anyone other than who Tanya told him to push, another innocent would die.

Kale would learn his place. Once Tanya had him back, that was the one thing she had absolute certainty of.

CHAPTER 35

G abriel could see the end game. Not the exact circumstances but the pieces were in play and there was only one logical ending. He didn't want to be around when it all went down. He was aware his actions had brought him to this moment. Some of them he regretted- deeply and some of them he did not.

His part in recent events was in some small way an apology. It made very little difference, but he wasn't seeking absolution. The best he could hope for, if he was still alive at the end of the day was to be able to sleep at night.

Vic Harris was one such apology. Gabriel hadn't had to destroy Vic's mind to discover where Cross had fled, but Tanya didn't need to know that. Once he extracted the information, he'd simply implanted the suggestion into Vic's subconscious that he was very tired and needed to sleep soundly for a while. Tanya had believed his lie. He hadn't worked with her for over ten years and not learned how to manipulate her.

Tanya might indeed discover where Cross was hiding but she wouldn't learn it from Gabriel. He might be a few decades too late, but he was finally accepting his parental responsibility. His sons might be dangerous, but in his opinion Tanya was more so.

Gabriel had one last task to accomplish. And then he could take Niko and walk out of this place. The thought was oddly liberating.

****

Vic sat on the cold concrete of his dark cell and wished he knew what was going on. What bothered him more than the lack of water or food or light was the lack of knowledge. He was in the dark in more ways than one.

Gabriel had at him, and that was a less than pleasant experience. Vic had worked with Cross for years, but never once had he pried into Vic's thoughts. Gabriel had no such ethics. It was a violation Vic had difficulty coping with. He could defend himself against any manner of physical threats, but he had no defense against something like that. Gabriel pried open his mind like a can of tuna and had a peek inside. Vic couldn't remember anything and had only just woke up a few hours ago. Vic was alone and confused as to what he had learned. He feared he had betrayed Charlie, Maizey and the entire Underground. But if that were the case, wouldn't Tanya have come to talk to him by now?

His head was pounding and his belly churning, either from lack of water or Gabriel's indelicate probing. He was having a hard time seeing a way out of this one. They hadn't killed him yet, so the fact that he was still alive gave him hope that Cross and the Underground had somehow eluded Tanya and the Department.

He was just drifting into a restless sleep when the cell door creaked open. He squinted, raised a hand to shade his eyes as he tried to determine who had come for him.

Instead of the expected security guard, he heard soft footsteps just before a cold nose pressed to his face. His visitor was Niko, Cross's dog.

"She knows you."

Gabriel stood in the doorway. Vic tried for an *I don't give a damn* front, but he knew Gabriel could see past it.

"She should. I spent a lot of time with Cross and her over the years." Niko sat down and put her head in Vic's lap. For some reason that made him feel better. He ran a hand over her head.

"What do you want?" His gut clenched at the thought of Gabriel prying his mind open again.

"Redemption?"

Vic screwed his face up in confusion. "Come again?"

Gabriel tossed a small rectangular object to Vic. It landed on the floor next to his hand.

When he picked it up he saw it was Coben's ID badge. He looked to Gabriel for an explanation.

"I wanted to apologize for any discomfort I caused you. I needed my probe to look convincing to Tanya. When I looked in your head I found out some interesting things."

Cold fear gripped Vic.

"Not only did you help Cross get out," Gabriel continued, "But you have, for the last several years, been an informant to an underground organization consisting of people like Cross and Kale. People like myself with abilities the Department would be interested in. You help shield them from this department."

"They are good people, Gabriel. All they want is to be left alone. To raise their children in peace like everyone else. Why can't you understand that?"

"I do. I do understand that, Vic," Gabriel said.

Now that Vic's eyes had adjusted to the light, he could see how tired Gabriel looked. His normally impeccable attire was rumpled, Vic might even have to say disheveled. His silvery hair was mussed and he needed a shave.

"I could never be mistaken for father of the year. I helped to hide the truth from one son and ignored what was happening to another. I can't go back and change that. What's done is done."

Vic held up Coben's ID. "What's this all about?"

"I decided to do something I should've done years ago."

"What's that?"

"Grow a spine. I told Tanya that you knew nothing more than what you already told us. Right now she thinks I broke your mind. She's trying to decide if you are anymore use to them." He indicated the ID badge. "That will get you out of here. I've cleared the way. You won't encounter anyone and the badge will open the doors. I won't stop you, and I won't tell anyone what I know."

Vic got to his feet. "How do I know this isn't a trap? An excuse for Tanya to kill me trying to escape."

"Since when does Tanya need an excuse to kill anyone? It's not a trap, Vic, I would ask you to trust me but I understand how ridiculous that would sound. Look at it this way, what do you have to lose?" Gabriel stepped aside and offered Vic the open door.

Vic put Coben's ID around his neck. "How did you get this?"

"I have other talents besides violating people's innermost sanctums. Coben won't know its missing for a few hours, but if I were you I wouldn't waste any more time asking questions when you could be getting out of here. Use the fire exits. All the alarms have been disabled. I would have arranged transportation but the department vehicles are easily traced."

"It's New York, I'll manage." Vic paused in the doorway. "I don't know why you're doing this, but thank you."

Gabriel shook his head. "Just do whatever you have to, to keep my sons out of her hands."

Without another word, Vic walked out of his cell.

CHAPTER 36

When Cross awoke, he couldn't remember where he was for a moment or two. In the tunnels. He was still in the chair next to Kale's bed. Someone had taken his glasses off and covered him with a blanket. He could hear no echoes of footsteps, no hushed voices. Only the sounds of the night greeted him. It almost felt as if they were alone.

Shadows, all that was left of his vision, greeted him, which told him nothing about the time of day- or night. Sitting up, he felt for and found Kale, still sleeping. He felt rested and decided to use his newly-learned sight. He was amazed at how simple it was.

Everything around him lit up in a subdued blue, not the bright blue/white he had experienced before. Apparently his new spectrum had its own limitations. He saw Kale stir as if he knew Cross watched him. Maybe he did. His brother braced his side with one hand and sat up. He gave him that well-remembered cocky grin.

"Hey," Kale said.

"How're you feeling? You look better, more with it than before."

"Yeah, I'm good. Wait. What do you mean I look better? How would you know?"

"Oh yeah, I forgot you don't know. Maizey taught me a way to see. Sort of."

"You can see?" Kale waved a hand in front Cross's face. Cross caught it and held it. "Not real sight, not like before, but yeah enough to get around on my own. It's kind of pretty, like blue energy surrounding everything. Only thing is, it taps me out if I use it for too long."

"That's kind of cool," Kale just stared at him for a long while.

Cross understood, he stared back. "I can't believe you're here. I thought you were dead, Kale. They told me you were dead." He shook his head as shame burned his face. "All the times you came to me, I always thought it was a dream. You know, just wishful thinking. If I'd known you were alive, I would've come for you. You have to know that, Kale."

"Which is exactly why you had to keep believing I was dead. If I told you anything else, Tanya would've brought you in years ago. I couldn't let that happen."

"I could've got you out. We could've both got out."

"You don't know Tanya. I do. Trust me it was better this way."

"Better for who? I spent all this time thinking my brother was dead. I thought I lost you. I did lose you," Cross tried to control the swirling emotions coursing through him and couldn't decide if he should be pissed, sad or relieved. He settled on a combination of all three. He should have known Kale would understand. Not only did they both have the psychic thing going on, but they were twins. They always knew what the other was thinking.

Kale put a hand on Cross's shoulder. The simple contact almost made Cross break down. "You never lost me," Kale told him. "You're the one who found me."

Cross took a deep breath to collect himself. "I don't plan on losing you ever again. Got it?"

Kale gave him the sideways grin again. "Yeah, man, I got it."

They let the moment hang there in the silence, content to simply be together again after all the time lost. After a while Kale started to look around the room. He tried to stand and found himself tethered to the bed by an IV attached to his arm. He pulled it out and put his hand over the small wound until it stopped bleeding.

"I'm pretty sure, Jude isn't going to like that," Cross said.

Kale shrugged. "I'm fine. Trust me, I've been in worse shape and I'm still alive. Come on." Kale motioned for Cross to follow him.

For a moment it felt like they were kids again, trying to get into trouble just to piss everyone off. "Come on where?"

"Outside. I want to go outside." Cross tried to keep up with Kale as he navigated the maze-like tunnels as if he'd been born in this place. Then he realized Kale was simply following his nose. Cross could smell the fresh air cutting through the stale air. Cross imagined if he had spent the last ten years caged inside, he would have been able to pick up the scent of fresh air just as easily. Still, he couldn't help but be impressed.

The tunnel exit opened in front of them. Kale picked up speed until he stepped outside and lifted his face to the gentle night breeze. The early November night was chilly. Cross wrapped his arms around his chest to ward off the cold. He realized Kale wore only a short-sleeve t-shirt and jeans and was barefoot.

"Aren't you cold?" Cross said.

"No way. This is great." Kale opened his arms and with his eyes closed and head lifted toward the night sky, he turned in a circle smiling blissfully.

Cross looked around at the dirty little lot that delighted Kale, and that pang of guilt hit him again. This littered, abandoned lot, with grass growing out if the cracks in the concrete and smelling of urine, was the best thing Kale had seen in forever.

Despite the guilt, it still made him smile. Kale was happy and that was an amazing thing. Cross just wanted to watch him for as long as he wanted to stay there. He watched until his sight slowly dimmed and left him in the dark again. He swayed with the sudden lack of visual input. Funny how after all the years he had spent in the dark, he had become used to the light again so quickly. Now the dark seemed all the more lonely to him.

He reached his hands out hoping to find something to steady himself with.

Kale's hand slipped under his arm. "Hey, whoa there, you okay?" he led Cross to the concrete steps. "Sit."

"Yeah, guess I overdid it with the sight thing. Damn, I'm in the dark again."

"You can't control it?" Kale sat next to him on the step.

"Working on it, but the bottom line is I'm still blind. I'll always be blind."

"What do you remember about that night?" Kale's voice sounded like he wasn't sure he wanted to know.

"You mean when we were fourteen? The night we tried to get out?"

"Yeah. Do you remember it?"

"Some of it. Some of it is like a story someone else told me. Charlie took away the blocks they placed and showed me the truth, but he couldn't fix the damage caused by the bullet."

"Charlie?"

"Oh, yeah. Sorry, you were really out if it on the way here. Charlie is Maria's father. He's our grandfather, Kale."

"We have a grandfather?" Kale sounded excited.

"Apparently. Anyway, Charlie has this ability to let a person see the truth. But like I said, there was a lot of damage from the bullet. What I remember most is more of a feeling than memory."

"Anger," Kale said.

Cross looked in his direction. "Yeah, exactly. Every time I think about that day, all I get is a lot of anger."

"You were pissed man. I mean more than usual. I know they messed with your head, made you into someone you weren't but I remember you Cross. You were always the other half of me. You used to tell me you were the better half," Kale laughed quietly. "The day before you went all postal..." Kale paused.

Cross heard the hesitation in his voice.

"What, Kale? What happened?"

Kale took a deep breath and let it out all at once. "You never showed them what you could do. You hid it. I didn't, because I thought Tanya would be happy if I did what she wanted."

"But she wasn't." Cross could remember bits and pieces.

"No, no way. She knew you were holding out on her. The day before, she beat me in front of you, to try to get you to do something."

Cross tried to remember that day. It was all a fuzzy picture in his head. "What did I do?" Cross hoped to hell he'd showed her something. He hated to think he had allowed his brother to take a beating because of his stubbornness.

"Nothing. You didn't have too. I *pushed* them." Kale sounded pleased. "Told them to leave us alone and they did."

"Holy shit. Bet Tanya wasn't too thrilled about that." Cross couldn't help but smile at the thought of Kale getting one over on Tanya.

"She wasn't. That's when you said we had to get out of there. You said if we didn't they were going to kill us, or make us kill someone else. Someone innocent. You said if she wanted to see what you could do, then you were going to fucking show her what you could do."

Kale paused, swallowed audibly. "We showed them all right. Together we killed a dozen of her people before Gabriel shot you. He was aiming to kill you. I tried to push you out of the way. Guess I wasn't fast enough."

"Hey, I'm still alive."

"But your eyes man."

"Kale, it's cool. You saved my life."

"Did I, Cross? They took everything away from you. All your memories, your eyes, everything that made you who you were. They programmed you into who they wanted you to be. They told you I was dead and gave you a lie to live. Exactly what did I save?"

Cross reached for Kale's hand in the dark. When he found it he held tight. "This. Despite what anyone did to us, despite all the lies, all the manipulation and bullshit, we found each other. Right here, right now, I have my brother back. You saved us."

"I missed you Cross," Kale said.

"Back atcha man. Right the hell back atcha. I would have looked for you, Kale," Cross said. "If I had known, if I had even guessed you were still alive –"

"I know. It's okay, Cross."

Anger at what had been done to them half a lifetime ago surged through him suddenly. "No it's not. They took your life just as surely as a bullet would have. The only difference is, the bullet would have been more merciful."

Kale put a hand over Cross's. His voice was one of reason, one of acceptance, and that almost made Cross angrier. He didn't want to be reasonable. He sure as hell didn't want to be accepting.

"I can't change what they did." Kale said. "Would I like to? Hell yes, I'd like to do a lot of things if given the chance, some of it good, some of it not so much. But one thing Tanya did teach me was you can't go back, you can only go forward. It might have taken us ten years, but we finally made it right."

"We might have found each other, but we haven't made it right. Not by a long shot."

Kale was silent for a while, and when he spoke again, he obviously decided he had questions of his own. "Cross, how old are we anyway? I've been trying to do the math in my head, but I lost track of time a long time ago."

Cross opened his mouth to answer and found he couldn't. The simple question brought the enormity of what had been done to them front and center once more. "We are twenty-four," he finally said. He heard sadness etched into the words and hoped Kale didn't notice.

"Wow, really? Damn we're old. Hey, didn't we promise each other we were going to get drunk and laid on our twenty-first birthday?"

"We're a little late for that. I've already gotten drunk and laid. Not necessarily in that order."

"So chicks go for the blind thing, huh?"

Cross couldn't help the smile that tugged at his lips. "You're still a pig, Kale."

"What's your point? Hey, come on. I've been locked up for the last decade. My experience with the opposite sex has been, shall we say, limited."

An unwanted image of Tanya seducing a sixteen-year-old Kale slammed into Cross's brain and every trace of humor he might have felt vanished. He knew Kale felt it too.

"It was my choice too, you know. It's not like she raped me."

Cross heard defensiveness in his tone. "I know."

"I don't think you do. I know what you think about it. I can feel what you feel, remember? The disgust, the anger. I feel that."

"But for her, not for you. Can't you understand that?"

"You weren't there. She was the only person I had contact with. She made it that way. I realize that, but it doesn't change the fact she was my jailer and my salvation in one package. She made me fall in love with her, so I would do anything for her, and I very nearly did."

They were both shivering now. Cross could feel Kale as he sat bunched up next to him, but neither moved just yet. "What did she want from you?"

"The same thing she wanted from you. The only difference was, she had a lot longer to try and get it from me."

"Tell me." Cross knew the answer, he also knew Kale needed to say it. He needed Cross to forgive him for the sin of trying to survive.

"She wanted me to do the things she told everyone I did. She wanted me to push people to do terrible things. Sometimes to themselves. Sometimes to other people. I refused and then she killed them anyway, in front of me – told me I was to blame for their deaths. She would leave their bodies inside my cell for days. Desensitization, she told me.

"That was bad. I would have nightmares they were still alive and talking to me. I could smell them, you know? She told me she would kill you if I didn't do what she wanted. But I could always find you, up here." He tapped the side of his head. "I knew you were okay. When she saw that wasn't working she started a more primitive, but effective method of getting me to cooperate with her."

"The beatings," Cross guessed.

"If you want to civilize it, you could call it that, but yeah pain is a very reliable persuader."

"You gave in?" Cross wouldn't blame him if he did. He couldn't say he wouldn't have done the same after only a few weeks at Tanya's hands.

"Once." The admission cost Kale. Cross didn't need to see to know the pain Kale was in. "She wanted me to *push* someone. She wanted me to have him kill someone else." He paused and Cross knew he was collecting himself.

"He was just some guy, I never saw him before. She hadn't given me anything to eat for days, kept me awake, and increased the beatings. She promised me it would all stop if I just told the guy to go home and kill his wife. She said I wouldn't be to blame, I was only the one who told him to do it.

"Even then I knew that was bullshit, but I was tired and hungry and hurt. So I did it. I *pushed* the guy. He did exactly what I told him to do. He went home and he beat his wife to death because I told him to. Tanya had it recorded.

"After that, Tanya was obsessed, but I swore she would kill me before I ever did that again."

Cross could feel the torment Kale had been in, the guilt that still ate at him every day. The conflicting emotions he still had for Tanya. "How old were you when this happened?"

Cross could feel Kale shrug, a quick up and down movement of his shoulders. "Maybe nineteen or twenty."

"She wore you down, Kale. You weren't thinking clearly."

"I was thinking just fine." Now Cross heard anger in his voice, anger at himself. Cross would have preferred that anger directed at Tanya.

"I was thinking if I do this one thing, I can eat, I can sleep, and I can stop wondering if someone's going to beat the crap out of me in the middle of the night. I understood what I was doing, Cross, and someone died because I wasn't strong enough to say no to her one more time."

Tanya was very good at her job and Cross very much wanted to hurt her. "You're strong enough now, aren't you?"

"Doesn't bring that guy's wife back."

"Always move forward," Cross reminded him. "So, now we figure out how to stop her. For good, right?"

He felt the slight hesitation. It was barely discernable, but he felt it. Even after everything Tanya had done to him Cross was certain Kale still had feelings for her. He didn't need to confront him with that fact, Kale was aware Cross knew. There were no secrets between them. What Cross knew, Kale knew. It's how they were made, it's what they were always meant to be. They were each part of the other.

"I can't help it," Kale said. His voice revealed his shame. "I don't know if I could bring myself to hurt her."

Cross understood. As horrible as it sounded, he could see how it must have been. Kale, young, alone, starved for affection, attention and Tanya as beautiful as she was deadly, grudgingly giving him both in small quantities until he was desperate for more. Kale would have done anything for Tanya.

He still would.

"You don't have to hurt her. I wouldn't ask that of you. All you have to do is not stop someone else from doing what needs to be done." Cross felt Kale's pain at the thought of Tanya being hurt, but he knew Kale understood.

"She told you she wouldn't hurt me if you did what she wanted. She lied to you. You have to know that. She used you."

"I know."

The admission changed nothing. "We'll get through this, Kale, me and you. I think we're overdue on some good luck for a change."

"We move forward," Kale said.

"Forward," Cross agreed. They sat in silence for a moment. "Could you do something for me?" Cross said.

"Name it."

Cross wasn't sure if he really wanted to know, but then curiosity won out over caution. "Charlie showed me the truth, which memories were fake, but not everything is clear. They all seem real to me."

"You want me to tell you which ones are real and which ones are fake?" Kale said.

"Yeah, do you mind?"

"Lay it on me, man."

"Okay. You already told me the tree house was real. What about camping? I remember Mom and Dad taking us camping somewhere when we were little, maybe six or seven? There was a campfire, tents, marshmallows, fireflies in mason jars – the works."

"Sorry, man, never happened. I wish it was true. I think I would have liked camping, but no, that one was implanted. Tanya would've never let us out of the department for that."

"Damn, really? That was a great memory. What about Dad? What about Gabriel?"

"What about him?" Kale's voice changed. The subject of Gabriel was obviously not one he wanted to talk about. "Let me make this easy for you, Cross. Gabriel wasn't a father. He said it himself to me more than once. All he was to us was a biological donation. Half of our genetic code. To him we were never anything more than an experiment."

"He told me he loved me. I think I remember that." Cross knew how that must have sounded, but even with Charlie's help, the memories and the truth were difficult to sort out in his head.

"He told you whatever would get him what he wanted at the time. A nice memory of the perfect family kept you docile, kept you in line. That's all they wanted." Kale's anger was obvious. Cross felt it too.

He sighed. "Okay, we never went camping and Gabriel flunked parenting 101. What about our mother?"

"She was the real deal, or as real as they let her be anyway. Maria did what she had to do to survive and to protect us. But I don't think she fully understood what the government intended to do with us. To her, we were always her children first. She protected us the best she could, and when they took that control away from her, she couldn't take it anymore."

"She killed herself," Cross said.

"The bastards killed her just as surely as if they pulled the trigger."

"She called you her wild child." Cross smiled at the memory.

"And you were her thinker. 'Always thinking, Cross, always thinking.' She used to tell you to stop thinking so much and just enjoy life, do you remember?"

"I remember." He was quiet for a long while after that. Cross remembered his mother's eyes, they were dark and gentle, her quiet laugh and the way she would kiss each of them on the forehead when she put them to bed at night. He didn't want to know if those memories were real or not. He chose to believe they were and moved on.

"One more," Cross leaned back against the steps and angled his face toward the night sky. He closed his eyes, not that the view changed – black was black, but it helped him think. "I remember us sneaking out at night. We would lie on our backs with our hands behind our heads and stare up at the stars. We would look for the constellations, Orion, Ursula Major, Cassiopeia, and The Seven Sisters."

He could almost see it again in his head, the night sky a velvet drape with the stars set like sparkling jewels within it. The Milky Way, Andromeda, the entire universe there just for them. The perfect backdrop for two little boys with impossible dreams. "We would tell each other the plans we had for the future. The things we wanted to do, the things that meant so much to us. It almost diminished their importance by putting it into words, – but we understood. We told each other everything under those stars."

Cross turned toward his brother, his blind eyes open. "Please don't tell me it didn't happen. Tell me that much, at least, was for real."

Kale's voice when he spoke again was quiet. "Yeah, Cross, that one's real. I remember it too. Many a great scheme was planned, looking up at those stars."

"I wish I could see them, just one more time. It's funny the things you miss when you know you'll never see them again. Most of the time I'm okay with it, but if I could have my eyes back just for one moment, my real eyes, I would want to see the stars again. I always wondered if they were really as beautiful as I remember them, or if time warped what I see in my mind." He let his head roll back and opened his eyes as if he were looking up at that star-filled sky. "Are the stars out tonight?"

"Yeah, they are," Kale said.

He sat up straight when he heard Kale move. "Just stay there like that."

"Why?" Cross was more suspicious than concerned.

"Trust me. Just do it."

Cross leaned back against the steps again and let his head loll. His weight on his elbows and his legs splayed out in front of him.

Kale sat behind him on the top step, one leg on either side of Cross. "Just relax. I think I remember how to do this."

He placed one hand on either side of his head. Cross felt Kale's fingers placed all around his skull, just the tips of them touching him.

Like a door being opened in a dark room, light flooded in. His dark world went nova. His eyes involuntarily squeezed shut at the assault, but then gradually the light dimmed, he opened his eyes little by little.

He was looking out at the night. He was looking out at *this* night. Cross looked through his brother's eyes and the light from countless stars set in the black velvet of the sky looked back at him.

It wasn't like he remembered it at all. It was better. The universe stretched out forever in that clear, cold November night. He could see Orion the Hunter, and the seven sisters clustered together for warmth, or protection. He saw the wispy swath of the Milky Way as it stretched into forever.

He saw two little boys planning for dreams they couldn't possibly know would never come true. It made him sad, but mostly it made him grateful. He had gotten his one chance.

"Thank you, Kale," he whispered. His voice thick with emotions he had trouble putting a name to.

"Shush," Kale told him. "I'm freezing my ass off here, so just shut up and look for as long as you want."

Cross shut up, and in the brilliant dark, two brothers stared up at the night sky and silently spoke the secrets of a lifetime worth of stolen dreams, while the stars bore them witness and kept their confidences.

CHAPTER 37

Despite Kale's protests that he was fine, Jude had restarted IV fluids and antibiotics on him. His fever was down and he looked more comfortable. Cross had gradually released his control of Kale's pain as Kale regained his strength. Now Cross was beyond exhausted. He was dozing in a chair next to Kale's bed until a voice in his head woke him. At first he thought it might be a dream, but he heard it again after he woke.

I need to see you.

No dream. Cross recognized the voice. He closed his eyes. *Get out of my head, Gabriel.*

I have something of yours I'd like to return.

After a moment of confusion, Cross realized what Gabriel wanted to give back. He could feel her presence through the mental connection his father had made.

Niko.

She misses you.

Where are you?

Outside the south 4ᵗʰ street station in Williamsburg.

Cross's heart rate jumped. That was the abandoned subway station the underground used to come and go. If Gabriel had tracked them here, the entire underground was in danger. Gabriel seemed to sense his fear.

Tanya has no idea where you are. Or even where I am for that matter. I came on my own. I'm unarmed and alone. Just see me. Please, that's all I ask. Let me say my piece and then you can do what you like to me.

Gabriel was right, Cross would be a fool to trust him. But he had Niko. Damn it. Trap or not, Cross owed it to Niko to at least try to get her back. But he was making a mistake. Cross felt that in every fiber of his being.

Stay where you are. If I sense anyone with you, I swear I'll kill you before they take me.

Fair enough. I'll wait for you.

Cross touched Kale's head and hoped he wasn't putting everyone he cared for in jeopardy for a dog. No, that wasn't fair, Niko was far more than just a dog to him.

He couldn't feel any deception in Gabriel's words, but the bastard could be clever. Perhaps clever enough to convince his son he was telling the truth when he was actually setting him up for an ambush.

Cross had regained enough of his strength that he was able to use his sight to navigate the twists and turns of the dark empty tunnels. It took him about twenty minutes before the exit burned a bright hole in the dark. A soft whining followed by a happy, frantic barking told him Niko knew he was there. No need for stealth. Gabriel would know he was there as well.

Cross entered the light and saw Gabriel trying to restrain Niko. His normally calm and composed guide dog was straining at the leash. Cross gave Gabriel a quick glance and then squatted down to Niko's level. Gabriel released the leash and Niko leapt at Cross.

She nearly knocked him over but seemed to remember her training at the last moment. Rolling over, she gave Cross her belly and whimpered with excitement. He hugged her, rubbed her belly and told her how much he had missed her. He was almost as excited as the dog.

"She missed you terribly," Gabriel said. "You can see me? Ah, a gift from your new friend."

Cross didn't bother to reply to that. He realized Gabriel knew about Maizey. He took a strong hold on Niko's leash. There was no way anyone was taking her away from him again. "What do you want Gabriel?"

"Is Kale all right? I know what Tanya had done to him. I would have stopped it if I could have."

"If you knew where I was, you know Kale is here and I'm betting you know exactly how he is. Stop wasting my time. You said you needed to talk to me. So talk."

Gabriel leaned against the brick wall behind him. Cross realized it was the first time he had *seen* the man since he was fourteen. Time had not been a friend. The dark hair he remembered had thinned and turned white. It surrounded his head like a fuzzy halo. His eyes were clear, but held a deep sadness. Or maybe it was guilt. If there was any justice in the world, Gabriel had paid for keeping his sons imprisoned. For trying to kill one and using the other.

"I know how you feel about me," Gabriel began.

"No. you don't."

Gabriel tapped the side of his head. "Yes. I do. And I deserve all that wonderfully cultivated hate." He looked down as if he couldn't take Cross's scrutiny. When he looked back up, resignation was all Cross saw. "I wanted to warn you, Tanya is closing in on you. You might want to think about relocating somewhere out of the loop."

Cross almost laughed at that. "You came here to warn me about Tanya?"

Gabriel took a deep breath and let it out slowly. "I did, but not like you think. Did you ever stop to wonder why it was so important that Tanya kept you alive all those years ago, why she kept Kale the way she did?"

Cross narrowed his eyes at Gabriel, trying to understand where he was going with this. "To use us. She bartered Kale's cooperation by threatening my safety. She watched me to see if I remembered my abilities. I know this already."

"You know only a small part of it. Tanya might be a lot of things but stupid isn't one of them. She has an entire building full of freaks, some more powerful than you. Why then would she risk everything, the entire stability of the program to retrieve you and Kale?"

"Because her ego won't allow her to lose."

"Maybe, but that's not the whole story. Tanya has made the department a lot of money over the years. Money she and Coben have grown accustomed to."

"Money? From who? For what?" Cross tried to understand what Gabriel was talking about, but he was coming up with nothing but blanks.

"The military. Tanya has been contracting out Kale on a limited basis for years now. He's agreed in part to keep you safe. He's also insanely in love with her. As sick and twisted as that sounds, Tanya made sure he was totally dependent on her. She orchestrated every aspect of his life and manipulated him to do what she wanted."

Cross put a hand out. "Wait, back up. What would the military want with Kale?"

"Really? You can't figure that out for yourself? Or maybe you just don't want to. Think about it. War has always been an economic shot in the arm for this country, but unpopular wars are political murder. A president who can prevent or peacefully side step what could be a bloody and long confrontation? That's pure political and economic gold.

"Put Kale anywhere near the enemy. Have him push whoever is in charge. All of a sudden a civil war breaks out between the powers gearing up to do battle with us. They take each other out and leave us to reap the benefits. We win by attrition. No American lives lost."

Cross opened his mouth. And closed it again as what Gabriel said made sense. "She's made him do this?"

Gabriel arched a brow. "How do you know if the absence of a conflict was simply that, or if the conflict was avoided by other means?"

"They paid her to have him do this?"

"Paid the Department, yes. When you started to get your memory back, she understood exactly how dangerous that could be. And how profitable. She managed to convince Coben it was worth the risk."

"What risk?"

"You, Cross. Tanya underestimated you when you were young. She thought you were hiding your abilities from her, but she had no idea what you and Kale could do *together.*"

Cross thought he understood now. "We're stronger together."

"She wants to use that. She thinks she can control that."

"What do you think?" Cross almost wanted Gabriel to challenge him.

"I think I know you better than Tanya." Gabriel had yet to move, but he watched Cross with great interest.

"Tanya's interest in us didn't seem to bother you before. If I remember correctly, it was you who put a bullet in my head with the express intention of ending my life. Now you want me to believe you have altruistic notions about warning me, helping us?"

"Altruistic isn't the word I would use."

"That I believe. So what's in it for you?"

"Tanya has grown tired of me. Or perhaps she's simply tired of trusting me. Either way I think you understand the limited lifespan of people Tanya has no further use for. I simply wish to disappear."

"You tried to kill me and you ignored what was happening to Kale all these years. Now that you realize you're the one in the crosshairs, you want to hide. Why even tell me? Why not just leave?"

"Maybe because I've changed."

Cross choked out a laugh. "Don't try to bullshit a psychic. You haven't changed. You're just scared. You're afraid Tanya is going to start to treat you like one of her caged 'specimens'. Your privileged life has ended and you don't want to end up down in the mud with the rest of us."

"Yes." Gabriel's gaze was unnervingly direct and honest.

"You want Kale to hide you from her, don't you?" Cross was baffled by Gabriel's gall. "Why should he, after what you've done to us? Why shouldn't we let Tanya do what she wants to you?"

"Maybe because I'm the only one who knows where you are. Maybe because I am sorry for my part in all of this. And maybe I don't like what I've seen. I still think you're dangerous, Cross. That hasn't changed."

"Then what has?"

"You're dangerous because we made you that way. I understand that now. But the power you bear is tempered by the kind of man you've become."

"You mean the kind of man you programmed me to become."

Gabriel shook his head. "No. Despite everything we tried to do to you, you are still a good man." He touched the side of his head "I know that. Tanya is the one who is truly dangerous. What she's done, what she plans on doing... it might be too little too late, but I want no part of it or her anymore."

Cross tried to see a trap, a lie, but all he saw was a tired old man. He saw no deception behind Gabriel's words. If he didn't help him, Tanya would use Gabriel to find the Underground. He understood exactly why Gabriel stood there so confidently in front of him. It was in Cross's and Kale's best interest to help him disappear. "If I ask Kale to do this, can I have your word that you will never be a part of our lives again?"

Gabriel gave a quick dip of his head. "Done. But before I disappear into oblivion there is one thing I would like to give you."

"Just go away Gabriel. We don't want or need anything from you. You can't start to be a father now. It's too late."

"Perhaps, but I'll try to assuage my guilt anyway." Gabriel held out a folded piece of paper.

Cross considered it with suspicion.

"Take it." Gabriel said.

"What is it?" Cross took the paper but didn't look at it.

"A chance. I grew up in rural Pennsylvania. My grandparents raised me. It was a good childhood, one I never appreciated until it was too late. I ran away when I was very young. Lived off the streets until the Department found me."

Cross opened the paper and read it. There were two sets of numbers on it. He recognized them as latitude and longitude.

"My grandparents died years ago. They left their farm to me but I've never been back. My sister has taken care of it. Your aunt. We've been in touch," Gabriel touched the side of his head. "Up here. She's like me, but she was smart enough to hide it. She'll take you in, if you want."

Cross looked from the paper to Gabriel's face. "Does Tanya know about this?"

"I never told her about my past. When she asked I told her everyone who mattered was dead. It wasn't a lie. She has no clue about the place. You and Kale and anyone you want to bring with you, would be safe there."

"Why? Why do this for us?"

"Does it matter?"

Cross tried to figure Gabriel's angle. "If you're lying, I'll kill you."

"You might have to wait your turn for that." He gestured to Niko and a sad smile spread across his face. "Take care of each other."

Without another word Gabriel Delancey turned and walked away. Cross wondered if he would ever see him again. Part of him didn't want to say goodbye. The other part hoped the view of Gabriel's back disappearing into the shadows would be the last he ever saw of the man.

Too much had happened between them for Cross to forgive him. But let him go?

Cross stepped back into the tunnels and let Gabriel go.

Chapter 38

Kale opened his eyes when he heard a voice in his head. He bolted upright, understanding immediately he wasn't dreaming.

Kale, I miss you.

He knew that voice, how could he forget it. Tanya had no psychic abilities, but Kale was used to listening for her thoughts over the years. It was like having a number on speed dial. If Tanya wanted to contact him all she had to do was think about him. Even here. Tanya called for him and he heard her.

He wanted to answer. Sudden longing nearly overwhelmed him. She was close.

You left me, Kale. Why would you leave me?

He knew he should ignore her, shut his mind off to her. He tried to do just that, but the side of him that he loathed, the side Tanya had created, was stronger. He missed her terribly. Despite the beatings, the isolation, the mental anguish she had caused both him and Cross over the years. He wanted her. He *needed* her.

You kept me like a pet, you beat me, Tanya. You hurt Cross. You would have killed us.

Oh, Kale, I love you, I miss you. I would never do that to you. It was simply discipline. You used to understand discipline. Your brother was the one who has caused all this trouble. Come back to me Kale. Come back now and I promise no one else will get hurt. Please Kale, come home.

No one gets hurt? Not even Cross?

Trust me. I just want you home safe. Come back to me Kale. Come home.

Home. He longed for that. The comforting quiet of his isolated room. Everything here was loud and big and *too much.* Kale didn't understand the rules here. Being back with Cross was more than he could've ever hoped for, but maybe Tanya was right. Maybe he needed to go to her. Maybe then everything would be all right again.

Cross would understand. They would all understand.

He squeezed his eyes closed for one moment trying to make a decision. When he opened them again he knew what he had to do.

Where are you, Tanya?

****

They had followed Gabriel to the abandoned lot and equally abandoned factory across from an old unused subway entrance.

"You're sure they're down there?" Robert said.

Tanya gave Robert a smug, self-assured expression. "I had Bernard put the tracker on the dog's collar when Gabriel came to see me. It was working perfectly. It would seem Woo was right to suspect he was up to something. He had no idea his little good dead would accomplish this entire underground's downfall. Gabriel had no idea we played him."

"Kale bought it?" Robert said.

"Please, as if there was ever any doubt." Tanya took her phone from her jacket pocket and smirked. "I own that boy. He understands that." Head down, she smiled as she sent a text to her man following Gabriel Delancey.

MISSION COMPLETED?

The return text read: I FOUND HIM.ONE SHOT. TARGET DOWN.

GABRIEL IS DEAD? Tanya texted back. She wanted to be sure.

Her man replied: I DON'T MISS.

She said to Robert, "It seems I was right. Vic did have information, Gabriel decided to keep what he learned to himself.

No one gets the better of me, Robert. Remember that. Gabriel has paid the price for thinking he was smarter than me.

"Kale will be back with us momentarily, and then we will take care of Cross. Coben will be pleased. Everything will soon be all neat and tidy again. Inform everyone watching the tunnels not to interfere with Kale when he comes out. Let him come to me."

Robert picked up his radio but paused before pushing the button. "What about Cross?"

Tanya pursed her lips. "In a perfect world I would want them both, but for once Gabriel was right. Cross is dangerous. I can deal with Kale, but Cross is fair game, along with everyone else down there."

"Even the kids?" Robert didn't sound concerned over the thought of killing children. He simply wanted clarification.

"Kids grow up. Kill them all. I want no one around to cause problems. We still have Kale as well as every freak at the department."

Robert unslung the sniper rifle and got into position. "Understood." He lay on his belly and rested the rifle on the low window sill. He put one eye to the scope and waited for Kale to show.

Tanya knew he was nervous. She could see the thin sheen of sweat on his face. He had every right. The people they hunted were dangerous and unpredictable.

"Trust me, Robert, this is all going to be over shortly." Robert's answer was to wind the rifle's strap around his wrist making it more secure on its perch.

Tanya watched with him.

The arrogance. Cross had thought they could simply walk out. She would make him understand no one ever got the better of her. And if Kale thought he had paid for his disobedience before, he would be in for an unpleasant surprise when she got him back. He would understand exactly the price of disobeying Tanya Santiago.

CHAPTER 39

U tah wasn't used to blending in. All of her life she felt out of place in her very up-tight, very upper class family. Often, she wondered if her parents took the right baby home.

This place was different. Hidden away in the dark. Away from the prying eyes of the city and surrounded by those who hid what made them different, Utah fit. She felt a peace here she had never known before. It would all be so perfect if she wasn't worried over Kale.

He tried not to show it but Kale was miserable. He was scared and despite being with his brother again, he was so lonely. His physical injuries were healing, thanks, in part, to Jude. But Utah could feel the conflict inside the guy.

She didn't go to him. She let him have the much-needed reunion with his brother, but she watched. Utah kept to the periphery and she watched Kale. They gave her a place to sleep, but with so much going on, Utah was left alone for the most part.

One night when sleep eluded her, she found herself in the deserted common room. With only the shadows for company, she tried not to think about Kale, when he materialized from one of the tunnels.

Utah felt his nervous energy immediately. She had no special abilities like everyone else here. She didn't need any. Kale's body language spoke for itself. He moved hesitantly as he walked into the common room. One hand was wrapped around his middle as if his stomach hurt him, the other clenched into a fist by his side. He looked brittle, as if he would break into a thousand pieces at any moment.

She didn't want to startle him, but Utah decided she had left him alone long enough. "Kale?" her voice had been soft, but it echoed off the empty walls surrounding them.

He jumped and turned toward her. For a moment Utah doubted her decision as terror filled Kale's face. He took a step back until he seemed to recognize her. "Utah, you're here? I didn't know you were here." He visibly relaxed when he saw they were alone in the common room.

"You've been kind of out it. I thought I would give you some time to get used to things. To be with your brother." She couldn't seem to think of one intelligent thing to say. Utah wanted to ask him so many questions, but mostly she wanted to hold him, stroke his hair and tell him it was going to be okay. She didn't think Kale had been held enough in his life.

The guarded, hunted look left his face and Kale's lips lifted into half a grin. Utah thought he looked so different when he smiled. "I should have asked. Jude's here, I should've realized you would be too. I'm sorry I didn't ask."

"Well, you've had a lot on your mind. It's no big deal."

"You saved my life," Kale took a step toward her. "That's kind of a big deal."

Utah bit her lip and worked up the courage to see if Kale was as dangerous as everyone told her he was. She slid off the table she had been sitting on, took a deep breath and told herself to trust her gut. This man would not hurt her. This man needed her. "They wouldn't let me near you. Jude took care of you, but everyone told me it was best if I stayed away from you. They told me you're a dangerous man."

The grin faded from Kale's face as he took a step away from her. "They're probably right."

"I said that was what they told me. I didn't say I believed them." Utah listened to her heart and took the step needed to take his hand in hers. He lifted his head and his eyes met hers. She felt the need in him to run, but she also felt her touch was not altogether unwelcomed. "If I thought for one moment you were dangerous, I would never have asked my brother to help you. I would have called 911 and walked away. Look, I might not be psychic or have any special powers like you, but I don't need any.

"See, my parents made sure I got a really good education. Top notch universities. They wanted me to study something I could make a living from, instead I took courses in the things that interested me. Things like human behavior. Do you want to know what I learned with the hard-earned and begrudged education my parents' paid for?"

"What did you learn?" Kale said.

"That people can be horrible to one another. They can manipulate and bend you until you don't even know who you were before they started. The can be cruel and heartless and totally without compassion to those they think beneath them."

"Okay, and this has what to do with me?"

"Your Tanya? She did all those things to you Kale. I know you can't see that, or at least you can't see it clearly. There're all sorts of labels and complicated explanations for what she did to you, but they don't matter, what does matter is how she made you feel."

Kale's expression hardened as he jerked his hand out of Utah's. "You don't know anything."

Like hell I don't.

Utah may have had doubts, but not anymore. Kale sounded like a petulant child denying the truth. In a way, that's exactly what he was. A child. The thought of what had been done to him, what had been denied to him, made Utah furious.

"Where are you going, Kale?" Her voice was soft, her tone gentle.

"Out. I'm just going out. Aren't I allowed or am I a prisoner here too?" Kale glanced around the room nervously.

"No, you're not a prisoner. You're free to come and go as far as I know. But From what I've been told you've spent the last ten years in one room. The only person allowed to see or talk to you was this Tanya. I gotta tell you Kale, I can't see someone like that taking a late night stroll, all by themselves in a deserted area of

New York. I don't care if you can do the glowing ball of light thing. You're not that brave."

"You don't know me. You know nothing about who I am."

"You're right. I don't know you. But I would like too. If you let me, I would like to get to know who Kale Delancey is. Not the guy who was kept locked up all of his life, but this guy," She gestured to him. "I would like, more than anything, to get to know the Kale Delancey standing in front of me."

All the anger that had been there a moment ago dissolved leaving Kale looking defeated. When he raised his head to meet Utah's gaze, his eyes were flat. She didn't like that. "That Kale doesn't exist."

Utah moved in quickly before Kale could back off again, she grabbed both his hands and held them tightly to her chest. "But he could. Don't you see, Kale? You've been given something most people would die for—a second chance. A do-over. You get to prove to all those people out there who think you deserved to be locked up, that they are wrong. You get to show them who you were meant to be. Who I know you are in here." She placed a hand over his heart. "I don't know where you're going, but I have a feeling that if you leave, you are letting that chance slip away."

Utah watched Kale closely. The edgy, guarded posturing, softened to be replaced by the conflict and uncertainty he was desperately trying to hide.

"I don't want to lie to you. Please don't make me." His eyes pleaded with her to let him go.

"I don't want you to lie to me either, so how about this. Before you do or say anything else, just listen to me, okay?"

He said nothing but gave her a quick nod. He wanted to be saved. Utah could feel it. She guided him to one of the benches and sat down next to him. "You don't owe this Tanya anything. I know you can't see that because she has you all twisted up inside."

"I don't want to talk about Tanya."

"Tanya is exactly who we need to talk about. Because I have a feeling she isn't anywhere near done with you." Utah didn't miss his nervous glance to the tunnel exit. "I know you love her. She made sure she was everything to you. She got you to do things by threatening that love and by threatening Cross."

"That's not how it was. You don't understand. She loves me." His words were almost like a plea. They held no conviction.

Utah gently placed a hand on his face and turned his head until he was looking at her. "That's not love, Kale. Not even close."

All the fight seemed to go out of him as he turned away from Utah. "I don't know what I know anymore. I don't know what I feel. All my life Tanya has been there. She could be horrible, brutal, but if you did what she wanted, she..." Utah could see Kale trying to find the words.

"She used you, Kale. She manipulated you. Kept you isolated and used your loneliness to get what she wanted out of you. If you played nice she pretended to give you what you needed- love. If you denied her, she hurt you." She turned his hand over and touched his bandaged wrist. "Love doesn't work that way."

"I know. I'm not stupid, I've always known but I don't know how to say no to her. Sometimes I don't think I want to say no to her."

"That's where you're going. Isn't it? Tanya's out there waiting for you."

Kale looked anywhere except at Utah. She stepped directly in front of him and forced him to look at her. A single tear rolled down his cheek.

"If you tell her no, Kale, then you can start to say yes to the people who want nothing more from you than what you're willing to give."

For the first time Kale lifted a hand and touched Utah's face. "People like you?" His voice held a note of hope that gave Utah the courage to do what she had wanted to do for days. She leaned in close. "Yeah. People like me." She kissed him and felt him melt in her embrace.

He broke the kiss and touched her lips with a finger. An expression of pure wonder lit up his face. "I have to go and do this. Tanya doesn't own me as much as she would like to think. But it's hard."

Utah touched her forehead to his. "I know." Her voice was a whisper. "But I think you're stronger than you give yourself credit for. Prove them wrong. Prove them all wrong, Kale. Then come back to me and I'll teach you what love is supposed to feel like."

Kale pulled back and held her face with both hands. He smoothed her hair, his eyes intent on hers. Then without another word he turned, and slipped away into the shadows.

When he was gone, a shadow that was Maizey stepped into the light. "You were here this whole time?" Utah said.

"I was prepared to stop him. I heard Tanya in his head. I was prepared to do whatever I had to do to keep him away from her."

"Why didn't you?"

Maizey stared out into the dark where Kale had disappeared into. "I'm not really sure. Something changed after you talked to him."

"He'll do the right thing," Utah said.

"I guess we will all find that out together. I'm not sure what you did Utah, but I am sure of one thing. I think you just might have saved us all with nothing more than a kiss."

CHAPTER 40

C ross was nearly back to the main hub after meeting Gabriel when a piercing pain in his head dropped him like a stone. A moment later he heard Gabriel's voice in his head.

Trouble! Tanya...

Cross got back to his feet as the sudden pain faded. He sought Gabriel's now familiar energy, but found nothing. In one clarifying moment he understood. Gabriel had been followed.

Cross thought he might be dead. And Tanya knew exactly where the Underground was.

Cross tried to contact Kale, but his brother was either ignoring him or blocking him. Either way worried Cross. He found Finn's energy immediately.

Tanya has found us.

Finn would understand the urgency without the warning being spelled out. Tanya had brought the fight here.

With Niko in tow, Cross ran full speed into the tunnel and found himself staring down the twin bores of a double-barreled shotgun. He tried to back up but only succeeded in falling.

Finn pulled the barrel up. "You almost got yourself killed!" He pulled Cross to his feet. "What's happening? Tanya knows where we are?"

"I should've been more careful, Gabriel called a truce. He gave me Niko back and said all he wanted to do was disappear. I don't know why, but I believed him. Tanya must have had him followed. I think she had him shot. I felt it. I heard him. He said it was Tanya."

"Okay, right. Now what do we do?" Finn said.

"She's got us outnumbered and outgunned. Charlie already moved a lot of the women and children out, but there are still some left down here."

"Are you trying to make a point here, because I gotta tell you, you're failing miserably and depressing me at the same time."

"You don't get it, Finn. It doesn't matter what Tanya throws at us because there's one thing she doesn't have. Me and Kale. She can't win. She has to know that."

"I hate to tell you this, but Kale is gone." Maizey walked into the room. She seemed calm but Cross could feel the turmoil simmering just beneath the surface.

"Gone? What do you mean gone?" Finn said.

"Trust him." Utah followed Maizey into the hub. "He'll be back. He promised."

Cross held up his hands. "Everybody be quiet for a minute." The noise in the room hushed to a level where he could concentrate. Kale didn't want to be found, but Cross found him anyway. It was almost like looking in a mirror. He would recognize his brother's unique signature anywhere. What concerned him was the other energy signature he found with Kale's. He opened his eyes. Betrayal and confusion vied for his emotion of choice. "No." The word was a whisper.

"He's with Tanya." Even saying the words hurt.

"I know," Maizey said.

"What do you mean you know?"

"I could've stopped him. I chose to let him go."

"Son-of-bitch! He chose her over us? Over you, his own brother? Why?" Finn was close to shouting.

A part of Cross had always known it would all play out like this. "He didn't. He didn't betray us. He's sacrificing himself."

"He's still protecting you," Maizey said.

"I know he's your brother, but are you sure he isn't going to flip?" Finn said. "He's been in Tanya's pocket all his life. That's not going to be an easy monkey to shake off his back."

"He isn't going to side with Tanya. You're just going to have to trust me on that."

"If you're wrong every single person in these tunnels will pay the price. The things Kale can do…"

"He isn't going to flip. I trust him Finn." Cross could feel Kale in his head so strongly it hurt. He knew his brother and he knew exactly what he intended to do. "He doesn't plan on coming back. He'll die to keep me safe. To keep all of us safe."

Utah's eyes went wide. "No. We can't let that happen. He's never had a chance to live his life. We can't let him die like this." She sent pleading looks to each of them. "We need to go and bring him back and we need to let this Tanya Santiago understand exactly who it is she's dealing with. She messes with one of us, she messes with all of us."

Finn raised his brows at Utah's words. "I sure as hell don't want to have to deal with her if Kale doesn't come back. I'm in." He stepped next to Utah and placed a hand on her shoulder. "I let Tanya have him once and did nothing to help him. Not happening again."

Danny King separated himself from the crowd and came to Utah's other side. He placed a hand on her other shoulder. "I get to help take down the bitch who killed my sister? Hell yeah, I'm in."

One by one the other men and women in the tunnel surrounded Cross and Utah in a circle, their hands connecting them, the things they could do uniting them. Cross felt it. They might each have their own reason but like Kale and him, together they were stronger. They were joining forces to save Kale Delancey not only from Tanya but also from himself. They shared a common goal.

Freedom.

The right to live without fear. The right to use what made them hunted, to feel the sun again without the fear of becoming caged.

If Tanya wanted a war, the people of the Underground were more than ready to oblige her.

CHAPTER 41

K ale had left Utah and walked to where Tanya waited. Her words still echoing in his thoughts. Cross was trying to get his attention, and he couldn't concentrate. His head was a mess and that was not a good thing when dealing with Tanya.

He had to do this. No one else could. He knew Tanya better than anyone. She was poised to take everyone in the Underground down to get what she wanted. And he was what she wanted.

Cross was powerful, maybe even powerful enough to stop her, but Kale didn't think that victory would be worth the lives it would cost. He made a promise to protect his brother. He couldn't stop protecting Cross now just because the power that had slept inside of him was finally awake.

Cross was only now learning how to use his talents. Thanks to Tanya, Kale had spent years honing his unique skills to perfection. He could this win this war before it even started.

As strong as her hold was on him, he didn't want that, not anymore. What he felt for Tanya was ugly and dirty. When Utah had kissed him, it was different. Scary, but in a good way, something he would've like to explore. Only that too came with a price, and it was one he wasn't willing to pay. Not anymore.

He just needed a little time to do what he had to do, and he needed everyone to leave him alone so he could do it. He didn't want to push Cross, or Utah or any of the new friends he'd made, but he had no choice.

Kale stopped walking and closed his eyes. He wasn't far from the underground, just outside the door, so he wouldn't need Gabriel's help. He could feel them, the people there, hundreds of them but he didn't need to *push* them all. Just the ones who gave the orders. He focused on Charlie, Maizey, Finn and Cross.

I know what I'm doing. Do not come out of the tunnels. Keep everyone safe inside. Give me twenty minutes. It will all be over in twenty minutes.

Charlie and Finn gave into the push without question or hesitation. Maizey fought back. He had never tried to push anyone like her before, someone who could do what he did. In the end he proved stronger. Her mind gave into the *push* and he felt her relax.

That left only Cross.

Pushing Cross was like trying to hold onto sand. His mind slipped out of Kale's mental grasp again and again, until he realized he was wasting time.

Cross, stop! Let me do this!

Let you die? I just got you back. No way. Don't do this Kale. We can beat her together.

She has the exits surrounded. She'll kill all of you to get to me. I know you feel that.

She can try. Not happening, man.

They need you to keep them safe, I need a few minutes. That's all I'm asking. Just a few minutes, and I can end this without anyone else dying because of me.

I'm not letting you sacrifice your life. Not for her and not for me. Stop protecting me, Kale.

Kale blocked Cross's thoughts.

His brother's last words repeated in his mind.

Stop protecting me.

No way. Kale thought.

Never.

CHAPTER 42

"Damn it, Kale!" Niko leaned hard against Cross's leg. He was upsetting her. He put a hand on her head in an effort to calm them both. Kale thought he could simply give himself up to that bitch without giving him any say. That was never happening again. Not while he still drew breath.

"What's wrong?" Maizey wore a content, almost sleepy, expression. She touched Cross's face lovingly.

He could feel a residue of Kale's *push* on her. He could sense his brother's energy covering Maizey's. Like a sticky sweet syrup it coated her own thoughts and only allowed the push to come through. Both Finn and Charlie had the same energy residue. They all lacked any sense of urgency. Cross shrugged off Maizey's touch impatiently.

"He's going to get himself killed. We have to help him."

"No, he said he could handle her," Finn said. "It'll be fine Cross. Relax."

Cross wanted to slap Finn's complacent expression right off. He fought the urge to scream at them all knowing it would do no good.

"He *pushed* you. Kale *pushed* all of you."

Maizey's languid smile faltered a little. He might have the best shot of getting through to her. To help her to overcome Kale's *push*, he concentrated only on her.

Every second was one less he had to try and save Kale, but if he let panic in, Tanya won. He ignored the fear and fought through Kale's *push* to reach Maizey. *Maizey. Wake up, listen to me and wake up!*

Maizey's thoughts still drifted, but Cross seized them before they slipped away. *Maizey, my beautiful Maizey. Please listen to me. Please see me!*

"Cross?" She blinked like someone coming out of dream. His vision clouded over and the last of his beautiful blue and white sight faded.

"Yes!" He took her face in his hands. She was only shadows and light to him now. "Do you see me? Can you hear me?"

"What's happening? What's wrong?" Her voice registered confusion, but Cross knew he had done it. He had broken through to the Maizey underneath Kale's *push*.

"Tanya."

"She's here." She understood immediately. "Where's Kale?"

"He's gone to her. He's still protecting me, only this time he doesn't plan on getting out alive."

"My God. He pushed me?"

"And Finn and Charlie. I thought I had the best shot of getting through to you. I was right."

"Who else do we have to help us?"

Cross grinned and held his hands out. "We're it sweetheart. There's no time to gather up the troops. You stay here and get everyone ready to move out. When Finn comes out of it, he'll know what to do." Cross started for the tunnel exit when Maizey grabbed his arm.

"Nice try, but if you really wanted me to simply stay behind and babysit, you wouldn't have wasted time waking me."

"There's no time for this Maizey. I don't want to argue with you—"

"Then don't." She pulled him in and kissed him hard and fast.

When she pulled back, his head was spinning. He didn't mind.

"Let's go get your pain-in-the-ass brother and bring him home. I really need to talk to him. *No one* pushes me."

"Not very good odds," he said.

"I thrive in the face of dismal odds. Besides I owe this Tanya of yours."

Maizey was right. He did want her with him. The fact that she was willing to go with him despite that neither might survive only confirmed what he had been thinking for a while. "I love you, Maizey."

"Of course you do." She took his hand.

Before they left, Cross asked Finn to look after Niko. Even under Kale's push, Finn agreed. He didn't understand why he was keeping her safe, but that didn't matter. Niko didn't like being left behind, but Cross couldn't let her go with him. Not now.

****

As soon as he emerged from the tunnel, Kale felt Tanya's men all around him. They were terrified, but held their ground as he slowly walked toward the dilapidated structure where Tanya waited.

For the first time in his life he believed Tanya's hype. He was the monster everyone thought him to be. Power surged through him, waiting to be called on. All it took to hold it in check was the memory of what she had done to Sybil. To Cross.

To him.

Kale felt no fear, no hesitation. He did exactly what Tanya had taught him to do. Exactly what he knew she always wanted him to do. With one small *push*, the men and women surrounding him dropped their weapons. They were lucky he didn't tell them to put the barrels to their heads and pull the triggers.

It didn't matter. She could believe she'd won. She could believe Kale was still her puppet.

Hell, maybe he was.

The wide, empty entrance to the building was full of shadows. He sensed her there, but he couldn't see her until he crossed the threshold. At the sight of her, all his plans, all his anger dissolved. Even in the shadows her blond hair glowed like gold in firelight. He had always loved her hair. The way it smelled like flowers and the way it flowed like warm silk as it swept across his body when she took him.

"I missed you, Kale." She held out her arms.

He closed the gap between them and fell into her embrace. As she wrapped her arms around him he sighed in contentment. He held on to her tightly, afraid if he let her go she would disappear. Afraid he would.

Tanya pulled back just far enough to kiss him. For a moment he forgot why he was there.

"You came to me. I wasn't sure you would," She caressed his face. "Why did you leave me Kale? How could you do that to me?"

He had an answer to that. Didn't he?

He fought to remember what had seemed so vital only moments ago. She was a drug to him. He forgot everything but her when she was near. Then his brother's voice sounded in his head, begging him to wait. To stop. Telling him they could do this together. Utah, Jude, Maizey, and all the people who were counting on him. His friends.

His friends.

He moved away from her, squeezed his eyes closed briefly. Despite wanting her, he took a step back. He needed to do this quickly or he would never do it at all. "You brought Cross in. You planned on using him like you used me all these years. That wasn't the deal. Cross is off limits. You changed the rules. I can't let you do that." Kale never felt braver than he did with those few words.

She undid him with a giggle. "Oh my. You can't let me? Since when do you tell me what to do Kale?" Her smile vanished replaced by an ugly sneer. Gone was the woman he lusted for. There was only a vicious viper poised to strike. "You have no rights here. You never did."

Tanya walked a small circle around him, as if judging his worth. "Let me tell you exactly what is going to happen here, Kale. You will either help me bring Cross back in, or you will help me kill him. The choice is entirely yours. You are mine, Kale Delancey, since the time you took your first breath to the time you take your last. I will dictate how you live and how you die, and you should thank me every day for that privilege."

Kale had heard variations of the same speech all his life, but this time he wasn't locked in a cell. This time she couldn't make good on her threat to kill Cross if he didn't cooperate. This time Kale had a choice.

But standing there in front of Tanya, he found it more difficult than he had imagined to make that choice.

He couldn't think! There was too much noise in his head, too many people crowding his thoughts. The world was so very big and so terribly intimidating. Not at all like he'd imagined it would be. He almost wished for his small windowless room, if only for the quiet it provided.

"Why do you always make it so difficult Kale?" Tanya took his chin in her hand and held it. He looked into her eyes. A small predatory grin played upon her lips. "Tell me what I want to hear, darling, and everything will be all right. Just say the words and Tanya will make it all better."

"Was any of it real?"

It clearly wasn't the answer Tanya wanted. "Was what real? What are you talking about?"

"I loved you. I still love you. Did you ever love me? You've said the words, but did you ever mean them? Did you ever feel them? Was any of it ever real for you, or was I nothing more than a thing to you. No more important than that girl you slaughtered in front of me."

Tanya made a face, annoyed with him. "For God's sake, Kale there isn't time for this. If I didn't love you, why would I be doing any of this?"

"I've asked myself that very question almost every day for the last ten years. I'm not sure what you feel for me, Tanya but I'm beginning to understand it's not love. It never was."

"I've had enough. I was going to forgive you. I was going to be lenient with you when we got back. But if you insist on making this more difficult than it has to be, fine. We can play it that way.

"I wanted to take Cross alive, but you need to be taught a lesson. You just killed your brother, Kale. Robert, take him and let's get on with this."

Kale knew Robert was there, hiding in the shadows. He could've pushed him, he could have killed him, but he had wanted to trust Tanya. He had needed to know.

He understood now.

The soft *spit* registered in Kale's ears, and then with a thought and a small flick of his hand there was nothing.

He took a moment to enjoy the silence in his mind.

Tanya stood exactly where she had been. Her unmoving eyes were focused just behind where Kale had been. He turned to where Robert stood, tranquilizer rifle aimed at where Kale had been and a dart with a red tassel suspended in mid-air. The bright orange explosion that had propelled it out of the firing chamber was frozen just behind it.

"That's new."

Kale turned. Cross and Maizey were framed in the doorway. His brother walked slowly toward him, apparently unaffected. Maizey, however, halted in mid-stride, with her wild red hair around her face like a fiery halo. Frozen in a moment of time.

"You just stopped time, Kale. How did you do that?"

"I didn't know I *could* do that. Why didn't I stop you too?"

"Same reason you can't push me, I guess. Can you unstop it?"

"Yeah, I'm not sure how I know that, but yeah I can. I thought I told you not to follow me. She means to kill you Cross. I didn't come here to be with her. I came here to stop her." Kale touched the dart meant to incapacitate him. It moved. He turned it around so it was aimed at Robert.

"You can't stop her," Cross said. "She'll kill me when she figures out I won't do her bidding. She'll never let you out of that cage again. You have to know that. This will never be over if she lives."

"I know."

"I can do it if you want. I know this can't be easy for you."

Kale passed a hand in front of his brother's eyes. "You can't see."

Cross caught his hand. "Everything has a price. But for the first time since I lost my sight, it's all perfectly clear. I'm not letting you do this alone. We finish what we started ten years ago, or we go down trying. We are stronger together." Cross gripped his hand.

Kale felt the power that coursed through him. Through *them.* "I'm not as brave as you," he admitted.

"You don't need to be. You saved me all those years ago. It's finally my turn to return the favor."

"I don't want more people dying because of me. Because of us." Kale wanted it to be over. He wanted to go someplace quiet and just *be.* Cross understood that. He was the only one who ever understood.

"I know."

"I can push her. I can tell her to forget about us. She can't look for us if she doesn't know we exist."

Cross shook his head. "Would that balance the scales? Bring justice to everyone Tanya has hurt?"

"Would killing her do that? It won't give you back your eyes, or me the last ten years. Why do we need to kill her, Cross?"

"Because she deserves it!" Cross yelled and his voice cracked.

Kale felt the emotions his brother had tried so hard to keep hidden come to the surface. They were like a raw wound, open and bleeding.

"She deserved it when we were fourteen and she tried to keep us in a cage. She deserved it when she used our mother, just to make us. God, Kale I'm trying like hell to understand you. I get that she was all you had all those years. I get the feelings you have for her, but are those feelings stronger than what we have? Are they worth the people in those tunnels who think of you as family now?"

Kale watched Tanya as Cross spoke. He was right, Kale knew that, but Cross was wrong about why. "No, she's not worth all that."

"Then kill her. Now. Or I will." Cross scooped the ambient energy surrounding them into his hands to form a glowing, surging ball of deadly light. The temperature surrounding them dropped as the ball of light in Cross's hands grew. All his brother needed to do was direct that lethal force toward Tanya. It was exactly the same way he had killed all those people when they tried to escape ten years ago.

It was the power Tanya craved when she tortured Cross.

"No! This is why. *This!* No more death, please. She's made me hurt so many people. Made me kill them." The memory sickened Kale. "I'm not like you Cross, I never was. I don't understand how you could kill her, as if her life means nothing. You're more like her than you know."

"I'm nothing like her." Cross stepped toward Tanya, still frozen in time.

"She uses people. I always knew she used me. It's who she is. She doesn't care who she hurts as long as gets what she wants. She killed Sybil King right in front of me. Put a gun to her head and blew her brains all over me, just to prove she owned me. To prove I would do anything for her."

"And you think I'm like that?"

"You've killed people to get what you wanted, to get out. Most of them never hurt us. Now you want to kill Tanya when there's another way."

"I killed them because I knew if we stayed we would end up dead, sooner than later. You knew that too. I don't kill because I like it, I killed to stay alive. I would still kill to stay alive, to keep the people I love alive. *Pushing* Tanya won't change her, Kale. Can't you see that? If she lives she will still hurt others like us. Other innocents like Sybil King will die because we didn't do the right thing now. Like you said, it's who she is. Some people don't deserve a second chance."

Kale heard the truth in Cross's words. If he didn't want more innocent blood on his hands, he knew what he had to do.

"I can do it," Cross said. The power seethed in his hands, waiting for him to call on it. "We can do this, just like we tried to do before. She doesn't get to win this time."

"No. It has to be me. But not like this. She needs to know it was me." Kale nodded toward Maizey as he took the knife from the sheath on Robert's hip. "Go to Maizey and hold her still. She'll keep moving when I start time again. You need to be prepared for Tanya's people in the courtyard. I pushed them. If something happens to me, the push will stop."

"Nothing's going to happen to you, Kale." Cross didn't want to, but he did as Kale asked. He let the energy still pulsing in his hands scatter above them. For one moment the abandoned warehouse, with its decay and neglect, was beautiful in the starry fallout. Cross wrapped his arms around Maizey protectively.

Kale embraced Tanya, with the knife positioned between them.

Get ready, he thought to Cross. Then he leaned in close and whispered in Tanya's ear. "I have loved you since I was sixteen. I will always love you."

With his thought, time returned. Tanya surged forward, only to be held in place. Her face registered confusion, and then anger. Kale heard Robert collapse behind him as the dart meant to sedate Kale found its mark.

"How? What did you do?" Tanya fought against Kale but he was stronger. He whispered to her and she calmed. He then moved away just enough so he could place the knife in her hand.

"I can't kill you, But Cross is right there is nothing good inside of you." Tanya stared at the knife, as if trying to figure out what it was she held. Kale knew her confusion wouldn't last long. He had mere moments to do what he had to do. The right thing, despite what his brother thought.

"You'll use me to get to them. You will always use me. I can change that." He stepped back and raised his arms out from his sides.

And then he *pushed* her.

"Kill me."

"No!" Cross screamed.

Kale kept his eyes on Tanya as the push took hold and her face went blank. She brought the blade up and down again in a deadly arc. Agony stabbed through Kale's chest at the same time he heard a single gunshot.

Tanya's face creased in pain and surprise. She teetered forward, pushing the knife deeper.

Kale fell on his back, with Tanya on top of him. After the first shock, there was only numbness.

He sensed Cross calling out to him. He felt his brother's grief but most of all he felt Cross's life. He had kept his promise. Cross would be safe now from Tanya. Everyone would be safe.

After all those years of being terrified Tanya would kill him, he finally understood death wasn't something to fear. It was to be embraced.

Kale struggled to take one last breath, and then he gratefully embraced his death.

CHAPTER 43

Searing pain in Cross's head crippled him. His chest was on fire as he tried to breath. Not his pain.

Kale's.

Kale!

The pain dissolved and the connection between them was severed.

Kale? Talk to me!

Someone's hands were on him helping to stand. Maizey.

Gunshots and screams from the courtyard.

"Kale's hurt." Maizey's voice was a forced calm Cross couldn't begin to feel.

"Where?" His hands searched frantically in front of him. "Where is he?" A soft unmoving shape. His hands found his brother's face. "Kale? God, Kale?"

A familiar energy appeared in Cross's mind.

"Vic? Oh thanks the gods, we thought you were dead!" Maizey's voice sounded relieved, but all Cross could think about was Kale so still beneath his hands.

"Not yet, sweetheart. Not yet and I would like to keep it that way." Vic's deep voice held no trace of its usual humor.

"Vic? What's happening? Kale won't wake up. What about Tanya?" Cross tried to contain his anxiety. "Where the hell did you come from?"

"First things first. We still aren't out of this. Maizey, can you handle the company coming in hot from the front courtyard?"

"My pleasure," Maizey said.

Cross felt a flicker in his mind. Kale. On the floor. He found his brother's limp hand and clasped it. Like a ghostly touch, the faint burning in his chest told him Kale was still alive.

As suddenly as it began, the battle in the courtyard stopped. Everything was calm. Quiet. That didn't make him feel safe. It scared him.

"What's happening Vic." Cross was having difficulty concentrating, despite the quiet.

"I shot Tanya. But not before she got Kale. We need to get him some help and fast."

"He's not dead. Just tell me he's not going to die, Vic." Cross sensed Vic kneeling on the other side of Kale. Felt his ghost touches in his head as he examined Kale.

"Why did he do that? Push her to kill him?" Vic said.

"He believed if he was dead, Tanya couldn't use him to hurt anyone, anymore. Particularly me. The idiot.

"I told him we could do this together!" Tears spilled down his face as anger dissolved and grief took its place. "I just got him back, Vic. He can't die now. He can't."

"I'm not about to let that happen. Not if I can help it." Vic pulled Kale into his arms.

"I can help," Cross said. "I can take some of his pain, share his injuries."

Maizey burst in, breathless. Energy radiated off of her in great spiking waves. "You're in no shape to share anything, Cross. He's near death."

"Do you think I care about myself?" The fourteen year old boy who didn't care who he killed surfaced. Rage bubbled through him, and for once he did nothing to dampen it. It right, it felt good. It felt powerful.

"Cross," Vic's voice made it through his wrath. "What are you doing? We aren't the enemy."

Energy seethed and whirled between his hands like a living thing. It wanted to be used. It wanted to be set free. And Cross wanted that too. He longed for it.

Maizey laid a gentle hand on his arm. "If you do this, love, then Tanya wins. None of us will walk away from here. No one but you. This won't save Kale. You will have made his sacrifice meaningless."

Cross flinched from her touch. "I don't care." But his words held no conviction. The energy between his hands lessened a bit in its intensity.

"Yes you do."

"After everything he's done for me, after all these years. Now, when he needs me most, I can't help him?"

"He's not dead yet, love," Maizey said. "If you take on his injuries you both might die. If you release that energy you've gathered, you will prove to all those people at the Department you are just as dangerous as they believe you to be."

"If he dies, I don't think I could live with myself. Maybe I deserve to die. Maybe I am dangerous."

"We need you Cross. Those people in the tunnels need you."

She was right. He hated it, but she was right. As his hatred and frustration drained away into defeat, the energy dissipated, leaving Cross groundless. He staggered and Maizey was there, her hand keeping him steady. "I don't know what to do," he admitted.

"Yes, you do. Choose life, Cross. Choose us."

He gulped down tears, fear and raw pain. Vic shouldered his way past them carrying Kale, Cross let Maizey take his arm and help him follow them down into the dark.

The dark, where hope and fear existed side by side.

****

Kale opened his eyes. Just little slits against the light. His mind was like a blank slate. No memory. He blinked and rubbed the grit from the corners of his eyes. His hand felt heavy, as if it didn't belong to him. He let it fall back to his side. He didn't know where he was and it didn't occur to him to be bothered by that. This wasn't his room at the department. To big, to light and airy.

Where am I?

Dead? Maybe. That thought didn't bother him either.

Little snips of memory began to flit in and out of his brain.

Tanya.

Had Tanya killed him? He tried to sit up because it seemed like he should.

A soft hand on his shoulder gently stopped him. "Let's just take it slow, okay?"

Kale stared at the hand, followed the arm up, and looked into a face he didn't recognize. A woman sat next to his bed. She had shiny brown hair pulled back from her face and very kind eyes. She was older than him, maybe fifty. He had never met her before. He was sure of that.

He wanted to ask who she was, but his voice refused to cooperate. A short raspy noise was all that came from his throat.

The woman took a cup from a side table and helped him to drink from it. Water had never tasted so good.

"I'm Ingrid. I know you have a lot of questions, but let me start by telling you that I'm a friend and you are safe."

Kale swallowed. "Cross?" The word came out this time but his voice sounded rusty, like it hadn't been used in some time.

Ingrid swept hair from his face. "He's here and safe. He'll be upset he missed being here when you woke up."

Kale closed his eyes and sought his brother. He needed more than this woman's word. Almost immediately he found Cross and he relaxed. He grinned as he understood that Cross had not only heard him, but was now on his way to wherever he was.

He must have fallen back to sleep. When he opened his eyes again, Cross was there holding his hand so hard it hurt. Kale didn't mind. It confirmed they were both alive. "Hey." His voice sounded more like the one he was use too, but still soft and weak.

"Don't 'hey' me," Cross said. He sounded like he was mad, but he was smiling. He was also looking directly at Kale. No dark glasses.

"You can see."

"Yeah, I'm getting better at it. God, it's good to see you awake. How are you, man? I mean really, how are you doing?"

Kale tried to hitch himself up a little in the bed, but didn't have the strength.

Cross offered a hand and helped him to sit against a pillow.

"Where are we? What is this place? Who's Ingrid?"

"What's the last thing you remember?" Cross relinquished Kale's hand and sat back in his chair.

Kale rested his head back against the pillow. Nothing came to him at first. But then images floated across his memory. One face stood out from the rest. "Tanya," he said, and that one image opened the flood gates. "Tanya." He remembered it all and closed his eyes. "What happened? I remember...I *pushed* her. I thought she killed me. I wanted her..." He opened his eyes and found Cross staring back at him.

"You nearly got your wish," Cross said. "There was nothing wrong with your *push*. Tanya tried to do exactly what you told her to do." Cross pointed to the bandages covering half of Kale's chest. "She stabbed you. Nicked a major vein. You almost bled to death. You should've bled to death."

"Then why aren't I dead?"

"Because a hell of a lot of people made sure that didn't happen. Jesus, Kale, I want to be furious with you. I told you we could handle her together. Why? Why did you think you had to do that?"

"I thought if I was dead, then you wouldn't have to worry about her using me anymore. And she couldn't use me to hurt anyone else." He tried for the cocky grin. "It seemed like a really good idea at the time."

Cross sighed and Kale knew he was trying hard not to smile.

"Okay, so that's the part you remember. I suggest you hang to something for the rest because it's a bumpy ride." He crossed one leg over a knee, but kept his eyes on Kale. "While you were deciding to be all self- sacrificing and noble, Gabriel was paying me a little visit. He gave me back Niko and told me all he wanted was to be free of the department. I didn't trust him, but I guess he was telling me the truth. Tanya had him killed."

"Gabriel's dead?" Kale wasn't sure how he felt about that.

"I felt him it." Cross tapped the side of his head. "Up here. I felt his pain and then I felt him die."

"Wow, I thought he was always *Team Tanya*, you know?"

"Yeah, me too. What he didn't tell me was that Tanya had finally caught onto Vic. He was the one who helped me. She had him roughed up, locked him in a cell. Probably would've had him killed. Gabriel let him out."

"Vic shot Tanya that night. He blames himself for this." Cross indicated Kale's injuries. "He doesn't like losing." Kale sucked in a breath. "Then Tanya is dead. Was this the bumpy ride you were talking about?"

"Part of it. Gabriel gave me something. I wasn't sure what to make of it, wasn't even sure I trusted him enough to use it."

"What did he give you?"

"A second chance," Cross said. "This place. He told me about this place. He grew up here. Ran away when he was a kid and never came back. But his sister stayed."

Kale thought about that. Little pieces were beginning to fall into place. "Ingrid."

"Yeah," Cross said, "Ingrid. She's our aunt, Kale. She's like us. You know- different. The Department isn't going to just forget about us because Tanya is gone. They know about the tunnels. They know everything. We couldn't stay there and be safe."

"Where exactly are we?"

Cross pushed out of the chair and went to the windows. He raised the shade and lovely, soft moonlight invaded the room. "Paradise, man. Paradise."

Kale struggled to see out of the little window, but all he saw were tree-tops and the pale light of the moon. But Cross was right, it was a far cry from his cold little cell at the Department.

"Gabriel told me no one at the Department knew about this place or Ingrid."

"So we're safe here?"

"You are very safe here." The voice from the doorway had them both turning. Ingrid stood there. She had a kind face, Kale decided. Soft and smooth, but her eyes were tough looking. Like she had fought a lot of battles and won them all. Then he remembered she was his aunt. His blood.

Family.

"I thought I told you to go slow with him," she said to Cross. She came and sat on the edge of Kale's bed. One hand touched his forehead. "For two weeks this boy has given me nothing but sleepless nights." She lowered her hand. "I won't have you putting him at risk now. I worked too hard to keep him breathing. Out."

"Wait," Kale realized what Ingrid had said. "Two weeks? I've been out of it for two weeks?" Cross turned back, but Ingrid shushed him with a look and shooed him out the door. Cross gave an embarrassed shrug.

Later, man. I promise.

Ingrid sent Cross a disapproving look. Obviously she had *heard* Cross's thoughts.

This is going to be interesting.

"Indeed it is." Ingrid said. "I told your brother he had a few minutes. He's had that and more. I know you have more questions, but you're weak and you need to rest. Everything will fall into place when it is time. Sleep. I'll know when you're awake. You'll be stronger next time. I promise." She kissed Kale on the head, pulled his covers up, and smoothed a hand over face. "Sleep Kale. No one can hurt you here."

Kale believed her and closed his eyes.

When they were outside Kale's room, Ingrid quietly shut the door and glared at Cross.

"I'm sorry, he needed to know. I needed to tell him." Cross looked, of all things, uncertain.

"Am I really all that scary?" Ingrid tried not to laugh. "It's okay, Cross. I'm not sure I could have done better if the situation had been reversed." She took his face in her hands and studied him with concern. "You need rest as well. You took far too much of his injuries. He is still too weak for you to give them back. They're yours now, you have to treat them that way."

"I'm fine," Cross said. "I'm great, now that I know Kale will pull through."

"Hmmm, he might pull through, but you, my dear Cross, are stubborn and just this side of fine. Get some rest. You'll be no good to anyone like this. You need to be strong for what is coming. You need to be strong for all these souls who, like it or not, look up to you now for answers."

"I don't have any answers. I'm just trying to do the best I can. I'm just trying to do the same thing they are. Survive."

Ingrid gave him a side-way glance. "Well like or not, those people look to you for answers, and I think we can do a lot better than just survive, nephew. Perhaps we might even manage to figure out how to live."

"There's more of them, you know. The ones still kept in cages back at the Department. I'm responsible for putting some of them there. I have to make that right. I can't leave them there."

Ingrid wiped a thumb softly across the bruised flesh under his eye. He was worn out and feeling guilty. She could feel that as easily as she felt the tears on his face.

"We won't leave them. I promise. But for now, you need to rest. I'll look after your brother." She led him to his room down the hall. Once he was lying on the bed, she placed a small sleeping spell on him. He would be angry over the deceit, but he would feel so much better in the morning if he slept without worrying about everything. She took his shoes off and covered him, dimmed the light and left the door opened a crack. He was sound asleep before she left the room.

With both Cross and Kale sleeping, Ingrid walked on silent feet through her house. She made sure Vic and Finn were settled in. She checked on every one of her charges and soothed raw nerves and left calmness in her wake. Only then did she go through her nightly routine.

All the locks were checked, the candles blown out. When she determined everything and everyone was safe and secure, she went to the back door and turned on the small porch light. The one she had turned on every night since Gabriel had run away as a child. Just in case he came home in the dark. Ingrid wanted him to know she had never forgotten about him. She still waited for him.

The light wasn't bright, just a small beacon in the dark.

A little glimmer of hope in the night for all those who were lost to find their way home.

About The Author

When not writing, Ann Simko works as a nurse at a level one trauma center. Her first novel Fallen was originally published in 2009, where it became the number one best seller for thrillers in her publishing house for almost a year. She writes thrillers, anything with a ticking-bomb type of plot, maybe with a wee bit of paranormal thrown in for fun.

She lives in rural Pennsylvania with her husband who puts up with her over active imagination, two scary teenagers who try to ignore her, three very large dogs, six cats and five extraordinarily large lawn ornaments otherwise known as horses.

Other Books By Ann Simko

COYOTE MOON SERIES
Fallen
Through the Glass
The Coyote's Song
Broken
And coming soon:
CROSS ROADS

Socrates's Child

VISIT: WWW.ANNSIMKO.COM

www.ingramcontent.com/pod-product-compliance
Lightning Source LLC
Chambersburg PA
CBHW061603170626
46811CB00001B/295